Praise for *KINK*:

'[*Kink* is] more about the transformative nature of kink as a practice, and the different modalities – kink as anticipation, as communication, as processing, as a mind-eraser, as an anchor, as a code, as freedom – it can unleash ... Ultimately, this seems to be the collection's point: to prompt a revisitation of the transgressive, a consideration, or insertion, of the self' *New York Times*

'This provocative collection will leave you tied to your chair ... [A] groundbreaking collection of short stories that explore desire, love, BDSM, and consent ...' *O Magazine*

'... Dive into this collection of short stories written by several renowned fiction authors. Set in places like therapists' offices, private estates, and a sex theater in early 20th century Paris, the stories explore various points across the sexual spectrum from love and desire to BDSM' *Cosmopolitan*

'In the introduction to their new collection, editors R.O. Kwon and Garth Greenwell declare that they want to take kink seriously. The fifteen stories that populate their anthology of literary short fiction certainly do that, investigating the intersection of love, desire and control in pieces that transport readers to therapists' offices, dungeons and a sex theater in 20th-century Paris. These narratives seek to analyze how gender and politics inform pleasure and power, and are written by the very best of the genre ...' *TIME*

'[*Kink*] is less a collection of stories than a journey through the spectra of human sexuality ... Some readers may be surprised, some may be bewildered, but all will be pleased by what they find between the covers' *Los Angeles Review Of Books*

'Fifteen writers explore power dynamics, self expression, and humanity through bends in desire. The stories ... are alternatingly funny, poignant, sexy, anxiety-provoking – like kinks, like life' *Vanity Fair*

'There's delight in *Kink*'s sensory abundance ... Each [story] is a portrait of the way sex can turn slippages and differentials in human society – between people trying to understand one another through language, between the strata of power hierarchies, between differing gender expressions – into a phenomenon only fiction can really get at. Kwon and Greenwell's *Kink* is ... an invitation to enjoy the sheer inexplicable fact that the body speaks a language we can't understand' **The New Republic**

'Provocative, poignant, and sublimely written' **Town & Country**

'... The characters in these stories illuminate the ways gender, politics, and cultural norms inform power dynamics – inside and outside the bedroom. The collection's strength lies not just in the diversity of the writers, but also in the experiences they're exploring ... Thrilling, provocative, and unapologetically kinky' **Kirkus Reviews**

'Greenwell and Kwon deliver on their promise to 'take kink seriously' in this enticing, wide-ranging collection that plumbs the depths of desire and control ... This visionary anthology successfully explores the range of sexual potency in the characters' power plays' **Publishers Weekly**

'... Stories about love and lust from a powerhouse lineup ... Edited by two writers whose work takes sex seriously, *Kink* makes a case for sex's place in literary fiction' **LITHUB**

'Intimate and wide ranging in every sense, the script-flipping, heart-skipping stories gathered here speak to and across one another, conveying truths of desire, experience, and selfhood as only literature can' **Booklist**

Kink

Stories

Edited by

R.O. Kwon &
Garth Greenwell

SCRIBNER

LONDON NEW YORK SYDNEY TORONTO NEW DELHI

First published in the United States by Simon & Schuster, Inc., 2021
First published in Great Britain by Scribner, an imprint of Simon & Schuster UK Ltd, 2021
This Paperback edition published in 2023

SCRIBNER and design are registered trademarks of The Gale Group, Inc., used under licence by Simon & Schuster Inc.

1 3 5 7 9 10 8 6 4 2

Simon & Schuster UK Ltd
1st Floor
222 Gray's Inn Road
London WC1X 8HB

www.simonandschuster.co.uk
www.simonandschuster.com.au
www.simonandschuster.co.in
Simon & Schuster Australia, Sydney
Simon & Schuster India, New Delhi

A CIP catalogue record for this book is available from the British Library

Paperback ISBN: 978-1-3985-0321-2
eBook ISBN: 978-1-3985-0320-5

Interior design by Lewelin Polanco
Printed and Bound in the UK using 100% Renewable
Electricity at CPI Group (UK) Ltd

Stories

Kink

Introduction

In late 2017, R.O. Kwon was at MacDowell, the artist's residency in Peterborough, New Hampshire, when she read Garth Greenwell's story "Gospodar" in a recent issue of the *Paris Review*, as well as a MacDowell library copy of Melissa Febos's *Whip Smart*, a memoir of her time working as a dominatrix in New York. Wouldn't it be wonderful, R.O. thought, if stories like these could live together in one book, in the kind of book that could sit on artists' residencies' library shelves? She asked Garth, whom she knew from an interview, if he'd like to coedit such a book, and he said yes.

Here is the book, with writing from some of the most exciting, groundbreaking, acclaimed voices in fiction today. These stories bring the full power of literature to bear on depicting love, desire, sadomasochism, and sexual kink in their considerable glory. A book like this hasn't been published in a long time.

Literature is the great technology for the communication of consciousness, and these stories are acute in their exploration of psychology. But they also recognize that all experience is embodied, and that bodies are always situated in the realities of history and culture, the crucibles of class, race, nationhood, and gender. By taking kink seriously, these stories recognize how the questions raised in intimate, kinky encounters—questions of power, agency, identity—can help us to interrogate and begin to re-script the larger cultural narratives that surround us. In many of these stories, kink can also deepen and complicate urgent conversations around how consent is established, negotiated, and sometimes broken.

Kink is often pathologized in popular culture, the attendant desires flattened, simplified, and turned into a joke, a cause for only shame. In movies, television shows, and popular books, kinky people are often also serial killers, emotionally stunted plutocrats, and other stock villains or exaggerated figures of fun. Instead of pathologizing kink, the stories in this anthology treat it as a complex, psychologically rich act of communication. Kink in these stories is a way of processing trauma, and also of processing joy, of expressing tenderness and cruelty and affection and play. The emotional dynamics of kink are as varied as those of any other human experience, and the stories here explore the whole gamut of human feeling, from exuberance to anguish. Rejecting reductive ideas of normalcy and aberrance, these stories allow for investigations richer than etiology, treating kink as one of the tools we use to make sense of our lives.

In *Life* magazine in 1963, James Baldwin said, "You think your pain and your heartbreak are unprecedented in the history of the world, but then you read. It was Dostoevsky and Dickens who taught me that the things that tormented me most were the very things that connected me with all the people who were alive, who had ever been alive." We hope that, in this book, you'll find fellowship; we hope it helps close some of the distances between our solitudes.

—*R.O. Kwon & Garth Greenwell, February 2021*

The Cure

by Melissa Febos

It happened in the summer. He was an old college friend. Someone with whom she'd always enjoyed a mutual attraction. They had nearly slept together once, and the episode had deterred her from ever trying again. She enjoyed their attraction the same way that, as a child, she had enjoyed the skin that formed on a cooling bowl of hot cereal: compelled by the physics of it, the surprising cohesion, the way a substance could be relied upon to change in a predictable way. One bite, two, and she gagged, pushed the bowl away. The same mutability that had attracted her then repelled her.

She had gone on a date with a woman. It had not gone well. The woman was a casual friend, and they had been talking for weeks on the phone at night, mostly while she had been traveling for work. Amid the characterless dark of hotel rooms, the sound of the friend's voice had seemed more familiar than it was and her longing to be home had turned romantic. On the coarse, neutered sheets of the hotel bed, they had had phone sex—something she'd never done before.

The date had not been acknowledged as a date, but at the candlelit table just a few blocks from her apartment, it had unmistakably been one. She had leaned into it, flirted with the confidence of someone who is risking nothing, still running on the fumes of longing, her unpacked suitcase at home on the bedroom floor. The friend had responded with ambivalence, and a tiresome conversation had ensued, snuffing out any erotic intrigue and stinging her with rejection. She was not even really attracted to her date! It was not even really a date. Which is all to say it was a typical kind of lesbian date.

Her friends were always complaining about the deficit of available women in New York—that was why they kept dating one another, and one another's exes, and one another's friends. It had seemed a ridiculous claim when she was younger and had lower standards. It was New York City! How could one run out of lesbians in New York City? But now, when she flipped through the profiles in the dating apps, it was a roulette of familiarity: a friend of hers, an ex of a friend, her own ex, her ex's ex, an obvious alcoholic, too young, too old, too many references to allergies or emotional triggers, too many misspellings, too many cats.

She left the restaurant upset, at first at her date, then herself. Even when she found a romantic prospect, why did it feel like her intrigues were always a few inches off the mark? They wanted her too much or not enough, and occasionally both. It is difficult to gauge one's own desire when one is calibrated to the desires of others. She had not even particularly wanted to have sex with her date, though she would have. She had just wanted her date to want her, to mistake that pleasure, even briefly, for desire.

As she walked home from the restaurant, she thought of something her therapist had once said to her: You can't get enough of a thing you don't need. She had rolled it around her mind for years, tugging at the riddle of its meaning, testing it against every kind of unhappiness. She couldn't get enough movie popcorn because it was terrible for her. She couldn't get enough episodes of the BBC crime dramas because they were an escape. She couldn't get enough money by working overtime because she already had enough money. She couldn't get enough approval from a boss whom she despised because she did not respect him. She couldn't get thin and fit enough because she still aspired to an absurd patriarchal ideal of female beauty. She couldn't get enough attention from a woman she wasn't really that attracted to because why should she crave it? These desires were insatiable because no need could be met— like fire, they grew when fed.

Not for the first time, she felt disgusted by how oriented she was to the interests and esteem of others. She enjoyed sex most when her lovers seemed satisfied. There was, of course, nothing wrong with this, except that it was to the exclusion of her own satisfaction. That is, her satisfaction was almost entirely contingent on her partner's pleasure. She had once read about a study that found lesbians to have an outrageously greater number of orgasms during sex than heterosexual women. This gave her a self-satisfied zing of pleasure, as if she'd given a correct answer on a game show. The reason offered for this was that women are socialized to be oriented to their partner's pleasure rather than their own. Reading this, her satisfaction dwindled. It was great that lesbians had co-opted the instinct for their own gain, however inadvertently, but still it depressed her to understand that women cultivated this instinct for men. Her whole life seemed defined by unfulfillable desires, by the effort to satisfy the interests of parties she didn't even care for.

When she got home from the failed date, she called her best friend to complain.

"I've run out of lesbians," she announced.

"You have not run out of lesbians," said her friend. "You are tired of pursuing the wrong lesbians."

"I called you for sympathy," she said. "I didn't call you for *the truth*."

"You have to stop looking for your self-esteem in a lover," said the friend, over a mouthful of something crunchy.

"If I wanted this kind of advice," she said, "I would have called my therapist. Are you eating a carrot?"

"A pickle. I think you should just go use someone."

"Like, for sex?"

"Mm-hm." More crunching. "Make it about *you*. Text an old college friend. Tell him to come fuck you. It will make you feel better."

"I'm gay," she reminded the friend.

"So what?" said the friend. "If I remember correctly, you're capable of enjoying sex with men. All the better to practice not caring about his feelings. You can stop if you don't like it."

Was that true? One of the things that she remembered about sleeping with men was that it was hard to stop even if you didn't like it. Inexplicably, it usually seemed easier to continue than to stop. Well, inexplicably to her then. One of the gifts of no longer sleeping with men was that she became capable of seeing clearly many terrible truths of it. It was easier to just keep fucking them, because then you wouldn't have to emotionally clean up afterward. It was easier to keep fucking them than to find out how awful they might be when sexually thwarted—a potential she had learned was hard to overestimate. Masculinity was a glass vase perpetually at the edge of the table.

In high school, she had once made out with a soccer jock at a party. She'd never had sex with a man and didn't want him to be her first. After she rebuffed him, he spread a rumor about the sex they'd had, alleging that she had made some bizarre erotic requests of him. It was a cruel and transparent reversal of his own rejection. Still, those details followed her for the rest of high school. She had been a relatively unknown character at the school and thus, to many, became defined by those humiliating fabrications. She knew it could have been worse. When a childhood friend had halted a sexual exchange with a boy, she had been raped.

For the last fifteen years, she had, somewhat smugly, considered herself free from the bondage of pleasing men. But if she was really honest about it, she had often had sex with women when she didn't feel like it, too. It suddenly seemed clear that she was not free from the instinct to please men, she had just opted out of having sex with them, mostly by virtue of the fact that she simply preferred sex with women. Like those people who took drugs that prevented other, more harmful drugs from working—it didn't cure their addictive behaviors, it just rendered the one option impotent. One had to learn how to not do a thing to really be free of it, she thought. Even though there were hardly any men in her life, she still functioned in ways designed to privilege their pleasure. Like craving the desire of people she didn't like and caring about every orgasm but her own. If she truly undid this instinct, extracted it at the root, perhaps she would really get free.

She texted an old college friend and invited him to come over.

While she waited, she imagined explaining this to her therapist and knew that her therapist would find it a very bad idea. Luckily, it was August, when all the therapists in New York City go on vacation, and she wouldn't have to explain until September, which seemed a long time away.

He had not been a pretty child (she knew from pictures)—gangly with incongruent features, and she could already see that he would not age well. He had thin lips and pale skin and dark hair that was already receding. But he was tall and broad-shouldered with strong cheekbones and a pretty cock. She knew that the window of time during which she had known him would be the one in which he was beautiful.

He was a nice guy, she'd always thought, by which she meant that he wasn't terrible.

He had arrived on her doorstep twenty minutes after she had texted him, an impressive time to travel from Williamsburg to Bed-Stuy on foot. Had he run? She imagined it and laughed and didn't explain as she led him into her apartment.

"Are you hungry?" she asked him. Normally she didn't ask visitors this, especially this late, but the fact of her intention to use him for sex seemed to demand a compensatory performance of consideration for his exploited body. To her surprise, he said yes, he was hungry. She had very little food in the apartment, having been out of town. She took a veggie burger out of the freezer and put it on a plate. She would have microwaved it for herself, but she took out a small frying pan and dripped some oil into it. As it cooked, she told him about her failed date.

A few months earlier, she had lunched with him. They had enjoyed the same attraction as ever, and she had not considered having sex with him. Now he stood in the room that served as her kitchen and living room and office, and she thought, *Sure*. She would fuck him, and if she didn't like it she would stop.

He was not a good kisser. As they backed toward her bed, she wondered if fucking a man would be similar to watching porn featuring men, which she sometimes did. That is, would she want to disappear him the instant she came? When masturbating to porn, she often closed the laptop before her orgasm had even completed its arc. Nothing was more grim than pornography post-orgasm.

His cock was not grim, thankfully. It was shapely and hard, and she liked the feeling of it on her thigh as he sucked on her nipple. There was a thrill as he penetrated her, owing in some part to novelty. Within a couple of minutes, however, it became the familiar tedium of being thrust upon. She knew what came next, and it was not her. Still, she dutifully turned over onto her hands and knees and let him fuck her from behind. It took a good five minutes for her to realize that she was waiting for it to be over. It took another five for her to work up the gumption to tell him to stop midthrust. But then, before she could speak, he sputtered to a finish and there was no need.

She wanted him to leave afterward. But he seemed to assume that he would be staying over, and she was very sleepy. When he curled up against her as big spoon, she scooted into him. This was a position she was used to, having been shorter than all of her past sleeping partners. But those people had been women. His size made her feel claustrophobic and overheated. His body hair prickled her unpleasantly, and his profusion of sweat repulsed her. A person only wants to be drenched in the sweat of someone she loves, and not always then.

With a calculated shifting, she nudged him away from her, and eventually he yielded, content to press his face into her shoulder. His breath shuddered against her neck, slightly congested, like that of a child.

———

In the morning, she dressed for work, and together they walked to the café before parting ways, each with a coffee in hand. She kissed him on the cheek, pretended not to see the moony look on his face, and walked purposefully toward the train. Confirming that he was out of view, she strode past the station and walked home. It was her day off.

When she closed the apartment door behind her, the pleasure of solitude was so great that she closed her eyes and leaned back against the door with a vocal sigh. She drank a glass of water and made her bed. Her bedroom, having been intruded upon by his ungainly presence, felt sanctified in his absence. She took off her clothes and lay on the taut blanket. She did not watch pornography; she thought about stopping him as soon as the sex became boring to her. She thought about stopping the moment it became an exercise in placation. The orgasm was deep and silent, the kind that opens a room in the body and then fills it with light.

When he called that afternoon, she surprised herself by inviting him over. He was eager again, like a dog before dinner—standing too close, mouth open. He commented on his hunger without prompting, but this time she didn't feed him. She handed him a glass of water and walked into the bedroom. They kissed for a few minutes. He had not learned how to kiss in the previous twelve hours. She thought about instructing him, something she remembered doing with men in the past. She decided not to perform the surgical tact required to teach him without offending his pride. This decision excited her. She turned her head away from his mouth and pressed her pelvis against him.

When she mounted him, it was exciting for only a couple of minutes. *I'm going to stop this*, she thought. *If he complains*, she thought, *I will never speak to him again*. He didn't complain. She climbed off him and walked into the kitchen. She returned with a glass of water. He was still on the bed. He reached out his hand, for her or the glass it was unclear. She gulped the water.

"I'm done," she said, not unkindly. "You should go."

In college, she worked for a year as a professional dominatrix. One of the activities that her clients routinely asked for was "teasing and denial." This usually meant a very slow hand job. Sometimes she would tie up her clients and pretend she was going to deny them an orgasm. Sometimes she would make them do it with their own hand. *Stop!* she'd shout at them. *Go!* But she always, or almost always, let them come at the end.

She considered whether this had anything in common with that and decided that it didn't. Like all of the things she did as a dominatrix—from inflated balloons to sensory deprivation to face-spitting—it was prescribed by the desires of her clients. Her interest in her old college friend was the opposite. It was the prioritization of her own pleasure that she found surprisingly erotic. She had imagined this exercise, this counterinstinctual conditioning as a kind of work, as that year she'd spent during college was work. She had not imagined that it would be pleasurable, that she would be driven more by her own pleasure than by any abstract objective.

After he left, she walked slowly around her apartment, observing it as a stranger would. She sipped the glass of water and touched her books, a photograph on the wall, the dishes dried in the rack beside the sink. She put herself to bed as gently, as lovingly as if she were her own child. She ran her hands softly over every inch of her body, as if she were washing it. This orgasm was a veil that drew over her, and when it ended, she was asleep.

The third time, he was anxious, sulky, his narrow mouth drawn like a tightened stitch. He was leaving the next day, he informed her. She did not feed him. She did not give him a glass of water. She told him to lie on the floor and touch himself. She lay on the sofa, where he only had a partial view of her. "Stop," she said. Then she masturbated to climax, not caring or even thinking about what noises she might be making. Afterward, she could feel him there, shimmering with desire and frustration. His frustration was not a problem for her to fix, though that idea rung familiar, like a song wafting from the window of a passing car. She sat up and looked at him, there on her floor with his cock in his hand. He was the last man she would ever have fucked.

He wouldn't call once he left, she thought. Or maybe he would call incessantly. She didn't care. Her not caring was voluptuous, sensual. It was a most substantial absence. It filled her like a good meal. She had had enough.

Best Friendster Date Ever

by Alexander Chee

In his profile pictures, he looked like a dirty-minded angel, blond hair sticking up, electric blue eyes, and a pink mouth that pouted beautifully. He was biting his finger, teeth bared, in one. It reminded me of an incident a long time ago, a Pride parade when I ran into an old boyfriend's old trick with said boyfriend, and while we were talking, the boyfriend turned his back on us. The trick smiled at me and slid a finger up the leg of the boyfriend's very short shorts, pushing in, visibly past his ring. I could see the finger slow and then slip forward. When he pulled it out, he looked at me and ran it under his nose with a grin.

The old boyfriend whipped his head around, uncertain which of us had just penetrated him there on the street. He wasn't mad, but I was, but also, I was completely turned on.

It was, after all, a championship piece of ass.

This boy, he reminded me of both of them that day.

I found him on Friendster, the first of what would be many giant electronic yearbooks for the never-ending high school that is life in the United States. On the outside chance you've no idea what I'm talking about, you joined the site, linked your profile page to your friends' pages, and soon you could follow a network out to, in my case then, 156,550 people.

My life felt smaller than that, though. I was living in Koreatown in Los Angeles in a sublet with friends in a four-thousand-square-foot, five-bedroom apartment, where we could be home and never see each other. One was an old friend, and the other two were his friends, who were now my friends. The building looked so much like a New York building it was constantly used for location shots. In 2004 Los Angeles, people took the Internet really seriously, most people I met had a blog, and my first summer there was the first time I was ever getting hit on over the Internet. I decided to hit back. It hadn't been a very romantic or sexual summer. The best I'd done live and in person was get blind drunk at a West Hollywood bar on vodka and Red Bull, like a sorority girl, buying someone a rose off one of those people that wander through bars with buckets of roses. Said recipient was said to be charmed, a friend of friends, and as such on Friendster, with some fairly amazing naked pictures of himself on his Friendster page. My birthday was coming up, I was single again, and while it was too gruesome to contemplate writing to the man from my blackout, I began paging through the pages and pages of strangers with their brightly colored snapshots and their witty or not-so-witty profile one-liners, until I saw this one. I sent him a very casual note and said something corny and low-key. *This is just a fan letter to say, You're hot.*

To my amazement, he wrote back. He was twelve years younger than me, just out of college in New York, but he was smart. A California Rimbaud, skinny and perhaps tall, in the photos.

He agreed to meet me while I was celebrating my birthday at the Silver Lake summer street fair. *Sounds like my kind of tragedy*, he wrote.

Fair enough, I thought.

We exchanged numbers, and I was excited, but on the day of, he became a little hard to find. We kept missing each other. By the time I met him, I was annoyed by seven missed calls, and no longer particularly interested. I finally found him across from an enormous Moonwalk.

In person, he was a little taller than me, probably about six one, and was dressed like the sort of boys I used to meet back in New York. From his appearance I was fairly sure there was an ex he wasn't over, that he read the *Economist* and had intimacy issues, especially after I noticed his glasses and rock-climbing shorts. I was about to give him the brush-off, but there was a flash of something in his eye that caught me, a fishhook notion. And it should be said, his skin was a miracle of smoothness to look at. He had the kind of perfect, slightly gold skin of some blonds.

I had friends with me—my roommates—and he had friends with him, and they were each watching us too intently. I said, "Let's get a beer," and we walked away from them all. The street fair had seemed like a good idea for my birthday in theory, but now that I was here, I found the bands dull, the people uninteresting, and the goods for sale unappealing. It was like the ugly stepchild of a really cool street fair somewhere else in time and place, just not here.

His friend group had vanished by the time we got our beers, at which point he admitted one of them was an ex-boyfriend who wasn't over him. I held back a laugh. My friends left next, saying they were going to go looking for a present for me.

We were alone. The beer was almost good enough to stay.

He mentioned a pilot show he was writing. I listened. The idea was pretty good, but he seemed nervous and a bit abrupt. We ran out of things to talk about fairly quickly. By the time my friends returned, I was relieved to see them. With wicked smiles, they tossed a paper bag on the table between us.

The friends in question, my three roommates, Peter, David, and Leon, had spoken to me about how I'd not gotten laid that summer in a kind of emergency conference before this. I pulled out the contents as they sang the "Happy Birthday" song.

Lube, single-portion-sized. Rubbers. Restraints, made of nylon and with clasps from a backpack, and Velcro. A few porno mags. Absurd enough to make it sexy. I laughed. It was a fairly direct editorial comment. I looked at their Velcro snaps and plastic hooks. Perfect for hiking and tying up vegetarians. Waterproof.

"Thanks," I said as they cheered.

They laughed and pinched my cheeks like aunties, blew kisses at both of us, and then removed themselves to another table.

My date reached over for the restraints. He tentatively put one on his wrist. "Hunh," he said. He seemed blankly quizzical, and I wondered what was going through his mind. I didn't know him well enough to know if he was hard to read.

All I was thinking was, *The real bottoms, you don't actually have to tie them up*.

————

The street fair mercifully came to an end, and a nearby party was suggested, so we went. I was on a date I knew had no future, but I gave myself some credit. I had just gotten out of a relationship with a closeted man so frustratingly asexual in its nature, and so tortured, I was a bit like a man on a fast who didn't know how to start eating again. I was trying. I was uncertain, but the terms of things around me were not. At the party I watched my date come in and out of view. I drank a bit, he got more interesting, but noticing this, and remembering the earlier disaster of the summer, I watched myself. He eventually vanished into a crowd of men doing blow in the other room. Boring people were often more boring on drugs, but I followed him in all the same, and after he pulled his face off a plate of blow, he said to me, "This is the best Friendster date ever."

I grinned at him then and thought, *Well, maybe now it will be*. But it made me sad for what it meant his life was like.

I took my turn, and when I looked up, didn't see him. I drifted downstairs. And then when I least expected it, and was thinking maybe I would just go home, he sat down near me and we each smoked a cigarette, him offering how he didn't normally smoke.

Check, I thought. *Economist*, climbing shorts, ex-boyfriend, in denial about smoking.

He was nervous again, or perhaps it was the blow. I had thought him indifferent to me by now, as I was to him, and while he was sexy, I was thinking right at that moment about how in order to have sex with him I was probably going to have to endure weeks of dull conversations. I was probably going to have to know everything I didn't want to know about him before we got there. I dreaded the ex-boyfriend story. I didn't like hiking.

"I really wanted you to have a good impression of me," he said.

"What are you talking about?" I said.

"Well," he said. "I just. I just did a bump."

"Hunh," I said. I shrugged.

"I just," he said. "I do this." And he made some kind of sound, like a child makes, and shrugged into himself. It was sweetly awkward.

"What," I said. "Don't worry about it," I said. "Whatever it is, just say it."

"It's your birthday. You just got restraints. Do you want to just go back to your apartment . . . and have a lot of sex?"

I laughed, surprised. "Yeah, I said. Let's go."

———————

The first person I ever tied up was my old boyfriend from the beginning of this story, who asked for it. He wanted me to be someone dirtier and more aggressive than I was then. He wanted me to be the person I felt myself becoming now, with my birthday date. Who was about to be the second person I was going to tie up.

There were twelve years in between these events. The age difference between me and him.

The absurdly large apartment's layout matters to the story. For this to really work, you have to understand that me and my three roommates had taken rooms all on one side of our five-bedroom apartment, and then on the other side off the kitchen there was what had once been servants' quarters: two smaller bedrooms that now doubled as offices. In between was a library, a dining room, a living room, a butler kitchen, and a pantry, and each bedroom had walk-in closets. The West Wing, as we jokingly called it, had its own bathroom. One of us could easily have had a guest there without the others knowing. We usually never heard one another when we were in our rooms, which were technically suites right next to one another. It was an incredible apartment, and I don't know if I'll ever live in another as odd and amazing in sheer spectacle.

I showed him around. The roommates were still at the party. I took him into the West Wing last, and in the room at the end of the hall, which I used as an office, we mutually realized the tour was over.

We stood for a moment in the dark. A futon was on the right, a desk on the left, books stacked on the walls where bookshelves should be.

I realized he was waiting for me to take control. That there was someone each of us didn't normally give ourselves permission to be. And that here was where they'd meet.

"Take off your clothes," I said.

He blinked and began immediately in a way that was touching, for how quickly it happened.

"Turn around," I said. He had a slim body, angular but athletic, almost completely hairless. His beautiful skin glowed blue in the sodium-vapor streetlights from outside the windows.

I fastened the restraints to his wrists behind his back and

raised his arms lightly, to make sure they were loose enough to allow him to move. I turned him back around to face me.

His dick was already hard. I tapped it with my finger and watched it bounce. His breathing was already rapid, from the calm of a moment before.

"Close your eyes," I said.

He did. He stood there, chest moving, eyes closed.

"I'm not going to fuck you in my bedroom," I said. "Just in case there's shouting."

"Okay," he said.

I turned and closed the door and went back to him. It was incredibly moving to see him like that. For all that the restraints were ridiculous, they did work. I stood close to him, close enough to feel the heat coming off him, his breath. I leaned in and ran my fingernail across his nipple. He jumped and gave a huffing kind of cry and I slid the nail down along his skin to just above his pubic hairline, where I pressed in again. "Hu-uh," he let out. And then I reached and pulled him in against me, reaching around to hold on where his wrists were joined. I hadn't taken off my clothes.

"I'm not going to take off my clothes," I said. "At least, I don't think I'm going to. But I don't think that's what you get this time. This time I'm not sure you even get to touch my dick," I said. "We'll see."

"Okay," he said.

I put my face near his and ran the tip of my tongue gently along his lower lip. His mouth opened with another gasp. His tongue met mine, and I pulled the cool wetness of it into my mouth, sucking for a moment. I pulled back slightly so that just our mouths touched. He lunged forward to keep the contact.

I pulled back again, and spat into his open mouth. It was halfway down his throat before he knew. He gasped and gulped on it, and his dick banged up harder. He opened his eyes to catch his balance, and I said, "Eyes closed," and knocked him backward onto the futon couch.

I pushed his mouth open and leaned down and licked the lower lip again. The magenta pout of him. I bit on it lightly. It was the only part of me touching him. He was breathing hard still. I let the lip go, sat back, and from above let the spit drizzle out of my mouth, like a fishing line in the streetlight coming in. He gasped again—"Hu-uh"—opened his mouth wider, and I just let it fall for a moment in a straight line, him gulping on it. Drinking me.

He was now completely fascinating. I leaned down and kissed him, and he reached back hungrily, noisy. "Uhmmm," he hummed into my mouth. I sat back and opened a condom, pulled it over two of my fingers, lubed it. He opened his eyes.

"I'm sorry," he said.

"What," I said.

"I'm not usually this turned on," he said.

He was apparently embarrassed of his emotions and responses. It made it even more fun to play him, then. "Can I have a drink of water?" he asked.

"Sure," I said.

I went to the kitchen and looked at the lubed condom on my fingers. I filled the glass from the fridge dispenser and returned.

"Stand up," I said as I entered, and he struggled to his feet. He looked expectantly at the glass of water. I held it waist high, so it wasn't too hard to stick it over his dick.

It was cold. He jumped in place. "Fuck," he said. He almost lost his balance and I steadied him as I thrust his dick deeper into the water. He was panting again. I held the glass to his mouth, letting him drink from it. When he was done, I put it on the desk. I kissed him hard again, and as I did reached underneath his balls and slid my finger back and forth gently across his hole, getting it slick. He was breathing as hard as a runner. I slid my wet hand over his dick, down the shaft and over the knob of it, running the rubber across the crown in circles before going back down the underside of the shaft and then continuing, under his balls and back toward his hole. I did this a few more times, luxuriating in the way he shook and shuddered and yelped. I kept him close, my teeth on his underlip, his fast breath against my cheek, and when I had established the back-and-forth rhythm, as I went back under his balls one more time, this time I pushed in.

"Aaa-aa-aah!" I let his lip go as his head flew back and I thrust inside him, his arms tight against the restraints. I slid out and felt him croon a little, disappointed. I made like I was headed back to his dick and instead returned inside him. He was slick and wet there, and it went in easily.

He crooned again. It was like feeding him, sticking something in there.

I got him on his back on the futon couch, his legs in the air, arms behind his back, and as I kissed him I worked his hole open with those two fingers, gently, feeling it push back against me like his mouth did as I kissed him and gently fucked his mouth with my tongue.

His face was wet and his eyes drunk on plain lust. His face was flushed, I could tell, even in just the blue lights from the street, and his skin had the sheen of his exertions on it. He was the most beautiful thing I'd seen right then, arms relaxed behind his back, yet also out of control. I tapped the crown of his dick lightly and he winced, his pouty mouth closing slightly and then hanging open again, his lips the larger from the bruising kisses. We'd been at it now for a while.

It would ruin it if he saw anything coming. I unzipped and his eyes focused. I drew out my dick.

"I want to see it," he said.

"No," I said. "You don't get to."

I drew the condom on and lubed it and covered his eyes with my hands, tipping his head back and up as I pushed inside him. The warmth of him slid over my dick, and as I slid down into him I spat hard again into his open mouth as he gasped. He swallowed and made a kind of low hum as I slid in. I slapped his face with my other hand, his legs falling down around my thighs. "Unnh," he said. "Hunnnh." I slid my stubble down over his right nipple as I shoved even farther, rubbing against it, and his head slammed back and down. "Oh, fuck," he said. I grabbed his dick, letting the crown circle freehand in my palm as I fucked him and ground on that nipple and he used his head to hold himself in place, pushing it into the couch. "Fuck, fuck, fuck," he said. And then "Hrnnnh," like he was in a hard cry, his arms thrashing underneath me, stuck under the weight of him and tied together by the stupid Velcro and nylon, somehow still holding. "Ah, fuck," he said. "Ah."

I sat back and pulled him onto the floor, onto me, turning him on my dick so that he lay full on top of me, unsnapped his arms into a new position and snapped them back again so they were over his head, arms straight. He lay naked and wet, me underneath him in my T-shirt and jeans still, my fly open, and I thrust up into him. He was groaning now, his hard dick bobbing on his stomach as I shook him. I bent my knees, forcing him into place so his legs fell out to the side in a V. His head tipped back beside mine and he reached for me to kiss him and I spat again, this time not caring if I hit his mouth, and it ran wet down our faces so he could slide his mouth over to mine as I ground into him and he ground back.

I made him cum with me inside him, which he hated after he'd cum. And so I pulled out and put him over my knee, his cum spreading down my jeans leg. I spanked him, and when I started to get bored I pushed him over onto the bed and stared down at him. He stared back, waiting for more. I shucked off the rubber and beat off over him like that, letting it splash down his leg when I came again.

I wondered if he'd ever let me do this again. When I had sex with people I didn't know, I became someone I only met when I had sex with strangers. I found that the people I met like this often loved it but hated me for doing it, for knowing it about them afterward, and it wasn't always true there'd be a next time. Even if it had been amazing, maybe especially so. There was the rich shame and the defiant pleasure, and it wasn't ever clear which would win.

The spell was off. I bent down, gave him one last short kiss, but I could tell we both were done. By then it was just a little more than boys done wrestling. I didn't want to cuddle him, and I felt the need to sleep alone. It had to be a little ugly like this, as what we'd done was more intimate than if we'd held each other all night. I felt exposed, more naked than naked. I was about to ask if he'd mind sleeping in the office when he said, "Do you mind if I sleep in here?"

"I was just going to ask you to," I said. We smiled at each other in recognition.

Whatever we were to each other, it was mutual from start to finish. We'd been at this for four hours. I said good night and went across the apartment to my bed.

———

The next morning I went in to find him awake. I sat down on the bed. He seemed gently friendly. He'd been reading something.

We went to Starbucks, had coffee, talked a bit. He was meeting friends to continue drinking, asked me to maybe come along. "No," I said.

"I get so crazy," he said. "The first time I did that, I went home with some guy who had me in a sling."

"Do you like it?" I said. I wondered if I should get a sling.

"I do," he said. "But I don't let myself, most of the time. None of my friends know me like this. I freak out. I can't admit it or something. I run away."

It was my second time tying someone up, I admitted, and I want to do it again.

The Starbucks we were at was in a corporate center in Koreatown. We sat outside, the traffic on Wilshire on our right, the corporate park in front of us. It was like we'd wandered onto the set of *Office Space* or something and made what he was saying more surreal, like the sunlight hitting his blue eyes.

I knew we would probably try to have sex again, as it had been that good, and that we also probably wouldn't. When someone says, *I freak out and run away*, what they are saying is, *I am freaking out and about to run away*. Life is easier when you take people at their word.

Also, it's good to be wary of people who are afraid of what they desire.

"See you later," I said.

———————

I went in to do the sheets. He had left his pot pipe and an empty cigarette box. As I took the sheets off the futon, I noticed the stains from the lube and cum. I saw broken wood strings hanging down from under the couch's front edge.

We'd broken the two-by-four that ran the length of the frame.

It became part of my legend with my roommates. The Bed Breaker. I would laugh when they mentioned it, but images of that night strobed through my head. For weeks after, I'd be somewhere and see the blue silk silhouette of him, bound and heaving, hard, sobbing with pleasure.

I sent him an email, he sent one back, we even ran into each other at the gym. It was hard to speak. Speaking was maybe the problem. We were like prisoners who'd used each other to break out, and now that we were in the wide world, there wasn't anything more to say to each other. I knew who I was now, or what I was. I suspected he did, too.

And when I replaced the futon, I got a stronger one, just in case.

Trust

by Larissa Pham

It wasn't that he *left,* she says when recounting the story, long after he did leave the city. It was that she didn't think he would come back. When she tells it, she laughs, putting her hand in her hair. It just happened! It is funny now.

Bristol, Vermont. Summer—the flies biting. Vermont is named for its green mountains, the man tells her. To her, they look like sleeping animals with soft pelts. With the windows of the rental car down, it smells like cows, so they roll them up. The light has a weight to it. She squints against the sun. They have come to the mountains to get away from the city, where life feels unbearable. She has just dyed her hair blond and it is parched and fine, like straw. Too yellow, also like straw. In the photographs he will develop later, her profile is like a smear of gold on the print, in front of the green mountains, in front of the hazy blue sky. After she dyes it this one time, she won't do it again. But that is far from now.

And the space in the mountains, at first, is dazzling. All this new ground. They love driving. They love feeling reborn. They love speeding on the country roads, passing cars by crossing the yellow meridian and zooming back into place. They love listening to the radio and even the static between the stations. They love especially knowing that they are not in New York. Now everyone is unhappy except for them. While the man drives, she reads him the names of wildflowers: baneberry, columbine, spikenard, jack-in-the-pulpit, milkweed, two kinds of asters, marsh marigold, harebell, blue cohoosh, all flowers she would not know if she has seen. His hand rests loosely on her thigh.

———

All kinds of colors are running through her head while he drives. Colors of plants and flowers. Colors she can name and not name. The weekend has the palette of a fantasy. She loves to daydream; she thinks she has the face for it—a small pointed chin, deep-set brown eyes above an ordinary nose and a sad mouth. Acne on her chin, thin eyebrows. It's fun, like right now, to imagine herself as a character in a book, directed by some unseen narrative. Letting her agency fall away, her hands empty and limp. In the heat of the sun, she is thinking about how in love she is, about how its intensity seems to make all the colors of the world porous and bright, like tube watercolors. The mound of her pelvis, fat and tender, pulses from the sex they had the night prior. She wishes she had more words for color, more words to describe how everything feels. She tests them out, like picking crayons from a box: Russet. Salmon. Periwinkle. Oxblood.

It's too bad that English doesn't have very many words for color, she says.

Then you read Virginia Woolf and you realize just how many colors there are, he says.

But they're mostly flowers, she argues. If they're not flowers, they're referents, all words that you can only believe in if you've seen them.

She considers: Violet. Rose. Forget-me-nots, which are also called bluets. Sally Seton's cut blossoms floating in a bowl of water.

Where else would words for color come from? he asks reasonably. He has a long, handsome face, hazel eyes, closely cropped dark hair. She likes to look at him, but not for too long. Things you can't see? he says.

Red is a word for a color that isn't a word for anything else, she says.

He lifts his hand from her leg—this panics her, the loss. Then he places it back, squeezes the meat of her, slides his fingers along the inside of her thigh. That's true, he says.

———

He is twenty-nine. A writer. She's twenty-two. Newly graduated from art school. Their birthdays are a week apart, which she dislikes because it means they have the same horoscope. She doesn't like to think of them up against the same challenges posed by the movements of the planets, or that if she uses a loophole of logic to perform some kind of practical magic on her own future, she categorically has to use it on both of theirs. The idea of their fates being so close together, like two filmy pieces of trash rubbing against each other in a bin, makes her feel exposed. When he asks, she reads his fiction. But she doesn't think he's talented—she finds his prose hackneyed, his style overly masculine. His criticism is weak, too: where she would push forward, he simply gives up. Because she wants to love him, she doesn't tell him.

Because to tell him the truth would be to endanger the possibility of being loved by him, and all she wants is to be loved totally, without reason or question or sacrifice. Love is her hands above her head. Love is a riding crop, a whip, a knotted red rope—all things that force her to relinquish the control with which she tightly grips the world. Because he is willing to dominate her, she is willing to try to love him.

———————

They met just two months before this trip. They were at a poetry reading in her neighborhood. He saw her from across the room and walked up to her and said hello. Had she been familiar with who was reading tonight?

Then they were drinking whiskey in the dark. Then they were in her apartment.

Next to the window, through which she could see the tiny new buds dripping in the mimosa trees, he bent her over, her body folded in half, arm twisted over her back. It felt good. She liked the pressure of his hand on her wrist, his hard cock, which was just like any other hard cock. She didn't have to think about anything. The second time they fucked, he came inside her and she thought, at least she had an IUD.

Did you know you came inside me? she asked, wiping off her leg.

I did. I'm sorry. I got so excited.

She wasn't as mad at him as she expected to be. For a violation, it didn't feel like much of a violation. Instead, they lay in bed and compared tattoos. He was covered in a menagerie: a whale skeleton on the back of his left arm, a rabbit on his bicep, a nautilus shell on his thigh, trailing tentacles. When she asked him what each tattoo meant, he didn't have any explanation. Well. This one was from some Friday the thirteenth, years ago, a crow's foot on his elbow. She touched it with thumb and forefinger, trying to feel the raised edges of the ink underneath the skin.

That one's my favorite, he said. But to her, it still seemed so arbitrary.

Up ahead on the road is a sign for an organic fruit-and-vegetable farm. Do you want to stop in? he asks, slowing down. Yes, she says, let's take a look. They pull into the parking lot. When she hops out of the car, a cloud of dust rises around her sandaled feet.

It's cool and beautiful inside. Goose bumps prickle up her thighs and arms. She thinks, *bounty*. She thinks, *plenty*. Simple words, but being in the country makes her feel simple. She imagines brushing the dirt away from a clump of roots, recalls how fine the threads can get—greenish white, haloed with earth. The market has purple-and-white-striped runner beans, hand-folded ravioli filled with soft cheese from the goats bleating next door. Nubbly heads of dinosaur kale, the long leaves dark, with pale stems, and peaches, and cherries, and soft stone fruits arranged in neat rows. She thought they'd shop together, but he wanders alone through the store, and surreptitiously, she takes a picture of him with her phone.

His tattooed forearms flexing over the bins. She always takes photographs of him looking away, or down. She's worried she will see one expression in person, but another expression in the picture.

———————

While booking the reservation for the car, a week before the trip, he had texted her and asked jokingly:

Will we hate each other by the end of this?

Of course not! she wrote back. *Do you think so?*

No, he typed.

Why would you say something like that?

He'd upset her. *Sorry*, he typed. *I was just joking.*

Well, now I'm nervous, she wrote back.

And he was nervous, too. He is still nervous. She's too young to rent a car; that's why he had to book it. He doesn't like knowing this about her; it makes him feel uneasy, like a predator. But there's no way that he could unknow it, her youth, her porousness—there's no way to go back to the time before they met. Sometimes, when he is with her, he wonders what he's doing, if there is somewhere else he should be.

We'll be fine, he wrote. *I'm looking forward to a weekend away with you.*

The car is red, a little red Kia. When he picked it up, he laughed out loud; it was like a toy, and so improbably colored. But he took it for a joyride anyway, driving the length of Eastern Parkway with the windows down, all the way to the cemetery in Bushwick, where he'd never been. It was amazing how good it felt, the wind in his hair, the radio on. For a moment— for many moments—all he wanted to do was to keep going, to drive into Queens, into Long Island, to drive all the way until he reached the very tip of the land, where the map ended in the sound and there was no road, only horizon. In this vision, he is alone. He parked the car and walked among the gravestones, his fingers worrying at the key fob in his pocket. Then he got back in the little red sedan and turned around.

She was waiting for him outside when he pulled up to her apartment. He could sense it, her pure and searching need. Her hair shone in the sun. He leaned out the window.

You came! she said.

———————

In the farmstand on the side of the road, he feels suddenly lost. It was his idea to leave town, to find a new place to be together in. He's dreamt of this often, of starting over. He knows there's control in making decisions.

Under his hands, the peaches are soft and ripe—some of them break skin at a touch, the flesh slippery underneath, wet and inside-looking. He wants to buy some, to bring them back to the girl, to slice them into wedges and place them on her stomach under the soft light of what he imagines will be their cabin, but the more he touches them, feeling for rot, the more they bruise under his hands. He picks up a brown paper bag of cherries instead, filling it to the brim. They'll eat them in the car for the rest of the drive, spitting the pits out the windows.

But for now, he wants to try this. Here is a project, the project of becoming close to someone. At the register, he pulls her close to him, holding tight the firm swell of her body, feeling the elastic of her panties under his hand.

She takes pictures on her phone and she takes pictures with their plastic disposable camera. The ones on her phone are just for her—for her to scroll through later, in bed, when the man is asleep and dreaming. The ones on film are an attempt at a different kind of architecture. The two of them trying to forge some kind of relationship, making an album of moments together. Every frame, she thinks, fixes them in time.

As he's paying, he slides one hand into her back pocket, possessively, and something leaps up inside her at his touch. She feels desired and chosen. Maybe she could follow him anywhere. Maybe it could be nice to do so. To say yes to everything, to fold her future into his future. Years from now, she'll remember this moment, this weekend, how her world suddenly seemed to shrink and grow at the same time. It was as though she were trying on a new dress that didn't fit but looked beautiful, and she wanted to be the kind of woman who wore beautiful dresses, so she kept it on.

They load the groceries into the car, and she climbs into the passenger seat. She lets the emotion pass over her in waves, like a drug she's taken too much of. It's too strong, all of it, and after a moment a second emotion bubbles up inside her—a stilted, phony feeling. She doesn't know him at all, not really. They slept together once, then again, and then suddenly, they were holding up a frame to all this. She thinks *suddenly*, as though she had nothing to do with it. She is prone to this, to disappearing within her own life. Everything seems to happen to her.

Telling a story, any story, years later, she laughs, says, I don't know, it just happened!

———

They are staying in a cabin a few miles outside of Bristol, Vermont. It sits on the property of a couple who rent it out to vacationers. When they pull up into the gravel driveway, they see two horses—a big, beautiful mare and a squat little pony—flicking their tails in a meadow next to the property. The youngish man who greets them isn't the owner of the property, he explains, but he works for them. He introduces himself as Jeff. He's a local who's lived in Vermont his whole life. Jeff shakes their hands, the man's first, then hers.

Wow, Jeff says. We don't get a lot of Asians up here! He looks her up and down, like she might suddenly change shape.

She smiles a little, in a trying-to-be-friendly way. Yeah, we're from New York.

The blond hair is nice, Jeff says. It's cool. Don't see much of that here, either.

Thanks, she says.

Well, the man says. Let's go see the house.

———

When she pees, as she does immediately upon their arrival, the sound of it is audible in the tiny cabin.

You should turn on the water when you pee, he tells her as she steps out of the bathroom to wash her hands. It's more considerate.

But it's the same sound of water either way, she says, confused.

No, one is piss and one is water, he says.

I can turn on the faucet if you want, she says. But she doesn't really mean it. She's an environmentalist.

They have sex before they even begin to think about dinner. The light is warm and falls onto everything in golden planes. In bed, she puts her hands above her head and waits for him to do what she wants him to do. She doesn't understand why he won't just take her, why he doesn't seem to understand what to do with her wrists. It seems to her that there's only one thing to do when someone puts her hands over her head. He is sweating above her, his skin flushed. The blood blossoms in a dark, rosy V from the center of his chest, up into his neck, coloring his narrow face. She can imagine it flowing through his body, moving toward his cock and away from his brain.

Do what you want with me, she says.

He doesn't say anything. She presses her wrists into the bed to give him an idea of what she wants. Though nothing he could do would ever be enough. What she wants is for him to understand her, to anticipate her every need. She wants to submit to him so thoroughly that he possesses even her desires, recognizing her so thoroughly that she never has to ask for a thing.

Please, she says.

There is this way she has of looking at him. Like something caught. She doesn't talk enough, but when she does, she talks too much, like a nervous child. He wants to hate this, her jittery vulnerability, the way she darts around difficult conversations, but he can't. He's tantalized by the edge of what he suspects is there—a deep and lonely desire, a void that he could fill. Romantically, he thinks, he wants her to show it to him—to hold still long enough to be touched in the heart.

Now she is beneath him. On her back, her small breasts are flat, the areolae dark against her skin.

Please, she says again.

Suddenly, he wants to hurt her. Not in the way she wants him to. He has an idea of what she wants. She wants him to be brutal and present. She wants him to pin her down and choke her out. She wants him to slap her and shove his fingers in her mouth and say dirty, unforgivable things. She wants him to do what he wants, but she wants those wants to be her wants.

He wants her to tell him, *Do these things to me*. He wants her to describe exactly what she wants, exactly how she likes it. Then he would be happy to do them. He would do all of them, and more; he has a perverse imagination that belies his calm exterior. But he needs to hear it from her. There is something closed off about her, like a peony that was cut too soon, a tight green bud, balled up, truncated before the ecstatic frill of full flower. He knows she doesn't like it when he is gentle with her; it makes her uncomfortable. He knows she is more in love with the idea of him than she is in love with the actual him, because she doesn't know him at all.

He wants to hurt her, to test her. He wants to startle her out of her shyness and fully open herself to him, like forcing a peony to bloom by cutting the stem on the diagonal.

In one motion, he puts his hand over her wrists.

Yes, she sighs.

He is not inside her yet—he is hard, his cock flopped up on his stomach, and he sees how she arcs her hips up to meet him.

Tell me what you want, he says.

I want . . . she begins.

He presses his weight on her wrists, he knows he is hurting her, he's pushing her, he thinks. He wants to hear her say it—wants her to voice the heady need she shakes off her body like rain.

What do you want? he asks her. With his free hand he strokes her, and she is already slick; she spreads her legs, she mewls, she is looking up at him without really looking at him. When he gazes into her face she can't hold eye contact. Her eyelids flutter shut. It's this he can't stand, can't understand—how she can pretend to offer one kind of vulnerability without offering it all.

I want . . . she says again.

Exasperated, he slides into her, too fast, a little sloppy—she yelps, and he can feel the tendons in her wrists stiffening.

Is that what you wanted? he asks. He thrusts once—slow. Watching her face.

Yes, she says, and he knows she wants it. When he puts his free hand on her neck, he sees her eyes close in bliss. He chokes her, applying pressure, and she makes soft noises of pleasure.

But he wants more from her, more from this, wants to be affirmed absolutely that this is what he deserves. That he could—what? Own her? It's good, the way their bodies move together. This is the language they both understand. When he releases her hands, she sighs, grabs her own small breasts, pinching her nipples, squeezing her tits together like a girl in a porno. He finds it touching. She is so young. He reaches down—grabs her jaw in his hand, runs his thumb over her bottom lip. She smiles. Sucks on his fingers, her cheeks going concave.

Who do you belong to? he asks, taking his hand out of her mouth. He cradles her face.

Without answering, she closes her eyes.

———

She knows what he wants her to say. She can feel it, too, jumping up in her throat—the way he fucks her is so *good*. She worries that the goodness will fill her up and make her say things she's not ready to say. It's here that she wants to stay, here in the rhythm of their bodies, her nails digging into his back, his cock inside her, moans spilling out. She forces down the urge to say anything she'll regret. Instead, she raises her knees, pressing them against her chest, taking him even deeper inside her.

Sometimes she wonders if all that takes place between men and women is a battle of will. She knows that a small, soft animal lives inside her, and that that animal wants to be loved completely, flat on its back, kissed and cuddled. She wants that, too, the same way she wants to be dominated, the same way she submits to being pinned down, pressing her cheek into his hand. But at any touch of softness, a wall goes up in her that she cannot navigate around.

Fuck me harder, she says. Easy to be like this: hard. And he listens. He places a hand on the back of her thigh, shoving her knee up, lifting his other hand to slap her with an open palm, and she turns her face into it as a plant turns toward the sun, welcoming the blow, a smile stretching across her face.

———

After sex, she pees without turning on the water. He listens to her wash her hands. It takes her a long time. By now, the sun has set, and it is cold in the cabin. They are hungry. He rummages in the fridge for the groceries they bought on the trip up. They don't talk much while he cooks and she inspects a bottle of moonshine they picked up at the farm.

Do you want to try it? she asks. She turns the weight of it in her hands.

Yeah, he says.

She opens it; it smells terrible, like gasoline. She pours a finger into the bottom of two glasses. It's so bad it almost doesn't have a taste, just burns.

They eat in silence and after, they sit on the couch together. Her feet in his lap. She makes herself drink more to feel more comfortable, overly conscious of their proximity.

Once, an old boyfriend of hers broke up with her because she was too vulnerable, or more precisely, because she was not vulnerable in the correct ways. He went so far as to write her an email. In it, he described what he perceived to be her character flaws. *It seems to me that you are less interested in actually being vulnerable with others and more enamored with the symptoms of your own vulnerability*, he wrote. This struck her as cruel. It *was* cruel. It was not untrue, which made it even crueler. Since then, she has been guarded, locking everything inside her like a series of nested chests. She is aware that this makes her difficult to love, but she doesn't know how to stop doing it.

———————

The man watches her. He pours more moonshine into her glass.

Let's get you drunk, he says. He is already drunk. It is making him mean.

I'm not wearing any underwear, she says suddenly. She has changed into a white dress with a handkerchief hemline; the fabric of it is thin, with a small abstract print. He pulls her onto his lap and yanks up her dress, as though he is going to give her a spanking. There: her smooth buttocks, rising like two little hills, her skin pale and untanned. Without the lacy apparatus of underwear to hide her nakedness, she seems neutered somehow, and precious, like a doll or Eve in Eden; but there is also something so pornographic about her audacity that for a moment the man veers wildly between the two axes, unsure of what to do next. She rests the side of her face on the arm of the couch, not moving.

You're not, he agrees. Little slut, he adds experimentally.

Yes, she says softly. She cannot see his face. Her eyes are closed. He cups a hand around her ass, smacks it gently, then again, harder.

How did you become the way that you are? the man asks her.

What? she asks.

I can't figure you out, the man says.

I don't know, she says. I think I've always been this way.

She cannot see his face, but she can imagine his expression, the serious, contemplative look he wears. She knows he is not smiling. There is a sharp edge to him now that she does not recognize, and it scares her. When she says she wants him to be brutal, she only wants him to be brutal in a cinematic, delicious way. She imagines getting whipped by long-stemmed roses stripped of all their thorns. She wants him to tie her up and fuck her but kiss her after, rub her body down with sweet-smelling oils. His fingers rest on her cunt.

No, he says.

She waits.

You want people to be open with you, but you don't open yourself, he says. He slides a finger inside her—she is wet; it takes nothing. She sighs.

He massages her, thrusting his fingers in deeper, and she twists in his arms. Suddenly, the dense heat of her around him, he remembers the sound of her pissing, imagines the warmth rising from inside her and leaving her body in a stream. There is something about her pain that is exciting to him; he wants to crack her open to see what is at the middle, like a peach.

———

She sits up, bracing herself on her knees, her skirt falling over her lap. She feels sticky. She moves to straddle him, leaning over and tracing the shape of his mouth with her tongue. This is her way of changing the subject, of getting what she wants. He is simple; men are simple. He dives into her, pulling her dress up around her hips, and she feels herself hardening, the parts of her he can access receding further and further away.

They fuck on the couch, her dress still on, the white hand-kerchief hem bunched around her waist. She won't look at him, and they do it doggy, her face mushed into the armrest. One of his hands is wrapped around her face, fingers in her mouth. *That's good*, she thinks. She doesn't want to say anything. She can feel him pounding away in her, too deep, too fast, and her mind twirls up into a beautiful, static void. It is quiet in the cabin. When he comes, he pulls out, jetting onto the small of her back. Overcome with sudden loneliness, she wants to cry but won't.

They have bought candles at one of the shops in town, to ward off mosquitoes, though the bites are already rising on her calves and thighs and will leave scars that last long after the summer is over. They leave them lit while they go to sleep, the flames guttering in the metal votives and the smell of citronella rising to cover the smell of their sex.

The next morning. Cold, bright. She feels delicate and hollowed out, like an empty seashell. The candles are burned through. When she picks them up, she is horrified to see that in the night, several moths flew toward the light of the flames and their bodies are trapped in the molten wax. Some of the moths are big, over an inch long, longer, their wings splayed open like autumn leaves. She shows them to the man, their ruined bodies, trapped in soft, translucent layers of wax. She is worried he is going to put his finger in it, deep into the mess of dead things, but he just takes the metal votives out of her hands and throws them away.

Weekend things. Vacation things. Breakfast, eggs from the farm, coffee he makes with a French press, sweet cold milk in a glass bottle making swirling white clouds in their mugs. They go on a hike up a mountain that Jeff recommends. It is strenuous, but they enjoy it. She likes that they can't look at each other while they climb, that they are having two discrete experiences in their separate lives. She likes the smell of her own sweat. At the peak, they watch the red-tailed hawks soar in slow circles, patrolling their territory. There are two, three, four hawks, all circling above the valley. Their bodies look sleek and dangerous; their wingspans huge, the feathers fanned out.

Their eyes are so sharp, they can see a mouse on the ground from here, the man says. One hawk suddenly swoops to the ground, moving swifter than she thought possible. He probably saw one just now, the man says. Dinner.

She is reminded of a time at a party in college where a girl, an economics major, was loudly talking about the two kinds of people in the world. *Predator and prey*, she kept saying. *That's all there is in this world.* The girl looked her dead in the eyes. *You're prey*, she said.

They lose sight of the hawk, descended into the forest. She imagines the mouse, killed, a little blood left in the dirt.

Below them, the valley is spread out like a meal. Rows of evergreens sparkling in the heavy sun. The mountains sloping off into the distance in one direction, each layer bluer than the last, tiny glimpses of the shimmering river below. They are so high up, and very small.

She climbs out onto a rock, where the ground falls away and trees jut out at an angle, to take a photograph. She wants to preserve this moment, it is her way. Historian and hagiographer of her own life.

You want a selfie? he drawls.

Don't be mean, she responds. Maybe it's better when they're not talking. When they're quiet, she doesn't have to worry about the shape the thing between them isn't taking. She takes a picture of all that stretches below her, bathed in light, carefully framed.

Come stand here, she says, dropping back onto her heels. I'll take a picture of you.

I don't want a picture.

Well, okay, she says, her feelings hurt again.

—————

When she gets out of the shower she's taken to rinse off the grime of their hike, the man is gone. Naked, she walks around the cabin, dripping water onto the wood floors, looking for a sign—his wallet, a note, anything. There's nothing. His clothes are still neatly folded on the bed, his bag on the couch, a paperback hanging out like a lolling tongue. This isn't alarming yet, she knows; the man needs his space, he's prone to disappearing. She's already lost him more than once in a museum. It's possible that he's just outside, taking a walk, waiting for his turn to shower. She towels herself dry and dresses quickly. When she opens the door, she's startled by how bright it is outside, and how hot, the heat rising in visible shimmers.

Outside, her hair still wet and pushed back from her face, she sees Jeff, getting something from the shed where she knows they keep the firewood, and garden tools, and whatever else it is that people in the country seem to always have around. Propane tanks? A lawn mower?

Hi, she says.

Hi, says Jeff.

She realizes the little red Kia is gone.

Did you see him leave? she asks.

Nope, Jeff says. Just got back from running an errand myself.

Oh, she says.

Did he run out on you? He shouldn't have done that, Jeff says.

No, he shouldn't have, she agrees.

She walks in a short, helpless circle around the gravel driveway. Oh, she says again. In the meadow, surrounded by small yellow flowers, the horse and the pony are twitching their tails at flies. The meadow overlooks a valley. The view is so pretty it makes her heart ache. When she comes closer to the animals, she sees that the big horse is wearing black mesh goggles to protect its eyes from the biting flies. There are too many flies all over its face, buzzing and squirming—it makes her skin crawl. She wants to wash its sweet, bony face, wipe the crust from its big, long-lashed eyes. The pony is squat, its body like a barrel, its legs like tree trunks. Its belly is so close to the ground. *Where could he have gone?* she thinks.

It is so hot. Her neck prickles with anxious sweat. The world is too large and too loud and bright, and she is alone. She walks up to the fence that separates the meadow from the rest of the property, reaching for the horse, wanting to comfort it as though in doing so she would comfort herself. Then she stops herself, feeling muddled and abject—she's scared of the flies, and worried, suddenly, that to reach out and touch another living thing would only make clear how alone she is now. She feels trapped without the car, without the man. There's no way she has of leaving this place. Was that all it took for her to feel free? Or is it that now, suddenly loosed into the world, she doesn't know what to do with herself?

She goes back to the cabin, stepping into the cool, dark interior. She makes herself a drink. Rummages in his bag for a pack of cigarettes, extracting one. She lights it as she's leaving the cabin, where Jeff is standing in the driveway.

He didn't tell you where he was going, says Jeff.

I was in the shower, she says. It is too easy for her to do this, to make herself available to strangers. She looks at Jeff sidelong, avoiding eye contact. He just left without saying anything.

Jeff lets out a low whistle. Well. He'll be back, he says.

Will he? she thinks. *His things are still in the cabin.* Sure, she says aloud, exhaling a stream of blue smoke.

If he's not back by—Jeff glances at the sky—dinner, you're welcome to come by mine. I went fishing today, got a good catch. You know, I could even take you out tomorrow. If you want.

Oh, that's so nice of you. But I'm okay. I'm sure he'll be back soon, she says.

Well, you could still go fishing, Jeff presses.

No, that's really okay, thank you.

Most of the folks who come through here do it. They go with me, out on the boat—they really like it. They love it. There aren't many people who don't go out fishing with me.

She imagines being on a boat alone with Jeff. You know, I'm not really into fish, she says.

Really? Jeff seems excited about the challenge she presents. It's very healthy. And it's not that hard to cook. You ever gut and scale a fish before? What you do is, you lay your fish down on a nice flat surface. You get a butter knife, and you grab her tail in one hand, and you scrape those suckers right off. Slow, toward the head.

Uh-huh, she says, breathing hard through her nose.

And then, Jeff says, you have to gut her. You need a sharp knife, you make a cut, right in her belly, and you slice right up toward her head. Reach in and pull the guts right out. And then you go up into her neck—now Jeff is miming, opening an

imaginary cavity with one hand and pinching with the other—
and you grab her gills with your fingers and slice 'em right off.
And then—

I'm so sorry, she says, cutting him off, throwing down her
cigarette and crushing it into the gravel with the heel of her
sandal. Thank you, that was very educational, but I have to—

She hurries back into the cabin. From the window, behind
the shades, she watches as Jeff stands alone, for a moment, then
shrugs and turns to walk up the hill, to the little house where
he lives. Then she darts into the bathroom and dry-heaves into
the bowl of the toilet. She flushes, walks into the kitchen, and
makes another drink, looking anxiously out the window, waiting for time to pass.

The first time he slept with a woman who asked him to hit
her, it felt like a window had opened inside him. He's not sure
what happened, exactly—that she saw something in him and
touched it, or if the thing in her was so powerful, it moved the
thing in him. All he knows is how it felt—where there was
blank space, a rupturing.

The man is driving back now, the sun setting. He has been
gone for some hours. He feels lightened now, and at ease, in
motion where it best suits him. When he leaves a room, he
leaves it completely. He is like this at parties, restaurants, his
day job. Today he got into the car and drove into town and,
like a curtain falling behind him, the rest of the world dropped
away. In the trunk of the car is pasta, some vegetables, a bottle
of wine, some cheese. He went grocery shopping and for a walk
through the town, browsing through the one bookstore, the

antique shop, picking up the knickknacks and turning them over in his hands. He almost bought one—a small porcelain dog. He'll go back to the house, where she is, and they'll make dinner, and then they'll make love.

When he pulls onto the property, she is standing there, a peroxide blonde smoking in the driveway. It is dusk; everything is shades of blue.

Where did you go? she asks. She seems near tears. Why would you do that?

Do what? he asks.

Leave without telling me, she says.

But I came back.

I wasn't sure you were coming back.

He sighs. He is unloading the groceries from the car. I just wanted to get some things for dinner, he says. We didn't have anything left. He pulls down the lip of the bag to show the long, deep-green neck of the bottle. I got you wine, he says.

That was nice of you, she says thinly. I still can't believe you did that.

Was it really so bad? he asks.

She follows him into the cabin. She wonders if Jeff has heard the crunch of gravel, heard the man coming back.

The man turns on the stove.

Yes, it was! she says. It was bad! I was alone, and I was anxious, and you took the car. The only thing we have to get out of here. I felt trapped. You trapped me here, she says accusingly.

He puts on a pot of water to boil, shakes salt into it. You need to calm down, he says. Please. I'm not going to go anywhere.

But how am I supposed to know, if you keep leaving? she asks.

The man turns to open the bottle of wine. I don't know, he says. She is surprised to see the expression on his face. He looks angry, stricken. I wanted to do something nice for us, he says. There's no reason to be upset. I don't see why you should be making me feel bad.

I'm not trying to make you feel bad, she says softly. I just want you to understand how you made me feel.

Pitch dark again, in the woods just outside of Bristol, Vermont. One light on in the cabin, a lamp beside the bed. She is tied to the bedposts by her wrists with a red rope. They are talking, in a way. She is naked. Under the golden light of the reading lamp, her stomach looks soft, like caramel. The man is naked, too. Their bodies are very close together. He touches her cheek, kisses her on the mouth. Her hands tied, she sighs in response.

He will be attentive now. Gentle.

Tell me, he says, his hand cradling the side of her face. Tell me what you want.

I want to trust you, she says.

She begins to cry. She is so fragile. She can feel her heart opening, and she does not believe he deserves it. It feels as though he is breaking something in her that has repeatedly been broken.

This is what he has wanted, isn't it? To force the quiet, tight bud to blossom. He has done it with peonies before, cut too soon in the season. He sees it now, the flower opening inside her. The hard, pale green outer shell unfurls to reveal a series of delicate petals, thin as tissue, all different shades of pink, the edges frilled. All of the layers opening, turning back to reveal more and more delicacy of all colors, densely packed, the edges of the petals like little curling tongues.

And he knows now that he cannot turn back. That he is responsible for this, for her, for making her think that she could trust him, that she could open her heart to him. And he realizes now that he has not stopped to consider, at any moment, the shape of his own heart, if it is a flower or a lock or a door, and if it is a door if that door is closed or open.

They are driving back to the city now. Feeling tender. Let's ditch this small town and go to the city, my dear, the man says jubilantly, pulling out of the driveway. Bright lights. They have left the keys on the kitchen counter. The sheets are stained with their sex. His hand is idly on her thigh again, while countryside zooms past.

Her heart, all of her, feels gutted and pure. She knows that a shift has taken place inside her; she can feel it. She will try. She knows that it is not safe, that it is never safe. But she is here, now, alive in the world, and there is so much to see. Streaks of green and gold. The road curves before them. She feels drained and content, like she has been crying for days and run out. No longer suffocating under the weight of inarticulable feeling. Though that's not to say that she has words for how she is feeling. Simply that she understands that she must accept it.

On the freeway, somewhere on the New Jersey Turnpike, the two catch sight of a flock of starlings, a dense cloud of birds peppering the bright blue sky. As they drive, the flock swirls and floats, ebbing into itself, undulating and widening and narrowing to a tiny point, then swelling huge again.

Look, she says to the man. Look.

They see three or four of these flocks, driving back to the city. Each time they encounter one, she wants to press her face against the glass; she wants to stop time. She wants to ask him to pull over on the side of the road so she can float up into the sky with them, too.

How do they move like that? he wants to know. And what is it called? They look it up. It is hundreds of starlings moving in something larger than individual units. Emergent properties. A system. The name for it is murmuration. It happens because each bird moves in response to the birds around it, in a ring of seven, all tightly connected, instinctively rippling in response to something sensed on the other edge of the flock.

How can it be learned? How can it be choreographed? She considers it, sitting next to him, who is with her but soon will be leaving, though she doesn't know it, how little time they have left. She considers her own instincts, and then the instincts of all living things, all that animals know without being told.

Safeword

by R.O. Kwon

After some discussion, they decided they'd both benefit from professional guidance. It was like doing yoga, they figured. Hazardous, at first, to go through the poses without an instructor's help. The woman who opened the door was shorter than her pictures had suggested she'd be. On her website she'd been dressed in black pours of single-piece latex; now, in a buttoned white shirt with rolled sleeves, a simple black skirt, and calf-high boots so shiny Paul could see his blurred reflection, she looked less like a Mistress Ava Adamson than she did like a normal person, almost.

"Hello, Paul," she said. She took his hand in a predictably strong grip. Dark hair cupped her jaw, the tips curving under her chin like a gladiatorial helmet. She was roughly their age: still young, as opposed to young, period. "And *you*," she said, turning to Jihyun, who was standing half a step behind him, her hand in his. "I'm so glad to see you. Come along."

She turned and left them. Still holding hands, they followed the dominatrix. Down the long hall, then they were in a dim room with flashing mirrors and—contraptions. Everything was an elaborate variation on something else, something he understood. A black padded massage table, but sturdier, buckle restraints hanging from its corners. A cross, but X-shaped, also dangling restraints. At the end of the room, something like a throne, high-backed, theatrical, gilded, the center of its seat cut away. Then what looked like a cat's scratching post, except that it was human-sized, and, again, equipped with restraints. A mess of whips and crops, canes and paddles, lined the walls. Jihyun's grip on his hand had gone loose.

"May I take your coats?" the dominatrix said, smiling. Tattoos shimmered through the thin fabric of her shirt.

She'd be right back, she said. As soon as the door closed behind her, Jihyun turned to him. Her eyes were wide and urgent. "The envelope," she whispered.

"Oh, right," he said, pulling it from his pocket. The website had instructed them to leave their payment—their "tribute," what the fuck—out in plain sight at the start of their session. "Why are we whispering? Where am I supposed to put this?"

"Maybe on that—that table?"

He smoothed out the envelope and left it on the modified massage table. This woman was making more per hour than most bankers he knew. Jihyun was hugging herself, looking down. She'd agonized that morning over what clothes she should wear, which was pretty funny, since, as he'd pointed out, she probably wasn't going to be in them very long. After five, six outfit changes, she'd ended up choosing the first thing she'd tried on, a slim wool dress with stockings, an ensemble at least fifteen degrees too flimsy for the day. But now, underdressed, clutching herself, she looked tiny, miserable. He closed his arms around her, warming her up. He almost asked if she was all right, but maybe it was insensitive to imply there was any reason for her not to be all right, and why would there be? Here they were, in a dungeon in Chelsea, a dominatrix on her way: What could be off about this? So he kissed the top of her head, the white pure line of her part, and hoped the touch would say what needed to be said, whatever it was. He was so tired, he realized, of not knowing what he was supposed to do or say.

So much was his fault. Like a jackass, he'd pushed her and pushed her. A month ago, he'd interrupted the back massage he was giving her—"harder," she kept saying—to ask if there was anything else she wanted to try in bed.

"Jihyun?" he said, after a moment. It was possible she was asleep, but it was even more possible she was pretending this wasn't happening. They were like two-thirds of a bar joke: he was an ex-Pentecostal, she was an ex-Catholic, and though she'd been with him for three years, she still refused to let him in the bathroom if she was so much as taking a piss.

"*Ji*-hyun," he repeated, running a knuckle up the long, knobbed curve of her neck. He was straddling her; she was lying on her stomach in her bra and panties.

"No, I'm fine," she said. "Thank you."

"Really, there's nothing?" he said. "Come on, there must be some fantasy you've never told me about. There's not even one other thing you want to try?" He'd brought this up as a joke, mostly, and also of course because he kind of wanted her to ask him what other fantasies he had, but now that she was being so evasive he had to wonder: Was she lying?

She twisted her neck to look up at him. "Paul," she said, too gently. "Are you bored?"

"No," he said. Quickly, before she had time to think, he said, "But you are."

Then came the denials, the expostulations, the what-the-hell-are-you-talking-abouts, and then, if only to prove him wrong, she pulled off his boxers and bounced on top of him for a long, athletic display of just how bored she was not. But after she'd fallen asleep, her head huddled under his chin, he lay awake, wondering.

A year married, three together. Say they had sex every three days, on average. Once every three days, 121.7 fucks a year, so 365 times they'd played hide the salami, the same stick in the same hole, the stick in the hole, the stick in the hole, the stick in the—who wouldn't feel bored? The fact that he hadn't, yet, meant nothing. He was an outlier. Recently, he'd eaten the same lomito every weekday for a month from the Chilean sandwich place next to his office, because it was good. Tasty, filling, reliable. Why mess around? Maybe he should make the straightforward effort and believe his wife when she said she was fine, but now that he was thinking about it he couldn't, not really. She was so kind to him that she couldn't be trusted.

Over the next couple of weeks, he brought up the question every now and then, teasing her, and though she brushed him off each time, he shouldn't have been as surprised as he was when, one night, she shook him awake. It couldn't have taken long—he slept lightly, fearfully, because anything could happen. He opened his eyes, and Jihyun was sitting cross-legged, her hands folded in her lap. "Fine," she said. "If you really have to know. I think it's gone, but it comes back."

"What?" he said, thinking she'd had a bad dream. It was only when he reached for her hands, her palms damp and electric, that he realized she was crying. "Jihyun, what is it? *What* comes back?"

"There's something a little wrong with me," she said, each word enunciated, as if she were reciting a speech. "You're going to hate this. Sometimes I really need you to hurt me."

The door flung open. Ava swept in, chattering, something about how she'd just gotten back from a trip to Buenos Aires, she'd hitched a ride on a Peruvian cargo ship, it was her new favorite way to travel, then, "Paul," she said. "What do you do?"

"I work in finance," he said after a moment, flustered. She was still looking at him, so he added, "I'm a vice president at a fund. It's too boring to talk about." This last bit he said with a laugh—it was his usual sidestep, meant to prevent the blank look people got when he mentioned his job. Oh, great, another overpaid bozo in finance. It was a lie, though. It wasn't boring at all. He loved it, the numbers multiplying, the rush of the transaction, the pure, exquisite logic of the math, all of it at his fingers and under his control.

The dominatrix let her eyes linger on Paul another long moment—it was stagy, her menace; she was an actress who'd said her lines too many times—then she nodded. Turning to his wife, she flashed a smile and said, "I really do love seeing couples. So often, my clients are these lonely guys hiding from their wives. This is so much nicer. Jihyun, I'd like you to get rid of your clothes."

So he'd been right. He got to think about that, how right he'd been, as Jihyun slipped out of her dress. She stripped down to her panties, a little black cotton thong, but then she hesitated. Thumbs hooked in the waistband, she looked up at Ava. "That's fine," the dominatrix said. "Good. Now. Come here."

———

That first announcement of Jihyun's had felt like a rehearsed speech, he'd realized, because it *was* a rehearsed speech, a set piece of pure bravado, nearly exhausting what she had to say. That night and over the next few days, he quizzed Jihyun and as she tried—halting, wincing, tearing up—to answer his questions, it was slow going. Jihyun wanted: to be beaten. She wanted: rules—control—punishment—correction—pain. Ropes. Blindfolds. Whips. Not always, but in the, well, the bedroom, yeah. It could take her all exasperating evening long even to begin to answer a question as basic as, Exactly what kinds of rules do you want? They were both second-generation Americans—his parents had moved from Montreal, which counted—and though they shared the immigrant's skepticism of psychotherapy, it didn't take a shrink to guess why she was so shy: what with the nuns, the Catholic boarding schools, the subsequent renunciation of the Catholic schools, the shame, the counteracting feminism, her quasi-Victorian and entirely Korean squeamishness with anything having anything to do with the body, and all this heaped for decade upon decade on top of the great hungry beast of sexual desire—well.

Worse yet, he blundered from the start, asking her why she

felt she needed to be hurt. "Why are people gay?" she shot back, suddenly unshy. "Why does anyone have a foot fetish? One of my earlier memories is of looking up words related to—to this, in the dictionary. It just happens, you know?"

No, he didn't know: that was the problem. His fantasies were confined to, oh, an occasional longing for a threesome. His memory of a certain sixth-grade teacher, the ponytailed Miss Hale. An unindulged appetite for pigtails, and, unoriginally enough, for Natalie Portman. "Is this—something you've done before?" he asked her.

"God, no," she said.

So—his idea—they turned to outside sources. Huddled together on their couch, they watched *Belle de Jour* and *Repulsion*. They watched *Secretary*, and they tried reading *Fifty Shades*, but soon dropped it; it was so badly written that it made her laugh. Also, they studied a different book, a sort of how-to manual with diagrams, titled *Screw the Roses, Send Me the Thorns*. ("You don't like roses?" "Oh, I like roses.") After closing the book, after switching off the movie, he asked her what she'd liked about what they'd read or seen. ("Do you want us to get a cane?" Head-nod for yes. "Do you . . . want to have mud thrown on you?" Head-shake for no.)

Just once, he asked why in three years she'd never told him any of this.

"I don't want to be this way," she said, turning toward him her pale, determined face. "I'd rather not be this fucked up."

By now, the right reply came automatically. "You're not fucked up."

The dominatrix had Jihyun bent over the black table, her ass soaring upward. With quick, rhythmic slaps, the dominatrix struck her well below her tailbone. "I'm warming her up," Ava explained to Paul, who resisted the juvenile urge to say he knew that, already.

Mistress Ava Adamson was attractive enough, he supposed, in a sturdy way that wasn't his thing, but some guys would be into it, with her strong calves showcased by the short boots, the clusters of muscles sleek in the low light. Big breasts, too, tucked away in that no-nonsense shirt. The dominatrix was more muscular than he was, admittedly. He used to work out a lot more, then one day he caught himself fondling the flat planes of his abs and stopped, embarrassed. What was the point of all these muscles? It was the physique of a bodyguard, miscast in the life of a—fund manager. Brawn wouldn't maximize the possibility that he and Jihyun would have long and happy lives; money would. He had no romantic illusions about money, but he understood its ability, so he went less often to the gym and spent those saved hours at the fund, instead.

In one of the dungeon mirrors, he caught himself looking worried. The high flushed forehead settling into its first wrinkles, the disappearing hairline, his entire reflection these days a memento mori. He felt old, and tired. This was the thing about being an ex-Christian: like that, your life expectancy went from eternity to seventy-odd years. A death sentence on you and on those you loved. He tried not to think about it; he thought about it all the time.

"Up," the woman told his wife. Her ass was alarmingly red, and all she'd had was a so-called warm-up. "Jihyun, turn around. Look at me. You know, don't you, that we're just getting started? And you can't do a thing about it. Scream if you like, and no one else will hear you. If you try to get away, Paul and I will stop you. You're not going anywhere."

Jihyun looked—glassy, as if, Ava's threats to the contrary, she wasn't entirely here. "Are you okay, Jihyun?" he said. "Is this what you want? Is there anything else we should be doing?"

She blinked a few times, and shook her head. "I'm all right," she said, the words sluggish. A glance at him, and back to the dominatrix.

"Poor little Jihyun," Ava said, in singsong. "You're such a very submissive little girl, aren't you?" She spoke over her shoulder to Paul. "Your wife doesn't want to be asked what she wants. What she wants is to be told what to do."

"How do you know what she wants?"

"For one, because your wife told me so," she said. Ava had required a half-hour phone consultation with Jihyun before the session. "Plus, you see how she can barely talk? She's so high on endorphins, they're scrambling her brain. It's beautiful to see." Smiling at him, Ava added, gently, "She's been like this her whole life. In all likelihood, she'll stay this way. People don't change."

Something inside of him flailed, upset. He hadn't even realized he'd been hoping that, somehow, all this would go away. That they'd have their little excursion into the foreign land in which he was expected to beat his wife, then they'd come back to their cozy, normal life in which they took care of each other. But the dominatrix was still talking. "Right now, she just wants to be good, isn't that right, Jihyun?"

Of course, if he'd known what to expect, they wouldn't have had to come here. A week ago, he'd stolen out of the office early to get to stores before they closed. First to an equestrian shop on the Upper East Side that, according to Yelp, was the best in the city. He selected a few sturdy crops and whips. On second thought, he also picked out a zippered kelly-green canvas bag, to hide his purchases. Next, he rode the subway downtown to a sex shop on Sixth Avenue, where he bought a gag, a blindfold, and handcuffs. They sold whips there, too, but he knew—from his research—that they would be badly made, too flimsy to be functional. One last stop at a hardware store for a length of rope, and he was back on the subway, going home.

Jihyun called to say she was running late at the office. He waited in an armchair, drinking his Laphroaig and trying to read the *Journal*, but failing: nervous, though he shouldn't be. He had it all planned out. He was going to astound his wife. He was Mister Fucking Poppins, and when she walked through the door and he greeted her with the canvas bag, and she unzipped it and said, "Oh," and sat on the floor, like a kid, he figured, or, at least, he hoped, that everything was going to be all right.

She lifted her head, and her eyes were shining. "You're sweet to me," she said. He smiled at her. Then, he frowned. *Sweet*, an adjective fit for puppies and, what, figs. Wasn't his role now to be mean?

Soon, he had his wife trussed to the four posters of their bed, facedown, crops lined up at her side. "Jihyun-girl, I'm—going to hit you," he announced, like an idiot. The back of her head, banded electric pink with the blindfold, nodded her assent. Shostakovich was playing, in case of neighbors. Her hair split away from her head like black wings, but he knew she didn't want to fly away, so he raised his hand and let it fall on her trouser-covered ass.

Things went well enough, as far as he could tell, at first. Per the instructions in *Screw the Roses*, he steadily increased the intensity of his blows. At some point, he started wielding the lightest of the three crops. He could feel the Scotch; still, his aim was good. Jihyun wiggled, and cried out a little, but the knots held—he'd studied that, too—and they'd agreed on a safeword, "red," if things got to be too much for her, and it wasn't natural, frankly, it terrified him, to hurt her, but it was like trying to speak in tongues for the first time when every other believing kid but him could do it, his father telling him all he had to do was loosen up, open his mouth, and let God in, let God work, so he gave it a try, jumbling together consonants until he was yelling out something that sounded about right, and since doubt was the work of the devil, he kept going, telling himself that what sounded like squeals of pain were actually squeals of pleasure, and, in fact, he was starting to feel pretty good, getting into a rhythm, crop down, crop up, like Romeo-plus-a-whip, when she squeaked, "Red!"

"What is it?" he said, at her side, pulling up the blindfold. Her face was twisting with pain.

"You-hit-me-on-my-*tail*bone!"

"What's wrong?" he said, desperate, fumbling with rope knots. "What did I do?"

"Don't you know? It's unsafe," she said, wailing until he finally got her free.

———

So now Jihyun was fastened onto the black table, bottom up. The heels of her feet were dry, haloed in white bits of skin. A strap. A flogger. A belt. A leather paddle. A crop. A Lochgelly tawse. A ruler. A wooden paddle. A Lexan paddle. ("What's Lexan?" he asked. "A kind of plastic," Ava said.) A rattan cane. A Lexan cane. "This is how you hold it. This is how to strike from the wrist. Make sure to avoid her kidneys." ("Where, exactly, are her kidneys?" "Right here," she said. "And here.") "Swing from the elbow. Now, from the shoulder. Try her thighs. Yes, she's tender there. You can hit harder, if you like. That's it. Again from the shoulder. Don't mind her—it's good for her. She likes it. Isn't that right, little girl?"

Jihyun was yelping, her toes curling piteously into the soles of her feet. But no pleading, no safeword. Her ass was tingeing from red to bluish, which worried him. At some of Jihyun's screams, Ava tipped back her head and let loose a big laugh. He glanced at Ava, fascinated. The dominatrix wasn't faking it—she loved hurting his wife. Was he supposed to enjoy it, too, and how much further was this going to go, and exactly how often did she want to be hurt, and if he couldn't keep beating her up, then what, and what about *his* needs?

With each instrument, after a few strokes, Ava handed it to him, guiding him. She ran long fingers over Jihyun's skin, pressing marks and ridges, inspecting. He hesitated, and she urged him on. At some point, he noticed she'd soaked through the cotton, and there was a small puddle under her half-covered crotch. So this was why Ava had had Jihyun keep her panties on. He hadn't even known that could happen outside of the porn film demimonde, let alone with his wife. They kept an economy-sized bottle of lubricant in a bedside table because of how slow her body could be, sometimes, often, to respond to his.

Jihyun was gulping, possibly hyperventilating. He stopped hitting her, but before he could get to her Ava was there, bending down until her face was level with Jihyun's, which lay flat to the side, her mouth open. She raised the blindfold and said, "Breathe. Deep, long breaths. Breathe in. Breathe out. In. Out. That's a girl. I want you to keep doing that. Okay? You're all right. Shh. That's a very good girl. You're okay."

With each word her voice got lower and her face closer to Jihyun's until her lips, almost whispering, were no more than another reassurance away from kissing his wife. Her dark hair swung forward, a curtain. Jihyun inhaled and exhaled, visibly obedient. His prick, infuriatingly enough, was perking up, interested. Something about the two women, one little, one Amazonian, almost kissing. He'd have felt self-conscious, but hey, they weren't going to notice. Another few breaths, and Jihyun said, "Okay. I think. I'm all right, Mistress."

Ava laughed again, the loudest yet. She stood and said, "Of course, you're all right. I wasn't asking you, I was telling you."

He was tired. His right shoulder hurt. He didn't want to hit Jihyun anymore—he wanted to get out of here. He wanted to untie her and take her home, soothe her and have sex with her, his wife, whom he loved. But he kept going. Finish the session, he told himself. He got through the next round of implements, through Ava's jerking Jihyun's head up by a handful of hair and informing her it was a lucky thing her husband was so nice to her. "If you were mine," she said, "I'd string you up by your toes." She got out a paper-wrapped package of jagged plants—stinging nettles, she said—and next he got through seeing her stick the stems *into* Jihyun. Now there were nettles sprouting from his wife's ass, then came Jihyun's gleeful screams, and Ava's laughter, and which of the two was crazier, he didn't know, but because he was finishing the session he got through that, too.

On Ava's recommendation, Paul and Jihyun stopped at a pharmacy on the way home and picked up arnica gel, a homeopathic treatment that was supposed to reduce bruising. Once they were home, Jihyun rolled off her stockings, wincing as the elastic rode over her skin. Then she grinned—she was in such a good mood. When she asked him to help her put the cream on, he sat on the couch and she crawled over him, positioning her ass over his lap. He smoothed the gel over the discolored, swollen mass of her, and she sighed.

He was applying the gel to her thighs when it occurred to him that she was in a classic spanking position. If Ava were in his place she would give Jihyun a few more smacks, now, for fun, to hurt her just when she thought she was safe. Paul raised his hand. From behind, his wife was unrecognizable. He raised his hand higher, then he put his hand back down to the couch.

"Up you go," he said, and she thanked him, patting his thigh as she pushed herself off his lap. She stood, stretching, and she moved away from him.

Canada

by Callum Angus

I've had only coffee to drink, and the back of my throat tastes like rubber hose left out in the sun. I realize, as I normally do late afternoon with the sun slanting in, that I haven't said a word since waking up. I clip my toenails, put on a new shirt, turn left from the driveway to reach the fields outside of town, but the only farmstands I find are locked plywood boxes relying on suburban faith in the rough-cut slots for folded bills. I choose two tomatoes: one for the veins peeking through reddish-green skin, the other for the pucker where vine meets fruit. On the radio, archipelagos. I can't see them from here, but the announcer says they're out there, new islands made by rising water, like kneecaps in a bath.

I pass the greenhouse where Jay works a double shift. Forty-two acres tented over by white canvas. Jay and the others are torching the tomato plants row by row because of too many whiteflies. It's a sterile environment, and I'm not allowed inside. Inside they still call him Jenny.

At home in front of the sink I say *goddammit* after cutting my finger trying to filet the branzino. Bleeding, I leave them whole but gutted in a casserole dish on top of thyme and stuffed with lemons. The kitchen smells briny, garden-ish as I eat them, along with tomato slices floating in oil and vinegar.

A single Canada goose flies low overhead, squawking in the late evening, mid-March, eighty degrees, Massachusetts. Most birds have left, but I still look to see where the geese are going, hoping what's left of winter is enough for them. I can't tell which direction she's heading in the growing darkness. The squawking lingers like she's doing loops; she's looking for the others, she's circling the town, she's a mixed-up squawk of feathers and loneliness trying to get to Canada. Maybe Earth's magnetic fields have flipped, scrambling the tiny crystals in her head like microwaveable popcorn.

I always knew I'd enjoy the plague when it came. Bugs—tiny, flying—devouring everything in their path so all that's left are hundreds of brittle seastars bearing shriveled fruit. These I pull gasping from their plastic pots, throw their stems away to be trucked to the landfill. The tops of the plants, where the tomatoes grow, I pluck and place into big metal coffins. They'll go to the landfill, too, but we have to keep the infested harvest separate; we have to marvel at the wilted balloon of each tomato, its red long sucked away. It's an even trade: the whiteflies take my job, and I get to watch their devastation unfurl row by row. I try to look sad like my cowork-ers, drawing out the day for a few more cents before they're un-employed, moving slowly from plant to plant like zombies. But I won't miss it. What's money when they still call you Jenny? I want to tell the whitefly not to stop at the fruit but to keep going for the heads, not as juicy as the tomato but riper, more rotten.

Still no Jay when I wake up at eight. The goose is back a little after ten. In between I do the following: masturbate, check my email, fry eggs and sausage, brew coffee, read a violent book by a Portuguese writer. I sit down to write but nothing comes. Mostly I write because the most interesting thing for me to be doing is writing. Other times it's watching birds.

Instead of writing I go to the bedroom and open the top drawer of the dresser. On my side, bras in nude and black. On Jay's side a collection of thick Lycra tank tops. I pick one out, shiny like a bulletproof vest, and scrunch my torso inside it. The bottom pinches the skin just above my belly button. My breaths become shallow puffs. I pull on a pair of straight-fit jeans and a button-up. Finally, one of his caps.

It's a relief not to be me in the mirror anymore.

The fuel gauge reads almost empty, but I don't fill it because I've decided the most interesting thing for me to be doing is driving a new road, not pumping gas; the most interesting thing right now is not unleaded or diesel, it's the sun setting across that field, it's the way the power lines cut a hole through the oak trees, it's the yellow film of pollen on top of a stagnant pond. But then it's also keeping my eyes on the road so I don't crash; survival often becomes the most interesting thing, while still being sort of banal.

I park at the college and walk down to the lake, an oblong amoeba carved from the dirt by backhoes in the middle of campus. A flock of geese hollow out the afternoon with their honking. The closeness of their feathered bodies makes me horny, and I start to count the string of eighty-degree days since Jay and I last had sex. I stop when it exceeds one equinox and a solstice. Jay's binder is itchy under my shirt, and the hot-cold sweat collects in my armpits.

Wanting to see them take off all at once, I watch the geese for a while, but they make no move to fly. I'm the only one standing by the water looking at the birds, and even though I don't have anywhere to be I start to feel conspicuous and sad, like I've lost a game I don't want to be playing.

_____

The bugs are gone or burning now, the last paycheck's been collected, and I'm sitting in my truck wondering where to go. After hosing down the greenhouse we sprayed a chemical foam over everything the whiteflies might have touched, and now the only thing appealing is dead, dried meat, so I buy two packs of jerky at the corner store before going home. Out front the rhododendrons bloom the third time this spring like nothing's wrong. The rain gauge is Seattle-full. Lawn moldy, worms drowned and decomposing. New England has lost its shit. On the kitchen table, junk mail piles up: debt collections, library fines, student loans, all auto-mailed in cellophane windows to my old name, husks of my former self collecting like the papery exoskeletons of dragonflies. I hear Nina's car pull in while I'm chewing jerky and it's with the salty-sweet tang in my mouth that I see her, chest flattened, dressed in my clothes. I pull her into the bedroom and tear them off her. It's been so long since it's been this natural, since I've seen my hands, stained green from the tomato plants, cling to her body like she's an ancient ruin in jungle country. I want to erode her stone by stone, make her fall apart.

Driving home I hit five green lights: Moss. Seaglass. Celery. Mouthwash. New leaves. I park at the quick-stop down the block from home and get excited-scared in my chest as I walk in. *DING* goes the welcome bell. No one looks at me. I'm pulling a ginger ale from the cooler when I see him, two aisles over, hair sweated flat, the hint of a beard starting on his chin. He passes by me on his way to the checkout, but I don't call out and Jay doesn't see me. He buys his miserable lunch and leaves, looking haggard from sleeping not at all or just in his car.

My invisibility feels like a passport. Suddenly everything feels open, like I could adapt to anything.

When I get home Jay's truck is in the driveway. I walk into the kitchen and he sees me. At first I think he might get angry. He's never said I couldn't wear them, and we've shared clothes before. But then a familiar look in his eye. It's been since before the sap stopped flowing, before I worried about losing the geese, that I saw that look.

We go to the bedroom, and I expect him to protest when I climb on top because he's tired, but the hormones make him hornier and his green hands are on me. It's disturbing to watch them creep like vines around my areolae. After we finish, I think about this coming back together, what it will look like for us with so much different and still the same.

Then I hear the squawking. Louder now, and even inside I know it's a flock. I rush to the window and their dark swarm appears in the triangle of sky between the barn and the sugar maple. North. Their V is pointing north. They no longer want even our winter warmth. I run to the kitchen to warn Jay that these last signs of seasons are fleeing us, but he's already heard. He's pulled out the bottle of champagne we were saving and popped the cork, saluting a birdless state, toasting the last of them with big gulps, their squawks petering out as they head away from this unseasonable heat.

———————

After sex I like to water the houseplants, share with them my body after fruitless mating and feel the heat of their little blossom breaths on my skin. Then the geese start up. I go to the kitchen window and there they are: going. Nina comes out looking like she's about to cry, and part of me wants to go to her and tell her we'll be fine without them. But these days all she cares about is that she'll never see a goose again. She goes back to the bedroom and shuts the door. The last goose passes over our patchwork of scorched fields, our dried-up lakes, our barren greenhouses. If geese can't hack it here, good riddance. Good riddance to the delicate snowberry, to black-footed ferrets, to salamanders that can't deal with rising water. I want nothing incapable of change. I want cowbirds and milfoil. I want kudzu and knapweed and snakeheads and cheatgrass and bark beetles. I want the false webworm—I want plants that can withstand a flood, insects that won't apologize for taking up space, things that shouldn't thrive but do because conditions are finally ripe.

Oh, Youth

by Brandon Taylor

The dinner party was almost over.

Grisha smoked out on the terrace, his shadow on the lawn. The other guests had stopped smoking some years before, or so they'd said when Grisha had excused himself. They had smiled and nodded, their dental implants slightly discolored from coffee and wine and life, the flash of their grayed canines. "Oh, youth."

The house was nestled near the milky blue pond in the heart of the arboretum—it belonged to James, who was a friend of Victor and Enid, and his second wife, Ramona, who Grisha sensed almost immediately was not. At the start of the evening, Ramona had opened the door for them, and Grisha had found himself involuntarily staring at her dark lipstick and the large growth on her neck. She had seemed to brace herself as she let them in, not saying *welcome* or *hello* so much as humming tightly at the back of her throat. It was a sign, Grisha thought, of how the night would go.

The air was cool and damp. Overhead, a field of glinting white stars. Quiet, except for the music streaming through a window somewhere around the front of the house near the garden.

"Here you are," Enid called from behind him. Grisha turned and watched her approach through the low cloud of cigarette smoke. She was a tall woman in her late fifties, beautiful in the way that certain women become later in life, as though all their years of plainness had been rewarded with a sudden flare of beauty. Her hair was naturally light, a soft gray cold color, and her eyes were quite close together, which made her gaze censorious and accusatory. "I found you," she sang.

"I wasn't hiding," he said. "I told you I'd be out here."

"That's a filthy habit," she said, plucking the cigarette from his mouth. She did not inhale, just let the filter press to the surface of her lips. He watched her watch him. A dark gnat landed on her collarbone. Her face was caught up in the pool of shadow between their bodies, and her expression became vague, inscrutable.

"So I've heard," he said.

"It's not personal, baby. Don't pout." She inhaled. Folded her arms and put her head back a little. "It's so bad; that must be why it tastes so good."

"You sound like a cigarette commercial," he said. He put his hands in his pockets and looked away from her. She came closer to him in the dark.

"You can't be old enough to remember cigarette commercials," she said. "What are you, twenty-five?"

"Twenty-five," he confirmed, smiling, feeling his face go taut.

"Do you know what I was doing when I was twenty-five?"

"No," he said. She blew the smoke up into his face. It was sweet and pungent. He breathed it in.

"Married," she said. "Married to Victor. Living in Portland."

"Another life," he said, laughing. In the car on the way over, Enid had leaned against her seat, squeezed her legs together, and said with a sigh, "Another life," when Grisha asked how long she had known James and Ramona. But then she glanced back at him and said, "But that was before Ramona. Claudia was still alive then. She was still okay." Truthfully, Enid had said it every week, before each of the parties they had attended, *Another life, another life, another life*, as though it were a standardized measure of time. Victor would lift her fingers from the center console and kiss them, and Grisha, in the back, fiddling with the buttons of his shirt, would look out the window and catch Enid's eyes in the wing mirror.

Enid held the cigarette close to her lips and watched him through the sideways drift of the smoke. Grisha saw the faintest smudge of her dark lipstick. He could hear the shaft burning: a soft crackle.

She started to say something, but then, seeming to think better of it, said, "You hate these parties, don't you?"

"No," he said. "I just don't know why you keep bringing me."

She nodded at this but did not supply an answer. He took the cigarette from her and took a drag. The taste of her mouth was in the filter.

"We don't twist your arm. You could say no."

"Where would the fun be in that?"

"Where indeed," she said with an expression of half pain, half boredom.

"It's not so bad."

"Amen," she said, taking the cigarette back from him and taking a long, slow pull. Grisha's eyelids tingled, and he took a step toward her. Enid's tone had been dry, but he did not know in that moment how to read its texture. She turned from him, and the light of the party lit a strip of her skin. She laughed a little.

Grisha held his breath.

"It's the last party of the season," she said. "You can tell by the light in the sky, you know. This exact hour, three months ago, there was still light in the sky, but now, well . . . it's all used up."

"There's still light," he said.

"The young are still idealistic. There's that at least," she said and dropped his cigarette, still burning into the damp grass below the terrace.

Grisha made a low, soft sound.

"I'm not going to fight with you," he said.

"Who's fighting?" Enid gave a little shrug, but then, as if tired of herself and tired of the circular, narrowing flight of their conversation, she gave a sharp nod. Grisha dug his hands into his pockets and made fists. His nostrils were burning. There was still smoke somewhere inside of him. He looked out over the lawn and saw the sad, diminished summer furniture. The blue plastic straps of the lawn chairs, the circular table, the dark metal of the low fence rimming the perimeter, which Grisha assumed had something to do with the hosts' small silver dog and coyotes, and which struck Grisha as so inadequate that he wanted to laugh, like it was a pun or a joke out of rhythm.

"I don't know what's so funny," Enid said, and she shook her head.

"It's nothing," Grisha said, but Enid was already walking back across the terrace. She slid the door open and left him there. He took out another cigarette and lit it. He sat on the edge of the terrace and crossed his legs. In truth, he'd wanted to get out of the party because he was tired of being asked how Enid and Victor knew him. It had been his least favorite part of these summer parties, aside from how Enid and Victor's friends touched him and ran their hands and eyes over his body like he was chattel. This question of how they came to know each other. Sometimes Grisha just let a long enough period of time elapse for the person asking to forget. Other times, he was vague and let them change the subject.

But it was a question that hung in the air of every room he entered with Enid and Victor. How the three of them came to be. In one sense, it had been boring and straightforward. They had contacted him via an email inquiring about his ad on a website popular with married couples of a certain age. They had exchanged pictures. Details. And that had been that. But on the other hand, it was impossible to be straightforward about such things. Particularly when Grisha suspected that they were only asking as a way to steal a little power for themselves because they knew, surely they knew. He had seen them, some of these very people, at other parties in other summers. They knew. They must have known, in the same way that Enid and Victor had known to come look for him in the first place. They were all a part of the same network of hunger and want, a collective of desire. Here this very night, Grisha felt that he might be laying the foundation for next summer's couple. And so they asked politely, gently, *And where did you three meet?* when what they wanted to ask was, *Might I be next? Or me? Or me?*

Earlier that day, they had gone swimming. Enid and Grisha. Victor had lain alongside the pool with a magazine. He hated the water. Enid and Grisha swam in lazy circles, gliding through the cold water. They had eaten a small lunch because of the party, and the swimming had been to train their hunger into a keener point. It had been Enid's idea, and he had gone along with it. Sure enough, he had found himself growing hungrier and hungrier the more they swam. He and Enid went into the house, trailing water across the floor, and in the bathroom, he'd peeled off his swimsuit and hers, and the two of them had pressed against each other in the shower. Enid had dug her nails into his sacrum so sharply that the pain of his skin breaking and the ache of hunger had been indistinguishable. They emerged to find Victor still beside the pool reading. Grisha had straddled his lap, taken the magazine from his hands, and kissed him hard. Victor had been beautiful his whole life. Grisha had seen the pictures. He was tall and lean. He ran every day. He was in his late middle age, and in tremendous shape. Grisha kissed him. Victor kissed him back, and when Grisha slid a hand into Victor's swimming shorts, Victor sighed and closed his eyes. He said, "What beneficence."

It had been that way all summer—the lazy easiness of their sex. The slowness of their days. They ate their lunches indoors, in the small nook beside the kitchen, where they had long, lateral views of the trees and the water. Grisha had been given a bedroom in the western side of the house, a place to store his books and his drafting table. He spent the morning watching the light come into the world, sketching, trying to get down the shapes that could be made into homes and monuments. What he wanted was to build something simple, something elegant, something dexterous, the sort of structure one brought all of oneself to, and which could change in a moment, in an instant, with the shifting of the light through its surface.

In the evenings, before dinner, they listened to music in the parlor. Enid preferred Schubert, for his sweetness, for the docility of his nature. Victor preferred Liszt, as performed by Martha Argerich. Grisha preferred watching the record spin, the smooth, rhythmic turn of its treads, the barely discernible undulation of its rim.

He'd lie on his back on the floor watching the record while they sat on the gray chaise, their arms linked together, watching him. And then, when the music turned, right before one song became another, he would feel, sure enough, the press of Victor's heel against his shoulder, and he knew that he was to come to them that night. Walk down the long hall that connected their rooms, pass quietly as he could into their bedroom, and stand at the foot of their bed, watching them. He was to come to them, put his hand over their mouths or their throats, or else slide between them in the bed and let them draw themselves up out of sleep toward the heat of his body, the sourness of their breath issuing out of their teeth and gums as they writhed and twisted until they were suddenly awake, their eyes startled by the shape of his body, by the suddenness of his presence. Sometimes he did not come to them. Sometimes he let them wake and find themselves alone with each other.

But now the summer was ending in the way that the summers always did. He'd say goodbye to them. They would pay him. There would be restrained, warm handshakes. Hugs.

Your generosity, your kindness, thank you, thank you, and just like that, the transaction completed, they would become strangers again. It had the crisp finality of a mathematical conversion. Money was clarifying that way, a useful boundary. Grisha preferred married couples. It was inevitable that they were anxious to get back to how they were. One party always wanted it slightly more than the other, and so one became relieved that it was ending. Like a spring pulled out of equilibrium allowed to snap back into shape. He had made the mistake of spending the summer with a single man two years before, and it had been a disaster. Carlton had been difficult to lose: he left messages, he sent letters, he sent flowers, he sent an expensive watch that had glinted up from its velvet box like the eye of a snake, he had emailed pictures of himself hog-tied and facedown, had told Grisha what it was that he wanted done to himself, had begged into the phone, begged like a crying animal until it was too pitiful to listen to the messages anymore.

Grisha blew the smoke out and over the lawn, and then he lay back on the terrace and closed his eyes. The wind blew westward through the trees.

Grisha's first summer couple had been Nate and Brigid Wollend five years ago. Nate had been Grisha's professor in Form II the spring of his sophomore year. Grisha had volunteered to be Nate's research page, which had mostly involved running over materials from the architectural library and having things copied and shipped—the work had been numbing and menial, but Grisha grew to appreciate its rhythm, its finitude. Fifty copies, front and back, black-and-white, twenty-five color copies arranged into these folders for a research review. Copy the last three pages of this write-up on flow dynamics.

Check these figures against the math from the consulting firm. Three coffees, no cream, two sugars each. Grisha found a kind of natural easiness to the work, to the scope of its demands upon his time and concentration. Then had come that thick day in late spring when Nate had asked him, as easy as anything, if he wanted to come up to the lake for the weekend, as a reward for all his hard work, for his steadfastness, for his errand running. Grisha had agreed with an eagerness that he now saw as foolish—how had he not seen it coming? How had he not known until the very moment Nate had turned to him on the edge of their dock and kissed him full on the mouth, how things would go? What he liked to think now was that he had let himself be snared. How else to account for it?

Under the weight of Nate's hand on his thigh, Grisha had gone still and quiet. The lake was flat and dark beneath them, and across its surface flicked the lights of other people's lives. It was still the cool part of the year, and Grisha had been wearing a lightweight sweater in a pale color, and Nate had been wearing a slouchy green cardigan. Where their skin touched, he felt warm and dry.

"I think we better not do that," Grisha had said with Nate's mouth still on his. "I think we better stop."

"Why? Do you not want to?"

"I don't know," he had said. "What about Brigid?"

Brigid had been in the house, built on an incline, made out of sharp angles and lots of glass and steel. Nate had laughed. "Oh, Brigid and I have an understanding."

"What does that mean?"

"You're not stupid, Grisha. Come on. I can make it so good for you. I can make it worth it, you know?"

But Grisha had not known exactly what Nate was referring to—he had known what Nate wanted, but not what he was offering. Grisha wanted so few things then. He did want things—decent coffee, food that went beyond what was free at campus events, drafting pencils, trace paper that didn't tear when he unfurled it, sweaters that didn't have holes in them, cigarettes, an apartment off campus. His life at the time was a series of minor discomforts that accumulated like grit in a socket until rotation was no longer possible. But he had no way of connecting the things he wanted with what Nate wanted, or it hadn't occurred to him to connect the two. He had thought that want was a closed circuit, sealed inside of a person, and what you made of it might become ambition or bitterness, but it was always stuck inside of you. There was his soccer scholarship, small and inadequate. But that, too, had felt coterminous with his own desires, not something that someone had offered him, though in that moment with Nate's palm on his thigh, it became clear to Grisha, for the first time, that it had been exactly that.

Grisha had laughed nervously then. Nate's face darkened, grew impatient. The dock beneath shifted and groaned.

"It's not a good idea," Grisha said.

"Boys," Brigid said as she came down the slope. She wore a lambswool sweater in a pale salmon color and blue shorts. Her voice was smooth and clear. Grisha tried to pull his leg away from Nate, but Nate cupped his fingers on the inside of Grisha's thigh and held him firm.

"Tell him," Nate said, looking back and up at Brigid. Her expression shifted, pinched slightly, and then she stooped behind Grisha and put her arms around his neck.

"It's okay," she said. She stroked his neck and put her face against his cheek. She smelled like flowers. Her arms were taut and firm. There was strength running through her, like a spring wound tight. "It's okay. There's nothing to worry about."

Grisha was quiet. Nate dug his nails into Grisha's leg. Brigid shot him a hard look.

"You're being a brute," she said. "He's just a boy. You're being a real bastard about it."

"The hell I am," Nate said.

"Do you not like boys, is that the problem?" Brigid asked. "You don't, do you?"

Grisha closed his eyes and tried to think, but the smell of flowers was in him, drowning out everything.

"No, I do. Well. I don't know what I like. I don't like anything," he said.

Nate snorted. He let go of Grisha and took out some cigarettes from his pocket. Grisha wet his lips.

"Oh, we've found something he likes," Nate said. He lit the cigarette with an impossibly elegant gesture, and something in Grisha grew hot and keen, like the end of a knife left in the sun. Brigid drew her hand across his chest in smooth circles in a gesture that Grisha thought of, with some mild anger, as maternal, as loving, as kind.

"He's just a boy," she said again, this time a whisper pressed to the nape of Grisha's neck. "Just a baby boy." Grisha could feel the press of her heat close on his back. He counted the freckles on her wrist and her forearm, watched the fine white hair shift in the wind. Nate's blue smoke was on them, hung in the cool air and seemed almost solid.

"He's not a baby," Nate said. "He knows what he wants."

"I don't," Grisha said. "I don't know anything." Brigid laughed at him, but he hadn't been trying to be funny. He had noticed that when he spoke to older people and tried to be honest about his thoughts or his feelings, they always laughed at him, as if he were telling some sort of joke.

Brigid kissed his neck, his shoulder, his cheek. She patted his chest and stood up. He felt the boards flex under them.

"Don't bully him," she said. "If he doesn't want it, he doesn't want it," and she left, going up the hill and then into the house, which, caught in the glow of the sinking sun, was a little bead of light among the dark trees.

Nate gave him the cigarette. Grisha sucked it down greedily.

"She's right, you know. I won't bully you. Hell, I don't know. I just thought we could have fun together. The two of us, I mean."

"I don't know about that," Grisha said. "You're my teacher. You're my boss. I don't know."

"I'm not your boss. I don't pay you. It's a volunteer position," Nate said. "Is that it? You want money? I can give you money."

Grisha narrowed his eyes, which stung from the smoke. He picked at his teeth with his thumbnail, swallowed.

"Money?" he asked.

"How much?"

"I don't want to talk about money," Grisha said, dropping off the pier into the cold lake. He held his breath for as long as he could, and when he emerged, Nate was gone.

At the party, Grisha spotted Victor leaning against the credenza in the front hall. When they had arrived, Grisha had seen the three of them in the circular mirror that hung above the credenza, which was adorned with small dark statues made of wood or ebony. The reflection had startled him. He had not recognized himself for a moment. He was tall and dark-skinned, which seemed even more prominent between Enid and Victor. The summer suit they had bought for him, elegant, cut slim along the line of his body, seemed like an oxymoron of a sort. He had grown up thinking of himself as ugly, as stupid, but here he was among all of the beautiful things in life—fine architecture, sumptuous design, elegant food on delicate plates, surrounded by an array of grayish-white people who smiled and said erudite things. It had surprised him, that was all. But now, here was Victor looking forlorn, looking tired. He wore a dove-gray turtleneck, and there wasn't a speck of hair or lint or dust on him. Grisha brushed his fingers across the velvety surface of Victor's sleeve and smiled.

"There's my boy," Victor said, putting his arm around Grisha, locking it at the elbow so he couldn't get free. Victor sniffed. "Smoking, how bad. You don't deserve that body."

Grisha flinched a little, but Victor just settled him closer while they leaned against the credenza. At the end of the hall that opened into the interior of the living room, they could see the backs of the other guests. Victor's hand rested between Grisha's shoulders. In his other hand, a glass with two fingers of whiskey. Victor lifted the glass, and Grisha took it. He sipped from it the way a child might. It was bitter but sweet, and it burned a channel down his throat when he swallowed. Grisha crossed his arms. He made a noncommittal sound. His stomach ached. The smoke had turned sour on his belly. He had been trying to quit now for some weeks. It kept coming back to him, nestling up to him like a faithful animal.

When he had stopped smoking at Victor's request, the colors of the world had deepened and grown richer. The blue of the sky outside of his room at their house, the green of the leaves, all of it felt supple and clear. When he had stopped smoking, everything had grown crisp and sharp. He could see. He could run again without heat in his lungs. The ache in his knee subsided. He ran long hours in the park. He became fleet-footed, agile again, as when he was gangly and fourteen in a Chicago suburb, dreaming of going pro with his friend Marshall, or at least to Northwestern. He turned away from the memory of Marshall's face, because it came, in his mind, with the memory of Marshall's mother, the long, dark pull of her stare in the rearview mirror as she drove them home from practice, all sweaty and tired and bruised up. Marshall had turned fifteen and then sixteen and then seventeen, and then something in Marshall's brain had burst on a rainy day in October. Marshall had died in the old clubhouse at the edge of the park fields where the two of them used to go sometimes, before practice, to smoke or beat off or test each other, feel the changing shapes of their bodies, how suddenly they'd become men, or something like men. That day, Marshall had gone there alone, to be alone, because of an argument they'd had in geometry. A stupid fight about something that Grisha could not remember, that's how unimportant it had been. He'd gone there all alone. Dropped dead. Right there. By himself, with the sound of the rain tapping on the window, on the roof. He had found Marshall. He had found him and run across the street to the small corner store, panting, doubled over. He'd said, "Call someone, call someone." But by then it was already too late. The doctor said that Marshall's death had been sudden and merciful. When he thought of Marshall now, he thought of Marshall's mother those years before, when she'd looked at him like she wanted something, and how slowly that look changed in memory from wanting to hating.

But he'd gone and smoked tonight anyway, knowing what it would do to his body, knowing it would make him sick.

He'd done it. Because he was stupid.

"Where are you, space cadet?" Victor asked, and his hand was moving around Grisha's side to his hip, in the way Enid's had done. "Are you all right?" His dark blue eyes were narrowed in concern. Grisha smiled, nodded.

"I'm fine," he said. His lower lip twitched.

"I've been tired myself," Victor said with a soft laugh. His palm was warm against Grisha's neck. "The summer's almost over."

"So it is," Grisha said with a brief smile.

"Can you believe it's been three months already? Where does the time go?"

Grisha pressed the rim of the glass to his gums and nodded. It had seemed like no time at all since he'd come to live with them.

Three months was no time. Three months was no life at all.

"Well, we're very proud of you," Victor said. "You're going to make a fine architect."

"Come on, Victor," Grisha said, shaking his head. "It's impossible. You know that."

"It's not impossible. Not for you," Victor said, and his eyes were damp, and glistening, which startled Grisha. Victor's thumb brushed Grisha's carotid artery. Grisha swallowed. Victor passed his thumb higher until it ran across Grisha's lips, and he kissed it. Victor's eyes grew darker, damper. "You're going to be magnificent."

"I'm going to be a corporate chump," Grisha said, trying to laugh, but finding his voice thick and raspy. Victor drew him in for a hug, and the two of them embraced in front of the mirror. Grisha put his chin on Victor's shoulder, felt the sudden tight security of Victor's arms close around him. It was different from what their bodies usually did together, and Grisha felt the curious, weightless sweep of what he'd felt when Marshall had hugged him those years ago. His body, which often grew hot and stiff with inflammation, felt whole and good and loved. That's what it was, he realized. Tenderness. Love. No one had ever been in love with Grisha before. It had never occurred to him that someone might fall in love with him. He had loved Marshall. He had even loved Nate and Brigid. But no one had ever loved him, or made him feel loved. He felt dizzy and hot and a little sad. He could smell Victor's cologne, dense and musky. Someone loved him. Someone loved him. Someone loved him.

"You're nobody's chump, kid," Victor said. "And if you ever . . . well, you're not."

"Thank you, Victor," Grisha said. "For everything."

"Of course," Victor said, laughing. "You sound so formal. Like you're heading off to war."

"Oh," Grisha said, and he was embarrassed to feel warmth in his eyes. "Oh God. You're right."

"We support our troops," Victor said, and Grisha pulled

away from him, blotting at his eyelashes with his thumb. "What? My jokes aren't that bad."

"No, it's me," Grisha said. He shook his head and tried to laugh it off. "I'm a real baby tonight."

"You are a baby," Victor said. "Positively fetal."

"And what does that make you?"

"Don't be mean, Grisha," Victor said, and his voice was hard. His eyes glinted. There was tension in his jaw. Grisha reached out and tried to brush Victor's cheek with the back of his hand, but Victor slapped his hand away.

"Come on," Grisha said, trying again, and Victor slapped his hand away again, so Grisha pushed away from the credenza, caught Victor under his throat, and shoved him with one quick motion against the edge of the archway. They were in the shadow of the foyer. Victor's eyes narrowed, turned dark. His mouth fixed itself in a stern line. "Look at you," Grisha said.

"Look at me," Victor said, and Grisha felt Victor's palm groping between his legs. Such ugly desperation.

"Don't be pathetic, Victor," Grisha said, but Victor was already pushing out toward him, pulling at Grisha's waist. Grisha felt hot. His mouth dry. He dug at Victor's lips with his free hand, pried at them, but Victor clamped his mouth shut. "Open like a good boy." Victor did not open, so Grisha pressed on his throat and leaned closer so that their noses touched. Victor's hands stilled on Grisha. He could feel the fingers, stiff, taut, like suspension wires keeping the two of them together. The noise of the party fell away.

Victor was breathing hard. A white foam beaded at the corner of his mouth.

"Open," Grisha said, low, and Victor did open, just enough for Grisha to wedge his lips apart. Grisha inhaled and spat into Victor's mouth. He snapped Victor's mouth shut, saw the wild, furious beat of the vessels in Victor's eyes. "Swallow," he said. The cartilage in Victor's throat rose and fell, and Grisha watched his pupils contract. He could feel it in Victor's body, could feel Victor plummeting down through himself into humiliation and then into pleasure.

"Is that what you're proud of?" Grisha asked. Victor's muffled groan was neither assent nor denial, but it left Grisha feeling damp and unhappy. He let Victor go.

Enid's laughter trailed into the hall.

"I'll see what she's up to. Do you want another?" Grisha asked. Victor was coughing, massaging his neck. Grisha felt a little guilty. A little sad about the redness. The bruise.

"No, I'll come with you," Victor said, his voice thready. He put his arm back around Grisha's waist and drew him along the hall into the living room, where the others were sitting elegantly on the lean, muscular furniture in its modern gray tones. Enid was near the archway, across the room, at the edge of the kitchen. She was talking brightly to three other women of relatively the same age and size as her. She looked up, saw him, and waved him over. Victor let out a low chuffing sound, like a laugh.

"Grisha," someone said at his left, and Grisha turned to see Ramona.

"Hello," he said. On the long gray couch, two men and two women, their skin a rich, deep tan. Open shirt collars, black dresses. The room had the inflection of a funeral or a wake. They were all laughing.

"Do you have a moment?" she asked. "I'd like your help with something." Victor let him go.

"I'll go see about Enid," Victor said, moving away toward Enid, across the room. Ramona's hand was on Grisha's elbow.

"I do," Grisha said.

"This way," she said. "Please, if you'd just come with me this way." She paused, glanced at him over her shoulder. Grisha felt a familiar tightening in his stomach, that stutter-step that comes right before recognition. He followed her into the hall and then into a small room off from it. The air was cool. The room was dark. Grisha held his breath.

There was just enough light down the hall for Grisha to make out the depth of empty space in front of him. The music from the front of the house was louder here. It was some cover of an old song by Jacques Brel. He recognized it because it was Victor's favorite. He had come to know things like that about Victor and Enid: Their favorite songs. Their favorite meals.

"Are you enjoying the party?" Ramona asked, and Grisha could make out the shape of her in the dark now, near the window on the far wall. He stood in the doorway.

"Yes," he said, "though I guess I'm getting a little tired."

"Nonsense," she said firmly. "I don't believe that's true at all." She was crouching near the wall, rooting through something.

"Would you like a light?" he asked.

"No, just a moment, just a moment. Be patient."

Grisha nodded, but then he realized that she probably could not see him, and that was just as well. Patience came easily to him. Waiting had become a habit, like smoking. Waiting had as much to do with his relationship with Enid and Victor as the sex. The room smelled faintly sweet and damp, like an ice cream store.

"Here," she said, coming back to him. She handed him something heavy and cold, one of those plastic coolers. "For the party. We made a dessert, and we forgot to put it out."

"Oh," he said. "Oh, of course." He carried the cooler into the hall.

"It's torte. With salmon roe. We thought it'd be a nice note to end the summer on," she said, smiling, and smoothing the front of her dress down. They stood in the hall very close to one another. Over her head on the wall was the black-and-white framed photo of her and a man not much taller than her and a small, sexless child. They were not smiling in the picture. She did not look like herself, so much so that Grisha wondered if it wasn't her in the photo but someone else. It could be that way, but he'd never asked.

"Sounds great," he said, lifting the cooler higher so that it didn't slip. She raised a hand to tuck a strand of hair behind her ear. She noticed him looking over her shoulder and she turned and saw that he was looking at the picture. She cleared her throat.

"That's his first wife," she said. "She died. Cancer. It was very sad. It was very hard on him. He was alone for a long time before we found each other."

"Oh. It's nice you ended up together " he said, but she didn't seem to hear him or care one way or another what he said.

"That's his first wife," she said again with a voice that was like tightening a screw. Something in that moment darkened and dilated, and it felt like time itself was opening up, making space. But she didn't say anything. She ran her hand down the back of her dress, gave him a tight a smile, and moved down the hall. After a few steps, she stopped and looked at him again. "It'll melt if you don't hurry."

———

The torte was beautiful—a matte crimson surface studded with clusters of orange salmon roe. It rested on a small transparent dais in the cooler, which had been filled with liquid nitrogen. It was as if it rested on a cloud. Grisha set the cooler on the coffee table in front of the sofa and stood up. The other guests gathered around, and he felt some small measure of pride though he had only carried it.

"It's gelato," Ramona said, standing near his elbow. "You wouldn't know it from looking, but it's gelato." She rested her head against his shoulder.

A man, whom Grisha presumed to be her husband, came across the room with a knife. He playfully jabbed it in Grisha's direction, and he said, "Watch your hands, young man." He winked at Grisha. He had dense, leathery skin hanging under his neck, and very pale eyes. His mustache was bristly and dark. He wore wool slacks though it was summer.

The man leaned down and cut the cake with a smooth, even motion. Grisha watched the long muscle in his forearm extend and contract. The man made small, encouraging sounds to himself as he cut the torte into sections, and Grisha watched the pale interior of it emerge. The scent of coffee lingered in the air, and he looked up to see Enid carrying a tray with small espresso cups and a small carafe.

"It'll go perfect," Enid said. She set the tray alongside the cooler, and the man leaned over and kissed her on the cheek.

Ramona put her arm around Grisha's back and clenched his shirt tightly.

"Yes, it will," the man said. "Thank you, Enid."

"How is Robert?" Enid said, sitting on the couch and crossing her legs. She was talking to Ramona, who did not answer her. "Ramona, Ramona." Enid's eyes went to Grisha's and he shrugged a little. "Well, James?" Enid's voice was tired. A person sitting next to her, one of the four from earlier, put a hand on her knee, and gave her a brief, narrow smile.

"Bobby's fine," James said. "He's somewhere in Oregon, last I heard."

"Last you heard?" Enid said with a little trill. "Ramona, can you believe him? The last he heard."

"Robert doesn't visit much," Ramona said. "He isn't like that. He does whatever he wants. He's always been that way."

"Not always," James cut in. "He wasn't always like that. It happened after his mother died."

Ramona's hand flattened against Grisha's back. He put his arm around her shoulders.

"It's a terrible thing to lose a mother," Enid said, leaning forward. She rested her chin on her hand. "How awful. Poor Claudia."

"You didn't know her," Ramona said.

"I beg your pardon. I did know her. I knew her well."

"You didn't," Ramona said. "You and Victor came here after she was already sick. She was different before."

"Enid did know Claudia," James said, and he turned the cooler in a circle, admiring his fine handiwork. "She sure did."

"You're just saying that," Ramona said. "You're just saying that to be cruel." She drew away from Grisha, and James looked up at her because he was kneeling. His eyes were large, to the point of seeming to swell out of his head. Enid was not smiling, exactly. She looked a little sad.

"Ramona," James said. "This is not the time."

Ramona pressed her hair flat against the back of her head and then crossed her arms in front of herself.

"There's nothing to get bent out of shape over," Enid said. "We're all friends here, aren't we? I didn't mean any harm."

"You didn't do anything wrong," James said. The man who had put a hand on Enid's knee moved from his chair and sat next to her on the sofa. He put his arm along the back of the couch. He was pale and lengthy like Victor, though lacking Victor's grace, the easiness of his range.

"I guess I just worry about Robert. I've known him since he was a little boy. I just worry," Enid said.

"Have him, then," James said with a brusque laugh, and he slapped the table. "Take him." He stood up with some difficulty, and Grisha offered him a hand. James squeezed Grisha's hand hard, and Grisha thought his palm might break. He pulled, and James came up and stood there, bobbling for a beat, for a moment, and Grisha saw a look of delicate fear thread through his face. If Grisha had let go a moment earlier, James would have fallen onto his face. Grisha knew it. James knew it. And in the span of time that they held hands standing in the living room, the secret knowledge flowed between them like a current. James let go. "We'll take yours. Where'd you pick this orphan up from, Enid? The bus depot? They're popping up a dozen a day. Like water bugs."

"He's one of Victor's," Enid said dryly. Grisha rolled his eyes. James stared into Grisha's eyes. He would not be put off until someone was ashamed of themselves. Grisha could see that.

"They've just been very kind to me this summer. I'm in architecture school. At the university," Grisha said.

"Oh, then you wouldn't have known Bobby," James said, but then, seeming to catch on something, "Do you know Nate Wollend?"

"Yes," Grisha said. "He was my teacher."

"Is that so? Well, he's a fine architect."

"He is," Grisha said easily, because he believed that to be true. Nate's architecture was conservative but very beautiful. There was a purity about his lines, and it was there even in his drafts, the clarity and precision of his lines. They drew the eye steadily and carefully into the structures he made. He liked to say that there was a quiet center of gravity in every building, the fossa around which everything else orbited. That was the trick of it. The center is not a mass but a void, and everything accrues to it, converges. It had all seemed a little soft-headed, a little tenderhearted to Grisha then, lying on Nate's bed at the lake house, feeling Nate's hand on his navel. It had seemed stupidly romantic. But he could understand it now. The simple elegance of it, which seemed almost beyond the point. It wasn't exactly what Nate believed. It was more the fact of his believing in it.

"He made this house, this very house. Years ago," James said.

"Oh, I had no idea," Grisha said, genuinely shocked and looking over his shoulder front and back and to the side, as if at any moment Nate might pop up.

"He was just getting started then. It's a beautiful house. A little small, but beautiful. My wife wanted something personal."

Grisha bit his tongue. James's eyes had softened. He had his hands in his pockets.

"It looks like him," Grisha said, which made James laugh.

"I wouldn't know. My business is in hearts, not houses."

Enid got up from the sofa. Ramona was handing out slices of torte on small plates. Victor was delicately massaging his neck by the sliding door. Outside, there was a wall of night. Grisha rolled his sleeves back to his elbows.

"Do you want help, Ramona?"

Ramona looked at him like he had slapped her. Enid paused near the chair where she had been previously sitting, across the room, near the archway. She laughed. Ramona handed him a slice of the torte.

"Enjoy," she said, and she turned from him.

James took Enid's seat on the couch, and Grisha went into the kitchen after Enid.

———

She was pouring a martini. She plopped a fat olive into it. When she saw him, she shook her head and laughed again.

"Aren't you just the best domestic a girl could ask for."

"That isn't funny," Grisha said hotly. He leaned back against the counter. He wanted to throw up because of how stupid he felt.

"Victor looks awful. Did you have a lovers' quarrel?"

"Enid," Grisha said.

"He's in love with you, you know."

"No one's in love," Grisha said, thinking of the moment in the hall, thinking of how stupid he had been to think, if for a moment, that Victor had felt something real for him, something detached from sex and want and desire, something not at all about the transaction flowing between them. It had hurt his feelings to realize the scope of his stupidity, how quickly he had let himself be fooled.

"Victor is in love," she said. "Victor is in love with you." She was singing it to herself, stirring her drink.

"Believe me, it's not love," Grisha said.

"He told me," she said, then, catching herself, "No, I guess he didn't tell me, but I can feel it." Enid stepped through the other side of the kitchen into the hall, where he and Victor had been speaking before. Grisha followed her into its low, dark channel. "He's in love with you. And he's mad at me that you're leaving." In the dark of the hall, she looked fragile. Her eyes were larger in the dark. Her lips were moist. She set her martini on the credenza.

"He wanted to ask you to stay," she said. "At the end of summer. He said, 'What if he stays with us? Wouldn't that be wonderful?'"

Grisha swallowed. She handed him the martini. He drank. Too much vermouth. He chewed on the olive.

"Wouldn't that be wonderful?" she said, and flung her arms out. "What do you think, Grisha? Would that be wonderful to you? Is that what you do?"

"I don't do anything that I'm not asked to do," he said.

"Well, Victor wants you to stay. You must be thrilled."

Grisha downed the martini and handed her back the empty glass with the toothpick in it. She looked down at it. She was close enough for him to put his arms around her, so he did. He held her close to his chest, and let her press her face against him. She closed her eyes. She breathed deeply. He could feel the ridged column of her spine. He could see the faded scar from the time when she was twelve and fell down a hill while hiking in Ojai. She had shown him on their first weekend together, turned around on the edge of the pool and let him see it under the strap of her top. She'd laughed. She was always laughing. He pressed his thumb there now, and she sighed. He felt love for her in that moment, and it was this love for her that let him ascertain the edge of her fear. She was afraid of being left, being discarded. Or else, she felt a fear of change sweeping toward her. A change in Victor, like a sudden outbreak of new weather.

"Maybe *I* should leave," she said sarcastically.

"There's no need for all of that," Grisha said. "I'm leaving in a couple of weeks anyway."

"Tonight. What if it were tonight?" she said. A flutter of panic, like a flock of birds alighting suddenly inside of him.

"Enid," he said. "Tonight? Right this moment? Are you serious?"

"You could just leave. You're young. You could just go. And it won't even matter to you," Enid said, and her voice had gone from wild to calm. The idea was gathering solidity in her mind. A plan was growing firm. Grisha shook his head.

"Enid, you know that's ridiculous. No one is in love with anyone. In a couple of weeks, we'll all hug and say goodbye, and we'll say what a great summer we had. And we'll pretend to keep in touch and then you will go back to your life."

"He wants you to stay," she said.

"He is being nice. I will explain—"

"I will pay now. I will give you your money—I would never dream of not. We've had such a wonderful summer, Grisha.

You're beautiful. Please, I would never think of not paying you what you deserve. But I can do it now, and you can go."

"What about my things?"

"I can compensate you."

"You want me gone that badly?" he asked. A strap of hot hurt pressed against his chest. "Why?"

"He meant it, Grisha. I saw it in his eyes. He loves you."

"He loves *you*," Grisha said. "With me, it's just sex. It's just summer stuff. Come on."

"He does. I know that. But he loves you enough to want to change our life for you."

Grisha pressed the back of his hand against his mouth. He could taste something metallic and wet. He closed his eyes. Is that what it was? Love enough to change your life. It was funny in a way, stupid more than funny maybe, that he felt, at this sudden prospect of losing Enid *and* Victor, losing the house with the great light, losing the tenor of their lives together, at this prospect of sudden and horrendous change, he felt himself wanting to dig his heels in and stay. A cold horror at himself: He wanted things to go on as they were. He wanted Enid and Victor to keep him. All summer, he had been waiting for the moment of escape, thinking that as long as he exercised his right to leave them, they held no power over him. The terms were clear. But now he had no power. Now the terms were in Enid's hands, and he could not expect her to think of him and what he wanted. He could not think of asking her to be merciful, not when she was the one who feared for her life. Not her mortal life. But her life with Victor. Her right to the procession of things as she had always known them. This was the end of his time with them. He could see it as clearly as Enid could conjure *another life*. *Oh*, he thought, his eyes beginning to sting. *Oh*. He had misplayed his hand greatly.

"Enid."

"Our life is not a toy for you to play with."

"I have not played with your life."

"But if you stay, you will be. If you stay, knowing what you know now, you will be—how can you do that?"

"This is unreasonable," Grisha said. "I promise you no one has ever loved me. That's not a problem you have to worry about."

"You are being selfish," she said. "You could go, and it wouldn't be anything to you. Right now. You could go, and have your money and your life, and leave my husband to me. You could go."

"I fucked you, too," Grisha said. "Not just Victor. You too."

"I don't love you," she said, and he winced because it hurt him to hear that. He did not love Enid, either, but hearing it called what it was, or, rather, what it wasn't, rang in Grisha's ears. He nodded.

"I know," he said. "I get that. I do."

"Didn't you have a family?" she asked. "What would your family think? Would you let someone into your family this way?"

Grisha bit the edge of his tongue, because yes, he'd had a family. Marshall had been his family. Not his mother or his father, who had been nice enough to him in that they had mostly ignored him and directed their anger, their heat, toward each other. His mother had been a boozehound and his father a shattered, withered man with a bad back and worse eyes. But there had been Marshall until there wasn't anymore. And there was, from the very back of his mind, a cowardly whisper: *you, Enid, and Victor*.

"No," he said, shaking his head with a smile. "Never."

"You are being petulant," Enid said. "You were never petulant before."

"You never told me to leave before. What about my things?"

"I will pay you for them. Mail them. Whatever you want."

Enid put her hand over her eyes. She sighed heavily. Grisha rested his back against the wall.

"Okay, if that's what you want," he said, offering her a chance to change her mind, but he knew she wouldn't.

"I want you to leave."

Grisha took the glass from her hand. He held it for a moment, admiring its lightness, and he lifted it to the light to peer through it. He saw the world distorted, a mass of shifting shadows and passing impressions. He turned it so that the curve of the glass fell upon the mirror over the credenza, which appeared at that angle, in that moment, like a silvered full moon, so full of light and nothing else. He did not see himself looking back through the mirror and the glass. He did not see anything except a white blur.

"Okay," he said.

"Do it now if you're going to do it," she said, and Grisha thought that she might be asking for proof for the both of them—if he did not do it now, perhaps he never would or could.

Grisha held his breath. He set the glass down again. She picked it up, pressed it to her lips, and realized too late that there was nothing left in it.

Impact Play

by Peter Mountford

When Gavin told his cousin Betsy that he was thinking of asking his girlfriend, Pilar, to move in with him, she said, "Wait, is she the woman you had an affair with?"

"Well, I was dating a lot right after the divorce," Gavin said, and told himself it wasn't a lie. Strictly speaking, it wasn't. Kind of. Gavin had shared tales of bizarre Tinder dates, and how he liked Bumble, and OKCupid lived up to its name and was just okay. But what he neglected to say was that all of this dating took place just after his separation from his wife, which also happened to be when he and Pilar briefly stopped seeing each other.

"But it *is* her, isn't it?" Betsy said. She spoke with that breathy, babyish inflection on the phone. If she weren't his cousin—and close enough to be his sister—she'd be a great candidate for a job in phone sex.

"Pilar is—it's hard to explain."

"You mean it's *unpleasant* to explain?"

He just groaned.

"Does she have kids?"

"A son, Iggy. He's with her three-quarters of the time. Seventeen. I've met him a couple times—he's cool. Plays guitar."

He heard Betsy exhale slowly into the phone. Out the window of his office, a cluster of mourners milled in front of the cathedral across the street, their black ties and dresses fluttering in a strong breeze. Then she said, "You've never lived with a kid—do you know what you're doing? Honestly, I'd prefer she was your mistress rather than someone you don't know."

Fair enough. Leading a double life had been so hard logistically, and it had been so stressful, so emotionally exhausting, but now he could see it was also much less painful than this honesty, this transparency. Melding his separate lives together was proving messy and chaotic, and he wanted to hold on to some of his secrets—if he told Betsy everything, she'd probably think he was a piece of shit.

"Wait—" she said before he could come up with a response. "Isn't she married?"

"They got divorced last year. Pilar is a mature person. It's very amicable." He hated the sound of himself, selling Pilar's worthiness, that whoever she was, she wasn't as bad as him.

Betsy wasn't exactly a paladin of marital perfection, either, but she had checked all the boxes with both divorces: years of counseling, compulsory date nights, and mirthless vacations displayed in Instagram-worthy snapshots—rictus grins revealing the drudgery underway. Bewildered and sweating at Chichen Itza, or leaning toward each other from distant chairs on a beach. But Gavin had concocted a Molotov cocktail for his marriage—he'd come home one day and announced to his wife of fourteen years he'd been having an affair for three years.

"Did I mention," he said, sitting back down again, "that my boss has been muttering about retiring soon, and I'm pretty sure the board expects me to take over? They like me."

"Nice change of subject," she said, and sighed. Their parents had been poor and crazed—dead, vanished, or in jail—and they'd spent five glorious summers together, a pair of only children. Their bond was by far the strongest in his life. "I'll get the whole story when you come down to see me. When is that happening? It's been like two years!"

"One year, actually," he said. "But yeah, too long—maybe this weekend?" In fact, he and Pilar were already planning to be in Portland that weekend. They'd been planning the trip for months, and the whole time Pilar had been campaigning to meet Betsy while they were there. She'd never met someone who knew him well.

"That's great," Betsy said. "Bring your girlfriend."

Betsy didn't know, and he would never tell her, that he and Pilar were going to Portland to spend a couple days with ten thousand fellow perverts at KinkFest.

To his horror—he tried to not even think about it—Betsy might have heard he was kinky. The day after the divorce finalized, Oriana had Facebooked a drunken screed revealing that he'd spent $1,100 on sex toys in the last year, according to financial disclosures. She wrote that he'd been secretly "obsessed" with a "fetish lifestyle." Seattle was just stodgy enough, even its arts community, that being a freaky two-timing BDSM practitioner could jeopardize his shot at taking over his boss's job. *Have you heard about Gavin?* people might whisper, wide-eyed, *the assistant curator of the Fillmore?* Oriana deleted her message the next day, but presumably a number of her two thousand Facebook friends—among them a lot of the Seattle art world, and Betsy, and some of her friends—had already seen it. No one ever mentioned it to him. But why would they?

———————

Almost four years before, his heart pounding in his ears, he created a profile on the website FetLife, but obscured his identity: his profile pic only showed his torso, and his biographical details were pithed for charm, not clarity. Among the upcoming event listings in the area he saw a rope-bondage tutorial. He scoured the potential attendee profiles, only signing up once he was fairly certain no one he knew would be there. Seattle was not only stodgy—it was also small. He'd spent twelve years as assistant curator at the Fillmore, and the top position came with a lot of public scrutiny. But he'd spent too long trying to smother his kink, and it wasn't working anymore.

He met Pilar at that first rope tutorial, which was held in a wealthy couple's brightly lit basement. Newbies were matched up, wide-eyed and thick-fingered. His rope work was disastrous, but Pilar was nice about it, even when he cinched a knot too tight and she lost feeling in her right hand. Aiming for casual, she talked about her work, but he was evasive.

She'd been designing headstones—"monuments" in that industry's parlance—for fifteen years, and had a thirteen-year-old son from a first marriage. Her son played bass in a thrasher band. "Thrasher music still exists?" Gavin had said, and she just smiled. Clutching a new coil of rope, he told her that he worked for a museum, and when she asked which one, he complained of being "already bewildered" by this unwieldy length of rope. They laughed a lot. It wasn't sexy. But it was easy and light, like tying up someone you know well.

They went for coffee two days later, and ended up at her two-bedroom condo just down the hill from the Fillmore. There, she showed him the toys she used on herself—her husband wasn't game—ones Gavin had seen in porn but never in real life. Nipple clamps, thick vibrators, plugs, a wide flat paddle. As long as he'd been sexually active, he'd fantasized about spanking women, tying them up, using blindfolds, gags. He and Oriana had been together since their junior year at Reed, and she had made a face when, ten years ago, he'd brought home a pair of fur-lined handcuffs that he picked up while in London for Frieze. She tried to seem excited, but she thought he might want her to use them on him, and when he said no, she grimaced. The following day he threw the cuffs out.

But Pilar took the toys as seriously as she took his veneer of confidence. She whispered things she wanted in his ear, things that, in the days and months ahead, led to furtive Google searches on his phone: *safer choking, orgasm control*. When he pinned her to the bed, she asked him to press harder. He learned to pull her hair at the roots, because he had better control and she preferred that pain. Sometimes after an intense scene, Pilar went quiet, distant. At first, he was insulted, thinking it meant he'd made a mistake. Then he learned to stay, wrap her in a blanket, and whisper that she was good and beautiful.

Pilar detested secrets; her family had nested secrets inside of secrets. The honesty was shocking at times. She told her husband whenever she met Gavin. Initially, Gavin also claimed that his wife knew, but after six months he confessed over post-sex scrambled eggs that his wife had no idea. Pilar told him to leave her apartment immediately—they were done. That was the first time she broke up with him.

The following day she texted to say she missed him. Two hours later he was tearing her underwear off her body as she presented her ass to him. She said he needed to match her honesty and he agreed to be honest with her. But he was terrified of removing the secrets supporting the rest of his life, and knew he couldn't control the consequences of that much exposure.

Over the next stressful two and a half years, she kept trying to end things, and he kept talking her out of it, until the breaking up and reuniting became a ritual, just like when she'd plead to not be spanked, and he'd spank her, and she'd thank him for it and beg for more. Along the way, he learned that she was addicted to BuzzFeed listicles, and she brushed her hair with terrible force. She learned that he liked to ravage her while she feigned sleep. She moisturized multiple times a day, head to toe. "It rubs the lotion on its skin or else it gets the hose again!" she sometimes taunted from the bathroom, aware that he hated *The Silence of the Lambs*. While they weren't paying attention, they grew together like trees that share root systems.

During the weekdays, Gavin and Pilar would meet at restaurants for breakfast or lunch and would talk about NPR news, earthquakes, and Brexit over breakfast. Their eyes connected, and their minds swirled with perversions. To a casual observer, they surely looked like old friends, even siblings. The only clue was that Pilar wore a stainless steel Eternity collar and a matching left-hand wrist cuff. The key to the collar and cuff sat snugly in his wallet.

Sitting there, he'd think about her back tattoo, a gravestone with her own name on it. A crow roosted atop, and a pair of butterflies rested in the grass below, near her pelvis. The date of her death on this "monument" was blank, and the epitaph read:

> *Impatient for it*
> *to end, but never*
> *ready to leave*

When fucking her from behind, he used to find the tattoo distracting. But he came to like it, enjoyed staring at the curvature of her hips, her shoulders, her jet-black hair. Even her stretch marks—none of it turned him off. He liked the meat of her, loved to kiss her soft belly—loved her lack of shame about her hunger. He loved the inside, too, wanted to burrow within and make a home there. He loved the sweet taste that flooded her pussy as she came. Sometimes, afterward, he'd lean against her, and plead with her not to break up with him anymore, but she would, again and again, until he finally told his wife.

———

By the time he told Oriana, the other, secret life he'd been nurturing with Pilar was bleeding into his secular life. For a prized solo exhibition at the museum, he'd argued overenthusiastically for a trans male artist who focused on the role of sexual pain in their work. His boss, Gertrude, arched an eyebrow and said, "Let's be honest, the board can only be challenged by a show once or twice a year before they grumble about feeling like they don't belong anymore." A concurrent spate of exhibits about poverty and homelessness had earned wary looks from the old guard. "Feels like politics over aesthetics," the vice president whispered.

When he refused to tell Oriana the identity of this "other

woman"—the words sounded like epithets in her mouth—she tried guessing: "That fucking gallery owner, right? Freckles!"

"I'll tell you later. I don't want you lashing out."

"I'm not going to fucking—oh Jesus, tell me she's not an artist."

The lack of information was driving her even crazier, so he told her.

She stared at him, dumbstruck. She said, "So you've spent three years fucking a middle-aged single mom—a goth, at that—who sells gravestones?"

He nodded. He hadn't quite thought of it that way, but yes.

"And you love her?"

"I do." He felt his separate lives colliding like two giant ocean liners at harbor, creaking against each other and then splintering, shattering. Would one manage to stay afloat despite this violence? Neither? He had no idea.

She sputtered, unable to think of what to say, until she said, "*Why?*"

No answer would make sense to her. After that, Oriana went eerily cool and explained that he was selfish, lazy, and a snob. Probably all true. She was also a snob, though. He might accuse her of enjoying her marriage to the assistant curator of the Fillmore Museum more than her marriage to the person who happened to hold that job. But he knew his betrayal of her was entirely his fault. It was so brutal, so cruel. There was nothing to be said in his defense.

So he said nothing. He just stared at her, and some secret part left him, some part he hadn't even known was there, maybe—it slipped out of his body and crossed over to join Oriana. And he worried it would never come back, that from now on a piece of him would be trapped over there, gazing back at him in disgust. What he and Oriana had created together—their terribly photogenic life—felt so impressive, so essential to their individual identities, and he quietly but totally destroyed it without even telling her something might be amiss.

"You need to get out of here right now," she said at last. He didn't plead. That was when he knew which boat had sunk, and which had not.

A week after he separated from Oriana, seizing with guilt, he broke up with Pilar—the one and only time he broke up with her. He dated widely, enthusiastically, but it felt desperate and sad, and he missed Pilar. So they started up again. Slowly, at first. She'd been dating, as well, and had also been disappointed by the experience. They just weren't very good at remaining apart, or holding each other at a distance. Now they were becoming accustomed to sleeping beside each other, which they'd never done before.

Recently, he'd invited her to an opening. But he knew that any number of Oriana's friends could be there—even Oriana herself. Pilar knew, also, and said it wasn't a good idea.

"Are we going to be hiding out, tainted forever?" he asked. But to be honest, he didn't want Pilar to see him as he was among those people, performing a charming version of himself, or obsequious with benefactors. Gertrude would be there, and she wasn't aware of his kinky side, as far as he knew. Best to keep everything neatly compartmentalized as much as possible. Oriana never showed that night—no doubt staying away from anywhere he might be.

In the ensuing months, he and Pilar began spending some nights at his postdivorce apartment. They began going out at night without feeling so paranoid. They visited a B&B/sex dungeon in suburban Seattle several times, as well as an awkward swinger's club near the airport, and two FetLife "munches" (innocuous dinners at well-lit restaurants where kinky people dressed in civilian clothes, ate drab pizza, and chatted about their mortgages, their cats' kidney problems). But in Portland they could go out together without scanning for familiar faces, or so they told themselves. And that was how they ended up with tickets to KinkFest.

Now here they were in Portland, without any plans to see Betsy—he hadn't spoken to her since that call earlier in the week. He'd become busy, he told himself. But wouldn't he see her? It was one thing to wander around Seattle, his shame dragging behind him like something he'd welded to his spine, but he couldn't let it destroy his relationship with his cousin— his only family.

Black curtains hung at the back of the conference center's lobby, which smelled strongly of an airport-style burgers-and-fries place. Once admitted past the first black curtain, everyone flocked past the drinking fountains and the row of bootblacks, waiting for anyone who wanted their shoes shined to KinkFest's "dungeon." Gavin and Pilar—both dressed comparatively normally, although her skirt was considerably shorter than she'd wear outside, and she wasn't wearing a bra—entered the double doors, flashing their wristbands, and found a hangar large enough to hold a 747 with room to spare.

He tried to soak it all in—the people, pieces of equipment (if you squinted, it might look like a vast sex gym)—but his gaze was hijacked by a hairless potbellied white man standing, eyes closed, while a woman—also white, with crimson Manic-Panic hair—sucked his cock. Wearing stockings and a short ruffled skirt, she was topless, head bobbing methodically like a Texan pumpjack.

Gavin averted his eyes instinctively, although the couple surely selected a spot directly in front of the entrance because they wanted to be seen by as many people as possible.

The hangar was arranged in two long walkways with shorter paths cutting between them every thirty feet or so. As Gavin and Pilar began to move down the closer aisle, he spotted a shapely woman with excellent posture wearing leg irons sauntering toward them, topless in patent leather pants, on a leash, and—this was what seized the gaze—her head was *gone*. In place of her head Gavin observed a giant orange balloon: cinched at her neck, twice the size of a beach ball. A shorter woman clad in latex held the end of her leash.

He reached out and clasped Pilar's hand, aware that his palm was sweaty. Hers was cool.

"I guess I would like to see Betsy while we're here," he said, surprising himself. "It's important."

"Being here reminds you of your cousin?" she said and laughed.

He laughed, too, shaking his head. They hadn't talked about whether or not to contact Betsy since they'd been driving past Olympia. "I don't know—it's just . . ."

"Hey, I get it."

He shook his head. "Let's walk."

So they began to wander through the hangar. "You want to see her alone?" she said. "I mean, I'd really like to meet her, but I guess I can hang out here, or go downtown."

Self-conscious about his sweating hand, he wanted to pull it back, but she held tighter. To their right, a beefy South Asian leather daddy in chaps was flogging a scrawny white guy.

"No, no," he said. "I want you to come, too. You should meet her. She should meet you. You'll like each other. I think. I hope."

And here: a cattle prod crackling against the thigh of a screaming woman.

"You sure you want me there?" she said. They were not looking at each other, but were staring at everything else. It was hard to focus on anything.

"I am, I am," he said, although he had no idea. In truth, he was terrified of the thought of the two of them together. They might say anything. Betsy could ask if Pilar would be moving in soon. And Pilar—she was disastrous at withholding information, and knew it. Everything would come tumbling out.

A man with a horse's head cantered down the aisle toward them, his weirdly long and thin flaccid penis swinging around like a prop.

Above them: a fleshy, naked woman suspended in a cage.

It was as if everyone there was vying for attention—as if the point of the dungeon was to exhibit yourself. Maybe everyone was, first and foremost, either a voyeur, or an exhibitionist? Probably so. Exhibitionist plus pony. Exhibitionist plus masochist. His life with Oriana was intended to be looked at, admired. He'd thought about that before, how he was, after all, a curator.

No curator was in charge here; the result was overwhelming, and somehow not remotely erotic to him. Ten minutes and he was full, couldn't take in more.

"You okay?" Pilar said, clearly not as overwhelmed as him.

Among the hip collectors and creators he knew, this kind of Utilikilt kink would have registered as sad and profoundly unhip. He nodded. "So many nerds," he whispered. "I'm guessing there's a lot of overlap with Renfair regulars."

"Maybe? I bet most subcultures look down on other subcultures. Like, I don't think these people would love Seattle's gallery scene," she said. "Besides, you're always worried about someone seeing you. But if someone saw you here, you realize they're just as much of a freak as—or freakier than—we are."

"Definitely true," he said. "I need my hand back," he said, hoping it didn't sound rude but knowing it did.

To his left, people were pushing needles through other people. There was gauze in large quantities, numerous boxes of surgical gloves, antiseptic, bandages—disposable paper on the floor. He glanced, despite himself, and saw black blood oozing from a puncture wound in someone's bicep.

"You want to go?" she said.

"I just need to sit down."

They sat on the polished concrete floor.

Although he couldn't see her body beneath her clothes, he was keenly aware that Pilar's ass and arms were mottled with dark bruises. She applied hot washcloths to her skin after a session, which darkened the bruises. Just knowing the marks were there was reassuring, calming. Also that her ass still bore red streaks after a recent caning. He soaked the cane in water, because she preferred thud to sting, and waterlogged rattan helped achieve that effect.

He looked around again. No cell phones were permitted, so those engaged in their scenes gazed at each other, not at anyone else or into screens. Everyone was here to celebrate and explore the range and volume of their aberrance. Here, in this place that would soon host the Northwest Quilting Expo. Everyone was sweating and bleeding and pushing their fluids into one another, shoving tongues and digits inside other people, tearing at skin, as if to flay open an entrance, and conquer this problem of being stuck outside.

"Would you like to leave, sir?" she asked again, more gently, and kissed his forehead slowly, wetly, in the way that he loved.

He nodded. "Do you think there's a—like, an IHOP, or something?"

"IHOP?" She laughed. "Gavin!"

He rolled his eyes. "I haven't always been a snob."

"Oh, it's fine," she said, the corner of her mouth twitching. "I'll bet they have crepes for people like you."

The last time he was in Portland, a year ago, he interviewed Marina Abramović onstage in front of three thousand people, and ended up spending more time with her than with Betsy, who he only saw once for coffee. But now here he was again.

Betsy had bought her cute little shotgun house in Northeast Portland with her first husband in 2001 before the real estate market went rabid. Her front yard was chaos: huge planters, some half-shattered, and raised beds colonized by weeds, an old white fence collapsing in on itself. The empty chicken coop was still out front. Pilar snapped a cell-phone shot of a rusted bicycle claimed by tentacles of ivy that stood nobly beside the house, waiting optimistically.

The doorbell sent a loud, abrasive buzz into the house. No turning back now. Pilar took a deep breath, almost visibly shaking. Her entire impression of him was based on what he'd done with her, or what he'd told her about himself. He heard Betsy stomping toward them across her hardwood floors. The door was flung open, and there she was, in a stained apron, sweat gleaming on her high forehead, an inch of gray roots showing, and he grabbed her in a hug.

"Hey, fucker, how are you?" she whispered tenderly as he squeezed her a bit too hard.

"Fine, fine," he said and pulled away. "This is Pilar, my . . ." he said and then hesitated before saying, "girlfriend." They interacted with so few adults, and almost none outside of the kink community.

Pilar held the orange juice and champagne awkwardly in the crook of her left arm as she shook Betsy's hand, and then they were inside, the house redolent of bacon, weaving between stalagmites of magazines and unopened mail growing between her threadbare furniture. Nothing changed here, other than a gradual accrual of ephemera.

Betsy and Pilar bustled into the kitchen and opened the champagne and were very quickly making strata. Betsy put Gavin in charge of hacking up the stale baguette, while Pilar put herself on egg duty.

"Sorry my place is a shithole," Betsy muttered as Pilar tossed the third eggshell into the paper grocery bag on the floor and Gavin took a long drink of coffee. "But I did remove the cat carcasses from the living room."

"I'm sorry about our last-minute invasion. We could have just gone to Tasty n Daughters, or something," Gavin said.

"Nah, eleven on a Sunday? Dude. Mick Jagger would still have to wait two hours." She inhaled, grimacing.

Both Betsy and Pilar were wearing all black—Pilar in a maxi-skirt and sweater, Betsy in yoga pants and a black hoodie—and they wore their dark hair at the same length, both pulled back into a rough ponytail. They were also roughly the same height. It had sort of occurred to him before, their resemblance, but it was a bit weird in the flesh. They were discussing tattoos: his cousin had a colorful floral tattoo peekabooing out from her neckline, hinting at a larger picture below.

Pilar's face and shoulders relaxed, as if merely meeting Betsy confirmed that Gavin existed, that others also knew him and loved him. It felt comfortable, too. And he realized with relief that this was what he'd wanted: for Betsy to see him, him and Pilar, and to accept them despite his very serious moral failings. And for Pilar to see him and his cousin, and see that he could love someone well, for a lifetime.

After a pause, Betsy said, "What brings you two to town?"

"I just—I was hoping to just . . ." he said. Even during the affair, he'd preferred to engineer omissions rather than generate lies. She laughed, gave him her look.

"Ack," he said. He'd planned a lie, but he was blushing so deeply he might faint. "Fuck—it's embarrassing."

"Oh, maybe you're in town for KinkFest?" Betsy ventured.

He barked a laugh and shook his head, then pointed the

remaining half baguette at her accusingly and said, "How do you know about that kind of thing?"

"I know things," she said. "I'm your older cousin. It's my job. Was it fun?"

"Sort of." He shrugged, still blushing, focusing on cutting the bread. "Really—how *did* you know?"

She was dicing a stack of ham slices into tidy little squares. "I guessed." She was also an inexpert liar. Oriana's Facebook post. He knew with thudding clarity.

"Did you see him on Fet?" Pilar asked, and then he wanted to die, but also wanted to stay alive long enough to flee.

"What's Fet?" Betsy said, and he couldn't tell if she was feigning innocence or attempting to draw out more information.

"FetLife dot com," Pilar answered, very matter-of-factly. He almost felt frightened on her behalf. There she was, collar and cuff glinting in the midmorning light. Nothing to hide. They had agreed not to overshare about their lifestyle, but they hadn't anticipated Betsy's line of questioning.

"And that's a—" Betsy began, and then said, "Well, sort of self-explanatory."

Pilar cracked the sixth and final egg, and Gavin said, "Oriana also—" but then he stopped himself. A few agonizing seconds later, he went on, "Oriana posted an accusation about me on Facebook, but . . ."

"Yeah," Betsy said and drew a deep breath, chopping the zucchini with focus. "I told her to take it down."

"*You* did?"

"Yeah."

"Oh." He almost teared up thinking of his cousin defending him. "Thank you." No one spoke for a while. All the more now, he actually wanted to just have out with it. After all these years. Maybe they could just clear the air?

But then the strata slid into the oven, and they were finishing the champagne at the kitchen table. Sitting there looking at them both, he realized he never wanted to leave. Pilar and Betsy were ribbing him for being too "fancy" and shallow—name-dropping some artist, or scoffing at something for being obvious—both in that same big-sister way that really meant love. Something he hadn't realized he'd missed with Oriana, until now.

He joined in, describing to their laughter abstruse essays he'd read about surface and depth in contemporary art, and the deep value of "shallow" art. How he bantered at donor's mansions cocktail parties, before the host dragged everyone outside to view his new helicopter pad on the south lawn, and everyone guffawed merrily at the big pink heart at the center of the pad—so subversive!

The alarm on Betsy's phone rang and she pulled the strata from the oven, dusted it in nutmeg. It looked amazing, smelled better. What the hell was he doing in Seattle? Career, yes, but he should be here, with people he loved. "Let's give it five minutes to think about what it's done, and then we'll eat," she said. "We need more champagne!"

Betsy poured, and Pilar said, apropos of nothing, "Neither of you had kids."

After a brief silence, Gavin said, "The bloodline dies with us!"

But Betsy didn't laugh. Staring at Pilar, she said, "Do you know why we didn't have kids? He's a pretty good liar, you know."

Pilar winced. "No, he's a terrible liar. Do you have the same reason? I guess it's the reason for many people—like, you know, their parents were so awful that the whole thing is poisoned."

"My mom, Gavin's aunt, wasn't so bad," Betsy pointed out. "Despite being wasted on vodka for a couple decades. And then she died, go figure." She had that hard, cold note in her voice, and Gavin hoped that Pilar heard it, too, knew to back off. "Gavin has shown you all of the skeletons. Right?"

Pilar hesitated, then said, "He's honest with me. Are you surprised?"

Betsy looked at her for a while, not answering, only appraising her—and it occurred to him that Betsy might think he'd told her their secret, the one so sacred they didn't even say it to each other. But then Betsy pivoted, and said, "How are you adjusting to being with this guy who has a million friends?"

"I've never met any of them," Pilar admitted, still impressively relaxed, like she didn't even notice Betsy's rising blood pressure. Surely she saw. "Anyone who has that many friends," Pilar mused, probably feeling the champagne, "maybe they don't have any real friends. You know? I have my, like, five or six friends, who I see pretty often, who I text with regularly, and whatever. But that's it."

It was true. No wonder Pilar didn't need armor; she never went into battle. Betsy was like that, too: ten to fifteen real friends, and she barely spoke to anyone else apart from the patrons of the municipal swimming pool she managed.

"You design gravestones?" Betsy said, surely in a bid to change the subject again. "That must be fulfilling. I'm serious. When our dad died, the planning was . . ." She just stopped and shook her head.

Pilar gazed absently at the cuff on her left wrist. "None of the people who come through ever send me a card to thank me. They never call or follow up. Honestly, I don't mind, but I think it's telling: they all want to forget the whole thing. I'm making a memorial, something to help them remember, and they just want to forget, because the memory hurts them."

"Maybe they just have nothing to gain from you anymore," Gavin said.

"Nah," Pilar said, and rubbed her cuff. "They're in their own well of grief. Meanwhile, Gavin is lost in a lake of people who want some kind of professional connection, but nothing more. And yet he's the only person who has devoted himself to me in, well, I . . ." But she didn't finish, thank God.

He knew then that he would ask her to move in, on the drive back. The board and the rest of his art community would learn to love or at least accept this goth mom, or they wouldn't, but if loving Pilar somehow ruined his shot at Gertrude's job, then maybe that was for the best.

———

"Iggy can have my office," he said, eyes on the road as they left Portland.

She grinned. "You're too drunk to drive, let alone ask me to live with you." Actually, the champagne had worn off, leaving him with a fuzzy headache. We need to think about it first," she said.

"I've been thinking about it. I told Betsy last week that I was thinking about it."

"So I'll be your little sex slave?"

He laughed. "Basically."

"Deal." Full of champagne and strata, she laid her head against the car door and dozed, her legs spread slightly.

Along that stretch of I-5, the car was buffeted by strong winds, and Gavin had to work harder to steer straight. Keeping his eyes on the road, he worried the radio for a station that wasn't country-western or Christian testimonials, a part of his mind still circling the secret that had almost come tumbling out over breakfast.

In part, he'd never told Pilar what happened with Betsy because he'd never told *anyone* about the unusually hot summer he spent with her and her mom in Eugene. He was ten and she thirteen. Late afternoon, heat bearing down on her south-facing bedroom, he was in his boxers and T-shirt, drawing on her floor, when he looked up to find her asleep, but she'd tossed the cover off and parted her legs. Dark pubic hair bulged in her orange sherbet underwear. His own mom was in jail, and his dad was nowhere to be found. Her own dad was dead, and her mother was out screwing the deputy mayor. So they were alone all summer. Of course Betsy wasn't asleep, but she wanted them both to act as if she were asleep. So he approached slowly, and when he touched her she pretended to stir, and then she lifted her hip slightly so he could pull her underwear down without "waking" her. He'd never seen a woman's genitalia up close. Listening to her heavy, fast breathing, feeling his blood surge through his arteries, he stared, and his rigid penis ached with longing for something about this, but he didn't even know what it was he wanted.

After that, they'd do this—her "asleep" and him "exploring"— maybe a dozen times that summer. Although unspoken, the boundaries of what happened between them were strict: he looked, he touched anything he wanted, and he put his fingers inside of her. Once, he tried to put his tongue on her, but she suddenly stirred, signaling disapproval, so he didn't try that again. When he was back the next summer, it was more of the same. It stopped the third summer, by which point he was entering puberty and she was fifteen. That third summer she'd turn away when he entered, or sit up and ask how he was doing. He understood she was telling him it was over.

But the pleasure sensors in his mind had been so aggressively stimulated that they wouldn't reset. He'd always be like this, with hungry hands and cock and heart, greedy for more, wanting to find someone who would hold him as tightly as he grasped them.

He was glad they'd done it, but never again had any desire to see her naked. He continued fantasizing about sleeping women, tied-up women, and he thought about releasing hot jets of cum into their pussies. And he jerked off at least three times a day from then on—even now he rarely made it through a day without coming two to four times.

His sexual appetite had astonished Pilar, but almost four years into their relationship she still wanted to give a backseat blow job, to receive the midafternoon quickie, hiking up her skirt and pulling down her underwear. Every other woman he'd dated, including Oriana, eventually asked him to cool it, but Pilar still wanted it all. If he was going to jerk off, she asked that he at least push the head of his cock into her mouth or her pussy at the last minute so it didn't go to waste.

Those hours Gavin had spent buried under the covers when he was on one side of puberty and Betsy was on the other had been the most intimate and joyous part of his life during those awful years. Yes, he would have to tell Pilar, maybe when she was tied up, belly down, facing away from him.

———————

At a gas station in Centralia, he peed and bought a big bottle of Smartwater. From inside he gazed at Pilar, awake again, leaning against the car, wearing her "Nasty Woman" T-shirt.

Her son, Iggy, was only a year away from graduating high school. Gavin's place was in the same school zone as hers, so when they moved in Iggy wouldn't have to switch schools in his senior year. The soundproofing was better in his apartment than hers, too, so Iggy could turn the volume on his guitar up a couple extra notches. They'd get used to this—get used to each other.

Now, back on the road north, the wind still shoving at them in gusts, he almost told Pilar about Betsy and those summer afternoons. But this secret was a tender, special thing, starting to burn now that it was the only one left between the two of them. The secret wouldn't last long, he knew, but he'd hold it tenderly until he finally set it free.

Mirror, Mirror

by Vanessa Clark

"I think I'd die if I don't find my destiny soon" were some of the first words he said. It was an afternoon in-call, and the boyish shyness of his voice betrayed that this was his first time.

"Okay . . . so, have you ever dated an escort before?"

"No, ma'am."

"Where are you calling from?"

"Um, Upper West Side."

Most of the men who used my phone service were a type: chasers, size queens for women with well-hung, functional cocks, like mine. Usually, my size was a kink in and of itself—these men didn't seek light domination, restraining, teasing, verbal abuse, and choking; not even me fucking and plowing them to death was the be-all and end-all. There was some of that, and how they'd *love* that, of course, but the service they sought was rarely the full thing. The fantasy that they craved, needed, obsessed over, was just to see it—they hardly needed to touch, or feel. Just seeing it would get them off. Sometimes, their basking in my beauty was enough to thrill us both.

As I kicked back in my office chair from my Village apartment, I caught some breeze from my loud window fan. I applied my dark hibiscus-red lipstick to pursed lips, already feeling myself and my freshly sculpted beat. Nancy Wilson's "Time Out For Love" played from my radio.

"I'd like to kiss you in front of a mirror," the stranger said in a newly husky tone.

"And?" I asked, as in, *Get to the fucking point, I don't have all day*.

"And, um, I'd like to go down on you . . ."

"So you're into *size*?" I asked.

He chuckled. "Yeah . . . I do have experience with that, I'll tell you that, but I think I'm ready to take more, and bigger, like you . . . Um, I'd like to make you come, I'd like to make you come."

"Mmm, so you'd say that you're a cocksucker?"

I almost thought he'd hung up on me—he was that quiet—but through the silence I heard him breathe so softly before his slow, simple declaration: "I am a cocksucker . . ." In that moment, I imagined him floating through the air on a cloud of the silence that followed.

"You've never called an ad before, correct?" I asked him, point-blank, I couldn't help myself. I laughed sweetly as I caressed my chest.

"You've guessed right, ma'am . . ." With a smile, I nodded. I ordered him to describe himself to me. "Well, I'm thirty. I'm single. I'm about five ten, one hundred eighty-five pounds. I haven't been intimate with someone in a long time. I'm tired of dreaming about it and masturbating in my sleep. I work all day and too much." He paused here, as if to take stock of the person he'd just described. "I think I deserve some fun time. Wall Street is stressful sometimes, ya know?"

"Uh-huh," I replied.

"Um, I might need a little bit of help and encouragement, though. It's been a while, but I want to get off to you, Teena, so bad. I'd like to get together with you now if it's not too late, or too early . . . I can make it in half an hour."

"Okay, I gotchu, but my afternoon schedule is full, I'm afraid. But I have a spot open for tonight?" I gave him the time and place. "Will that be all right with you?"

"That's fine with me. I'm familiar with that area, and that joint."

"Great. Can you spend one hundred fifty dollars?"

I crossed my legs, and he gently confirmed: "Yes, I can."

———————

The moon was high and full, the sky cloudless. The city was muggy as balls that night, thick with the New York funk. I passed by the strip clubs and porno shops, pimps and hustlers, trade and drug dealers, that littered Times Square back in the 1990s. From the distance, I knew it was him, waiting for me in front of Sally's II, a drag transsexual nightclub. Sally's looked swanky from the outside, with its glitzy marble structure and lit-up marquee. The lobby of the twenty-four-story Carter Hotel was conveniently connected from the inside by way of a catwalk, its huge, red neon sign clear as forever in the dark. As I got closer, I had to stop and blink—was he for real? I couldn't believe it—ha! He was dressed as if it were 1980 and we were going to the prom. Whatever planet he was on, well, I didn't mind it. The nostalgia made me kind of horny. But—thirty my ass; he had to be north of forty, and no taller than five two. I wouldn't put it past him to be married, actually, with a wife and kids somewhere. They usually were. They'd promise they were single, but there was usually a picture of their wife and kids in their wallets.

But still, this white boy right here, I appreciated the effort in his black suede shoes, highwater dark blue pants, matching jacket, and shiny silk white vest with ruffles. He even wore a fucking black bow tie that matched his cheesy grin.

"You look—you look even more beautiful in person, ma'am!" he gasped, eyes lit up. I knew I looked good in my skintight white dress that hugged the curves of my body, low-cut, showing off luscious breasts, a slender belt of gold cinching my waist, white pumps I'd stoned myself, sparkling. I wore a long, black, dark, and lovely wig that rested just above my collarbone. I glowed with the dew of makeup and humid city air. He stared me over, again—could you blame him? My hips, my bust, my ass, no foam or padding here, I was *real*, as real as the Tiffany diamond studs in my ears.

I smiled and petted his damp cheek with a creamy white acrylic nail. "You've been my dream all along, Teena . . ."

"Chile." I laughed, batting my falsies.

He was on a cloud, this one. As harsh as it may have seemed, I had to burst that bubble and bring him back to earth real quick. One hand on my hip, the other extended, meaningfully, waiting. With a big smile, he took my hand. He turned it over to stroke my palm with his thumb. I blinked, thinking, *Bless his heart, this fool, but what the fuck is he doing, and who the hell does he think I am?* When he seemed about to knit our fingers together in a tight embrace, I cleared my throat and raised my brow to remind him why we were here. He blushed, let go of my hand, and nodded. He removed his wallet from his pocket.

I counted the cash; exactly one fifty. Mr. Big Spender took the door handle from the doorman and held it open for me, ushering me in. My voice went from deep to high as I chirped, "Why, thank you, dear!"

Sally's II, formerly known as Sally's Hideaway before it was damaged by a serious fire in 1992, was like a disco-cabaret love child. It held a circular bar, two flights above the street, and a small lounge, up another flight of stairs at the side of the bar. The low-ceilinged lounge area consisted of dozens of small cocktail and pool tables, where some cross-dressers could be found laughing like hyenas, toasting to nothing but the rhythm. There were mirrored disco balls hanging from the ceiling, strings of flashing rainbow lights illuminated the expansive dance floor packed with men grinding on one another under a rain of confetti to the *thumpa-thumpa*. This was my illusionary world, my safe haven, my home.

My date didn't seem taken aback by anything or anyone. I figured that he'd been here before, even though I could also tell that no one here knew or recognized him—no one greeted him with a wink, a smile, or a hello. He had a charming, cool air about him. I saw in his confidence a clear respect—he knew that all the customers and performers here were contour specialists, self-made stars, show personalities; we were liars, cheaters, scam artists, frauds, blackmail extortionists; we were victims of circumstance, battling AIDs; we were leaders, role models, and survivors. We were a family daring to be beautiful, amazing, electrifying.

I met eye to eye with a few of the glamazons who also stood many inches taller than my boy. They were decked out in dramatic furs; wild, feathered, showgirl headdresses; ridiculous sky-high pumps; catsuits; and radiant, rhinestoned costumes. Some were practically half-naked, as epic and divine as hell. And my boy didn't seem at all out of place. I had told some of the gorls I'd be bringing this strange boy along for freewheeling fun, and they smiled and waved me in with a loving "Hi-eee, bitch!" and "We still on for our silicone appointment tomorrow?" and "I want to be as pumped as you, Teena, gurl, you look sickening!" as still, my date was ignored, as if he weren't even here, like some cuckold. He couldn't stop smiling; he *loved* it.

After I blew kisses at the emcees, the Dolls, politely, my date once more took me by the hand, and this time he pecked it a most sophisticated kiss that said, *I'm ready when you are*. I checked the time on his clearly expensive, shiny gold Rolex wristwatch, as did he. With a wink, I led us to the back dressing room. It was dark and seedy, setting the mood perfectly. All of the girls had clearly just left, fully painted and ready for showtime. Hairspray and that heavy, waxy, powdery, and vanilla-ish essence of drag makeup and strong cocktails perfumed the air.

There was a mirror here, a mirror there, mirror, mirror, everywhere—we couldn't miss or hide from our reflections even if we tried.

He stood there, as boyish as ever, gawking at me all over. I went to him.

Now he was hard; his average cock rubbed against my tucked crotch as I leaned in to kiss him. His lips were so small and skinny, mine naturally overtaking his, as a moan and quiver escaped him. I sucked them whole with my tongue flickering, moist; his breath was sweet mint that I craved, sucking the taste from his mouth. I pulled him in closer and tugged at his bow tie, a collar and a chain.

I sucked his bottom lip with a tug, letting go. "*Get on your knees,*" I growled deeply. I pushed him back away from me as I glared; he looked overwhelmed with glee and a little touch of fear. "Who's a dirty pig?"

"I'm a dirty pig, I'm a dirty pig . . ." He shivered, finding his balance then looked down on the filthy, sticky floor, catching his breath. The look in his eyes was so needy, so eager, it was hard to tell if he was euphoric or ashamed. I smirked.

"Say it again," I demanded.

"I—I'm a—d-dirty—p-p-pig."

His stutter! Oh, that was so fucking *hot* that I knew I had to give him what he wanted. He blinked, and I undid my tuck, everything hanging out beneath the hem of my skirt. He looked up at me, more like a puppy than a swine, still on the floor, where I wanted him. "You're such a good boy . . ." I cooed as I petted that chin, smooth and shaven clean. When I lifted that chin up, I smiled at his sorry lips stained with hibiscus.

His Adam's apple bobbed as he gulped, taking in the sight of my cock. He looked me deep in the eyes and I spat—not on my cock but my left pump, saliva shining against the rhinestones, twinkling like his eyes. "Cocksucker. You're a bootlicker, too, aren't you?"

Did I even have to ask? Oh, he was a fast one! He was so

quick when I ordered him to lick my spit. There was no way this was his first time, fast and professional as he was, working his tongue around every crevice of the jewels. I stepped back and laughed high and mighty as he pouted. My legs began to shake under the pressure of the pumps and excitement. I needed to sit down; I wasn't going to let him see me fall. I moved to a chair, where I began caressing myself from waist to tummy as my nasty pig kept on licking. Once he licked me dry, I leaned over to spit on the floor, grinding my heel into the dribble to let him clean that, too. He cuffed his hands around my ankle, loosening, tightening his grip and holding as he licked and licked with a pant and groan. Did he know his thirty minutes were almost up?

He froze immediately when I ordered him to stop so he could unzip his pants and reveal himself to me.

He wore silk black panties, fishnet stockings, and a dainty little black garter belt that held them up high. When he pushed the panties down, his shiny metal cock ring, hugging at his base, against all that pubic hair, flashed. His mouth gaped open, drooling, as I began to caress my cock. I ordered him to clean that shit up—"Lick your own spit, bitch." He broke his gaze away, doing as he was told, Barbra Streisand's "One Less Bell to Answer/A House Is Not a Home" booming from the front of the club. I felt a surge of optimism, of romance, run through me, wonderful and weak.

I lifted my skirt, caressed my balls, wagged my cock like a tease to *oh, I should be happy* . . . He opened his mouth wider, only to stop to kiss the tip of my cock head, swallowing a pearl of precum. I gasped in shock at the sweetness of this, at the warmth of his mouth on my skin. I smiled, I closed my eyes, feeling his thin lips soft as rose petals against my brown skin. He thought I was in control, yet I wasn't. I watched him jerk himself off, his doleful eyes crowning at the head of my cock, taking me whole into his mouth. Slowly he sucked, his tongue dancing fast; my palm found the back of his head, running my acrylic nails through his shiny hair, greasy with pomade. His eyes watered as he inched his way down my shaft, as his throat opened, and by his command and pace and control alone, my cock dove deeper into that throbbing wet hole. Base deep, his lips trembled, jerking himself so fast the sight gave me whiplash. He bobbed faster, and harder, so confident and sure, his passion rising so high, so brilliantly. The vibration of his moan against my cock made us cum in unison. He pulled back only to push forward, again and again. He finally opened his mouth, showing off his tongue slick and gooey, holding me in his mouth.

"Rise!" I ordered.

His dick was limp and wet in my palms as I held it, and he gasped as I squeezed. Our lips met in one wet, sloppy kiss, our tongues swapping my cum back and forth, mouth-to-mouth, as if we were old lovers, tender and holding hands. Together our hips rocked together, slow dancing as if on prom night. Then, suddenly, we let go. We gulped.

"Will I ever see you again, Teena?" His usual shyness was there, but he also sounded sad and weary. He waited for my answer.

He smiled when I took his hand, as if there was hope, when I was only looking to his wristwatch to check the time again. Our thirty minutes had ended. I pouted and sighed. "Well, there's always the next appointment, sugar. You know which number to call . . ." I joined our fingers in an embrace.

When he took my free hand, we kissed again, our hands knotted ever more, and this time it felt as real as life could be. Were we really this fucking lonely? Face-to-face, mirror to mirror, we saw each other for what we were. As the audience in the other room applauded the end of the act, onward we kissed.

Reach

by Roxane Gay

I enjoy tormenting my wife, Sasha. I do it because she lets me. Sasha lets me torment her because she enjoys it. We play little games, share mutual interests. She likes watching me chop onions before I fuck her over the kitchen counter so that she can taste their bite and cry without cause. I like watching her humiliate herself for me. There is a balance between us. "Annie," she'll say, while we're sitting next to each other on the train, on the way to work. There's always urgency in her voice, and I know what she's going to say before the words fall from her mouth. I'll turn to look at her, then look away, quietly observing the other passengers—the way the man across the aisle from us adjusts himself when he thinks no one is looking, the way the woman in the row in front of us keeps jerking her head, trying to stay awake.

While I'm watching all this, I'll turn toward my wife, my needful wife, slide my hand across my left thigh to Sasha's right, squeezing gently, slipping my fingers beneath the hem of her skirt. She'll clear her throat and look out the opposite window at the passing scenery, a light pink blush spreading across her face. She'll pretend to be somewhat disturbed. But she'll brush her thumb across my wrist and lean closer into me. We'll stare at each other in these moments, and the rest of the world recedes. All I see is my wife, her legs spreading ever wider as we pass through the unknown.

Later, always, I smell her on my wedding ring.

Sasha enjoys these torments because she appreciates the view from the bottom. She told me this on our third date. She was kneeling on the floor of my apartment, smiling up at me on the couch, my jeans around my ankles. "I don't care what you think of me," she said, with a little laugh. "I like the view from down here." And with that, she swallowed the length of my cock, continuing to laugh. I could feel the vibrations of her throat muscles at the base of my clit. It was a curious sensation.

Sasha carries her secrets in tight knots along her spine. When she's lying in bed, her back facing me, I can see their outlines in the dark. Sometimes I reach for her to trace them with my fingertips. She shrinks away, curling herself tightly. I withdraw but continue to watch. Sometimes, after we've shared a bottle of wine and we're on the couch watching television, she'll dance around her secrets, try to share a part of herself, but she never gets too far. I don't push. I don't want to complicate the games we play with our histories.

We married after dating for only seven months. I proposed to her after a free jazz concert in Central Park. We were sitting on a bench, where she was trembling and smoking a cigarette. It was cold and windy and miserable. I put my coat around her shoulders, knowing it would smell like tobacco for weeks afterward. It was not a moment. I didn't make promises I couldn't keep. But after I asked and showed her the ring, she took a long drag on her cigarette and answered, "I'm going to say yes because I think you have the capacity to hurt me the way I need you to."

People think they know Sasha. When they see her, they think she is a thick, energetic woman who is always in a good mood. I see Sasha with her arms bound behind her back so tightly that her elbows are touching. There is anger in her eyes, and her lips are swollen. She is seated on a wooden chair, her breasts thrust forward, a thin silver chain between her nipples. I am standing, one boot on the chair between her thighs, only a few inches away from her cunt. She looks right through me as she tries to inch forward, create a point of contact between us. I simply smile. I hold myself back. And then I don't.

Sasha wants me to take her somewhere—a place she has no vocabulary for—a place neither of us has been. I can hear it in her cries when we're fucking, or I'm stretching her limbs across our bed, or we're crammed into the antiseptic space of the train bathroom. I can always tell that we're not quite there yet. It creates tension between us. Tonight, I wait for Sasha to return home from work. She is late, as usual. I never know where she goes after work. I don't ask. I am in our backyard listening to the night when I feel her cool hands on my shoulders. Without turning around, I say, "You're late."

"I know," she replies and returns to the house.

I finger my belt buckle and stand slowly. I find Sasha in our bathroom, undressing. She smiles at my reflection in the mirror, unraveling her hair from the two platinum hair sticks she uses to sweep her hair up most days. When she sets them on the counter, the sound echoes through the room. She quietly slips out of her dress, and I glance at the scars along her upper back—scars for which she offers no explanation. Lower, there are scars I have given her.

The thin, slightly braided scar just above the crack of her ass, that runs the width of her back, I gave to her in Miami. We were staying in one of those boutique hotels in South Beach. We came back to our room after a night of strolling Collins Avenue, drinking mojitos, dancing to *la musica Cubana*, pretending we were people different from ourselves. She quickly undressed, splashed some water on her face, and crawled into bed with my straight razor. She crossed one leg over the other, the tip of the open razor pressed into her knee. "I once saw this movie," she said, trailing her hand along the empty space next to her.

I knelt at her feet, pressing my lips against the exposed soft spot of her inner ankle. I slid my hands up her muscled calf, slightly gritty with sand. She uncrossed her legs. I lay atop her, letting her feel the full weight of my body. Sasha's chest tightened, and her breathing grew labored. I kissed her roughly, sliding my tongue into her mouth, across her teeth. I freed the razor from her grip, set it on the pillow next to her face. My hands, still rough with sand, slid between our bodies, up her torso, around the outer curves of her breasts. She arched upward, and I moved my lips to her neck, tugging at the taut skin with my teeth until she gasped loudly.

I turned Sasha onto her stomach and lay next to her, one of my legs draped over hers, my mouth at her ear, whispering to her about all the things I would do to her that night and every night thereafter. I called her the names she likes to be called—whore, slut, mine. I took the razor and slid the dull edge along her spine and across her back, navigating the tightly knotted secrets and scars. I stopped just above her ass, pressed the sharp edge of the razor at one end of her back, and quickly drew it across. She hissed as tiny droplets of blood appeared. I tossed the razor aside and inched her thighs farther apart. We had seen the same movie. I raised her ass toward me and slid my cock inside her. It seemed like all the muscles in her body tensed. She reached back without ceremony, digging her nails into my skin, urging me deeper. Afterward, I told her I loved her, the way I always did. I touched the drying blood. She sat up, wrapped the sheet around herself, and lit a cigarette. I watched the silhouette of smoke curl around her. Sasha, a life-long Johnny Cash fan, smiled at me and whispered, "Love is a burning thing."

I want to know the stories of all her scars, but I'm not sure I'm willing to pay the price for that knowledge. Sasha continues to stare at my reflection. She is an expert at holding a gaze. She won't break—not for anything. She's that way about many things. And I like to find a woman's breaking point before she finds mine. In this way, we are at cross purposes. She turns around and leans back against the bathroom counter. I pull my belt free from my waist and wrap it around her throat. She arches an eyebrow, feigns boredom. Sasha is very good at pushing buttons.

I cast my eyes downward, and she reaches forward, unzips my slacks, slides a hand into my boxers. Her touch is cold, and I shiver as she begins sliding her hand up and down along the length of my cock and then behind the base of it, her fingers glancing against my clit. She is neither gentle nor rough. My jaw clenches, and I clear my throat. I don't want to give her the satisfaction of knowing how much I enjoy her touch. When Sasha brushes her lips across the tip of my cock, before wrapping them around, then pulling away, moving lower, flicking her tongue against the wet slit of me, I stop her, push her away. It is a rough, unkind gesture. Still holding the end of my belt, I start walking away. When there's a tug, she starts to crawl after me, tentatively at first, then faster to keep up.

When I stop at the foot of our bed and turn to look at her, she is less smug than she was before. "You have not come close," she says.

"To what?"

"You'll know when you get there." She sits cross-legged, waiting for my next move. We are, I think, very large chess pieces. I cup her chin with my hand, pulling her mouth open. I slide two fingers deep, to the warm soft at the back of her throat. She tilts her head back, her hands holding my ass as I begin to slide my cock in and out of her mouth with slow, deliberate thrusts. Every now and again, she closes her mouth slightly, letting her teeth graze against my shaft. I slide my fingers through her dark hair, closing them into tight fists. Sasha brings one of her hands to my cunt. I grunt, try to twist away, but she is steady and unforgiving, sliding her fingers into me as I slide myself into her. I thrust harder, faster. She makes muffled coughing sounds. After I come, I stagger. Sasha wipes her lips with one thumb. She swallows. She waits for my next move. I'm not sure, but I think I hear her say, "Check."

Sasha hates having her pussy licked. Nothing gets her angrier than when I tie her down and lie between her thighs, lavishing my tongue across her swollen pussy lips and hard nub of a clit. She won't speak to me for days afterward, but she also never uses her safeword to stop me. When pressed, she says that it bores her and lacks purpose. But she comes when I put my mouth on her, and it's the only time she makes any real sounds—high-pitched moans that she utters at a staccato pace. I pull her onto the bed and slide my hands up her inner thighs. The muscles flex. I press my forehead against the mound of her pussy, breathing heavily. She smacks my forehead, but I push her arms away, sliding my tongue inside her cunt before drawing it up toward her clit. Sasha digs her heels into my back, just beneath my shoulder blades, far harder than necessary. When I look up, I see her head turned to the side, tears of anger threatening to spill over the crests of her eyelids. Sasha hates losing control.

"Do I have you where you want me to have you?"

"Fuck you," Sasha says. It is a wonder she can get words out through teeth clenched so tightly. I thrust two fingers inside of her, deep and hard. She winces. I slide my fingers out, then drag them up her body, between her breasts, leaving a damp trail. I straddle her waist, squeezing her breasts together. There will be bruises here. I reach over to the night table and fumble for a pair of handcuffs. Defiantly, Sasha throws her arms above her head. I clasp the cuffs around each wrist. Sasha shrugs. I slide off the bed and tell her I'll be back. I wait in the hallway just outside our bedroom. I can hear frustration in her breathing. She mutters unkind things about me.

I go to the den and turn on the television, loud, letting her hear it. Twenty minutes later, I hear footsteps. "Now we have a problem," I say. She stands in the doorway, her hands cuffed in front of her. She looks lonely, abandoned. She is beautiful. I stand and quickly close the distance between us. Clasping her throat with one hand, I force her against the wall. I slap her face, once, then reach down between her legs, where she is wet. I turn her around and kick her legs apart. One of her cheeks is pressed against the wall, and her eyes are tightly shut. I rub my hand across her ass, pulling my fingers along the cleft before smacking that ass once, twice. She makes no sound. I smack her again, hard enough that the palm of my hand tingles. She stands on the tips of her toes, offering herself to me. I spank her until my arm is heavy and the muscles in my shoulder burn. We are both sweating. She is raw. Strands of her hair are plastered against her face. When I scratch her reddened ass, it leaves white streaks.

This time, when I slide my fingers inside her pussy, she moans loudly. "That's fucking right," I tell her. I call her my bitch and tell her I want to hear just how much she wants this. She raises her arms over her head, her cuffed fists resting against the wall. To every question I ask, she gives me the answer I want to hear. I twist her nipples with the fingers of one hand and stroke her clit in tight, fast circles with the fingers of the other. Her head rocks from side to side. I want to overwhelm her with stimulation. We are loud and vulgar. Our damp bodies come together and fall apart with sharp sucking sounds. She is liquid heat around me, and I want to reach into the marrow of her with my lips, my fingers. In moments like these, her rough edges fade. Her arrogance retreats. Her body feels incredibly small and fragile. She is truly mine. I sink my teeth into her left shoulder, biting through the sweat and skin, then circling my tongue over the indentations. I kiss the back of her neck and slow the rhythm of my hips.

Suddenly, I want to be gentle with her. As if she can sense what I'm thinking, Sasha says, "Don't," her voice hoarse, almost trapped. The tension in her body begins to slacken. When she comes, I can feel her pussy pulsing around my fingers. Her body heaves with sobs, and slowly, she falls to the floor. I look down at her, smiling. She is clearly tired, but she knows what to do. Her face shines; her lips are slightly parted. She lowers her mouth to my boots. She affords me the proper gratitude. She moves her lips upward as she pulls my pants around my ankles. She takes the most sensitive part of me into her mouth until I can hardly stand. And when I am spent, I am the one leaning against the wall. She lies at my feet, bent and slightly broken, her arms wrapped around my legs. I touch the top of her head. Before long, I will help her up, carry her to bed, hoping I have inched closer to that place she might never let me reach.

Gospodar

by Garth Greenwell

It would have made me laugh in English, I think, the word he used for himself and that he insisted I use for him—not that he had had to insist, of course, I would call him whatever he wanted. It was the word for master or lord, but in his language it had a resonance it would have lacked in my own, partaking equally of the everyday (*Gospodine*, my students say in greeting, mister or sir) and of the scented chant of the cathedral. He was naked when he opened the door, backlit in the entrance of his apartment, or naked except for a series of leather straps that crossed his chest, serving no particular function; and this too might have made me laugh, were there not something in his manner that forbade it. He didn't greet me or invite me in, but turned without a word and walked to the center of what I took to be the apartment's main room. I didn't follow him, I waited at the edge of the light until he turned again and faced me, and then he did speak, telling me to undress in the hallway. Take off everything, he said, take off everything and then come in.

I was surprised by this, which was a risk for him as for me, for him more than for me, since he was surrounded by neighbors, any of whom might open their doors. He lived on a middle floor of one of the huge Soviet-style apartment blocks that stand everywhere in Sofia like fortresses or keeps, ugly and imperious, though this is a false impression they give, they're so poorly built as already to be crumbling away. I obeyed him, I took off my shoes and then my coat and began to undo the long line of buttons on my shirt, my hands fumbling in the dark and in my excitement, too. I pulled down my pants, awkward in my haste, wanting him and also wanting to end my exposure, though it was part of my excitement. It was for this excitement I had come, something to draw me out of the grief I still felt for R.; he had left months before, long enough for grief to have passed but it hadn't passed, and I found myself resorting again to habits I thought I had escaped, though that's the wrong word for it, escaped, given the eagerness with which I returned to them.

I made a bundle of my clothes, balling my pants and shirt and underthings in my coat, and I held this in one hand and my shoes in the other and stood, still not entering, my skin bristling both from cold and from that profounder exposure I felt. *Ne ne, kuchko*, he said, using for the first time the word that would be his only name for me. It's our word, bitch, an exact equivalent, but he spoke it almost tenderly, as if in fondness; no, he said, fold your clothes nicely before you come in, be a good girl. At this last, something rose up in me, as at a step too far in humiliation. Most men would feel this, I think, especially men like me, who are taught that it's the worst thing, to seem like a woman; when I was a boy, my father responded to any sign of it with a viciousness out of all proportion, as though he might keep me from what I would become, a faggot, as he said, which remained his word for me when for all his efforts I found myself as I am. Something rose up in me at what he said, this man who still barred my way, and then it lay back down, and I folded my clothes neatly and stepped inside, closing the door behind me.

It was a comfortless room. There was an armoire of some sort, a table, a plush chair, all from an earlier era. These spaces are passed from generation to generation; people can spend their whole lives amid the same objects and their evidence of other lives, as almost never happens in my own country, or never anymore. And yet it was impossible to imagine friends or family gathering there. I stood for a moment just in front of the door, and then the man told me to kneel. I could feel him looking at me in the clinical light, inspecting or evaluating me, and when he spoke it was as if with distaste. *Mnogo si debel*, he said, you're very fat, and I looked down at myself, at my thighs and the flesh folded over them, the flesh I have hated my entire life, and though I remained silent, I thought Not so very fat. It was part of our contract, that he could say such things and I would endure them. I wasn't as fat as he was, anyway: he was larger in person than in the photos he had sent, as you come to expect, larger and older, too; he was as old as my father, or almost, anyway nearer to him than to me. But he stood there as though free of both vanity and shame, with an indifference that seemed absolute and, in my experience of such things, unique. Even very beautiful men are eager to be admired, wherever you touch them they harden their muscles, turning their best angles to the light; but he seemed to feel no concern at all for my response to him, and it was then that I felt the first stirrings of unease.

He neither spoke nor gestured, and the longer he appraised me, the more I feared that having come all this way I would be told to leave. It wasn't the lost time I would resent, but the waste of the anticipation that had mounted in me over the several days I had chatted with him online, an anticipation that wasn't exactly desire, as it wasn't desire that I felt now, though I was hard, though I had been hard even as I climbed the stairs, even in the taxi that had brought me there. He was an unhandsome man, though in the way of some older men he seemed solid in his corpulence, thick through the chest and arms. His face was blunt-featured, generic somehow; it was clear that he had never been attractive, or rather that his primary attraction had always been the bearing he had either been born with or cultivated, the pose of uncaring that seemed to draw all value into itself, that seemed entirely self-sufficient. He would never be called a faggot, I thought, whatever the nature of his desires.

Then, to my relief, *Ela tuka* he said, come here, having decided to keep me, at least for a while. When I began to rise he snapped *Dolu*, stay down, and I moved across the space on all fours, the carpet featureless and gray and coarse. When I reached him, he took my hair in his hand and lifted me up onto my knees, not roughly, maybe just as a means of communication more efficient than speech. I had told him I wasn't Bulgarian in one of our online chats, warning him that when we met there might be things I wouldn't understand, but he had asked none of the usual questions, he seemed not to care why I had come to his country, where so few come and fewer still stay long enough to learn the language, which is spoken nowhere else, which even here, as the country shrinks, is spoken by fewer people each day; it's not difficult to imagine it disappearing altogether, the language and the country both. We'll understand each other, he had said, don't worry, and maybe it was just to ensure this understanding that he had taken me in hand, firmly but not painfully guiding me to my knees.

He let go of my hair then, freeing his hand to move down the side of my face, almost stroking it before he cupped it in his palm. It was a tender gesture, and his voice was tender too as he said *Kuchko*, addressing me as if solicitously and tilting my head so that we gazed at each other face-to-face; his fingers flexed against my cheek, almost in a caress. I leaned my head into him, resting it on his palm as he spoke again in that tone of tenderness or solicitude, Tell me, *Kuchko*, tell me what you want. And I did tell him, at first slowly and with the usual words, reciting the script that both does and does not express my desires; and then I spoke more quickly and more searchingly, drawn forward by the tone of his voice, what seemed like tenderness although it was not tenderness, until I found myself suddenly in some recess or depth where I had never been. There were things I could say in his language, because I spoke it poorly, without self-consciousness or shame, as if there were something in me unreachable in my own language, something I could reach only with that blunter instrument by which I, too, was made a blunter instrument, and I found myself at last at the end of my strange litany saying again and again I want to be nothing, I want to be nothing. Good, the man said, good, speaking with the same tenderness and smiling a little as he cupped my face in his palm and bent forward, bringing his own face to mine, as if to kiss me, I thought, which surprised me though I would have welcomed it. "Good," he said a third time, his hand letting go of my cheek and taking hold of my hair again, forcing my neck farther back, and then suddenly and with great force he spat into my face.

He pulled me forward, still holding my hair, and pressed my face hard into his crotch, hard enough that it must have been as uncomfortable for him as for me; any pleasure we took would be an accident, or a consequence of some other aim. Which isn't to say that I didn't feel pleasure; I had never stopped being hard, and when he said to me Breathe me in, smell me, I did so eagerly, taking great gasps. I had felt it before, too, when he spat on me it was like a spark along the track of my spine, who knows why we take pleasure in such things, it's best not to look into it too closely. He was feeling it, too, I could feel his cock thicken against my cheek, then lengthen and lift; there had been no change in it during my long recitation, that catalog of desires I had named, but now at our first real touch he grew hard. He kept one hand at the back of my head, gripping my hair and holding me in place, though there was no need, as surely he knew; but with the other he was reaching for something, as I could tell from the shifts in his balance and weight, and when he pulled me away from him, he slipped it quickly over my head. It was a chain, I realized as I felt it cold against my neck, or rather the kind of leash you use with difficult dogs, and immediately he pulled it tight, letting me feel the pinch of it. This didn't excite me, it was part of the pageantry I was indifferent to, but I didn't object; I assented, though he hadn't sought my permission or consent. And then he took another chain, this one shorter and finer, with little toothed clamps at each end, which (using both his hands, letting the leash fall free, since after all I wasn't an animal, I didn't need to be bound) he attached to my chest. It was the first real pain he had caused me, it made me suck in my breath, but it wasn't too much pain, and not unexciting; a thrill ran through me at this, too, and at what it promised.

Dobre, he said when he had finished, good, though he was speaking of his own work now and not of me. He took up the larger chain again and pulled it tight, twisting his wrist to gather up the slack, which he wrapped around his curled fingers until they were nearly flush against my neck. He was putting me on a short leash, I thought, though I was thinking more of his cock, which I was eager for now, perhaps because of the pain at my chest, which was more than pain, which was excitement too, as was the tightness of the chain around my neck, in which I felt the strength of his arm keeping me from what I wanted. Whatever chemical change desire is had taken hold and I was lit up with it, so that after all I did strain against the leash, he had been right to make it so short. It was a kind of disobedience but a kind he would like, and even as he tightened his grip on the chain I heard him laugh or almost laugh, a slow, satisfied chuckle. It was a sound of approval, and I glowed with it. She wants something, he said, still chuckling, and he lifted his foot to my crotch, feeling my erection as I knelt before him, she likes it, and then he used his foot to pull my cock down, letting it go so that it snapped back up, making me flinch. Then his foot moved lower and he placed his toes beneath my balls, which he fondled roughly, flexing his ankle until there was not quite pain but an intimation of pain. He was dulling my pleasure, I thought, not removing it entirely but taking off its edge.

But he didn't take off its edge, not really, and when there was a slackening in the leash I lunged forward, like the dog he called me. There wasn't anything special about his cock, it was solid and sizeable and thick, but none of these to a remarkable degree, and he had shaved himself there as all men here do, which I hate, the bareness of it is obscene somehow, I can't accustom myself to it. But I was eager, and as I took him in my mouth I felt the gratitude I nearly always feel in such moments, not so much to him as to whatever arrangement of things had allowed me what as a child I thought I would always be denied. It was large enough that I didn't try to take all of it at once; eager as I was, there are certain preparations required, the relaxation and lubrication of passages, a general warming up. But immediately his hand was on my head again, forcing me down, and when it was clear that the passage was blocked, he used both of his hands to hold me, at once pulling me to him and jerking his hips forward in short, savage thrusts, saying *Dai gurloto*, give me your throat, an odd construction I had never heard before. This was painful, and not only for me, it must have hurt him, too. But I did give my throat, I found an angle that gave him access, and soon enough I relaxed and there was a rush of saliva and he could move however he wanted, as he did for a while, maybe there was pleasure for him after all. As there was for me, the intense pleasure I've never been able to account for, that can't be accounted for mechanically; the pleasure of service, I've sometimes thought, or more darkly the pleasure of being used, the exhilaration of being made an object that had been lacking in sex with R., though that had had its own pleasures, pleasures I longed for but that had in no way compensated for the lack of this. I want to be nothing, I had said to him, and it was a way of being nothing, or next to nothing, a convenience, a tool.

He stopped moving then, taking his hands from my head and even from the chain, which fell superfluous and cold down my back. *Kuchkata*, he said, not *kuchko* anymore, the vocative that had softened the word and made it tender to my ears; no longer addressing me but speaking of the object I had become, he said Let the bitch do it herself. I obeyed it, the order he had spoken not to me but to the air, I forced myself upon him with a violence greater than his own, wanting to please him, I suppose, but that isn't true; I wanted to satisfy myself more than him, or rather to assuage that force or compulsion that drew me to him, that force that can make me such a stranger to myself, it is a failing to be so prone to it but I am prone to it. He let me do this for a while, setting my own pace, and then there came the shift in his balance that meant he was reaching to the table beside him again, choosing some new object. He struck me with it a moment later, not very hard but hard enough that I jerked, interrupting the rhythm I had set, and he placed his hand on my head again, taking hold of me as if I might bolt. It was another prop of the sort I had always laughed at before, a cat-o'-nine-tails, a kind of short whip with several strips of leather hanging down; the one time it had been used on me before the man had been timid and I had felt nothing at all, except to despise him a little because he used it only for show. This was something else, and though I had jerked more from shock than from pain there was pain too, less in the actual blow than in the moment after, a sharp heat spreading along my back.

He said a word I didn't understand then, which from his tone I took as something like steady, the kind of mixed reassurance and admonishment one might give a startled horse, and his grip on my head softened, he flexed his fingers again in that gesture that was almost a caress. I was surprised at what I felt then, which was outsized and overwhelming, gratitude at what seemed like kindness from this man who had been so stern; it was something I hadn't felt before, or not for a very long time. I began moving again, having frozen at the shock of the first blow, brought back by his caress or perhaps there had been a very slight pressure from his hand, I'm not sure. I took the whole length of him, and I felt his hand rise and fall again, this time more gently, and since I had warning it didn't interrupt the motion I had fallen into, it became a part of that motion; we fell into a rhythm together, and as his strokes grew quicker and more intense so did my own. Soon enough I was in real pain, my back had grown tender, and I realized that I had begun making noises, little whimpers and cries, and they too became part of the rhythm we had fallen into, his arm rising and falling and my own movement forward and back, and with that movement the swinging of the smaller chain at my chest, the ache that had grown dull but that shifted as I swayed. Then he broke our rhythm, suddenly pulling me to him and thrusting his hips forward at the same time, his grip tight, and as he ground me against him he struck me several times quickly and very hard, and I cried out with real urgency, an animal objection. But I couldn't cry out, the passage was blocked, and with the effort I began to choke, the mechanism failed, and I struggled against him; I tried to wrench my head away, I even brought my hands to his thighs but he held me firm. He struck me five or six times in this way, or maybe seven or eight, they were indistinct as I struggled, moving incoherently, at once pushing myself back from him and flinching at the blows. Then he was still, and though he didn't release me, he drew back, letting me breathe and grow calm again. *Dobra kuchka*, he said, again not addressing me but praising me to the air, and his hands were gentle as he held me, not constraining but steadying, a comfort for which I felt again that strange, inappropriate gratitude.

I was cold as I knelt there, I had broken out in a sweat. The man was breathing heavily, too, he had exerted himself, the rest was as much for him as for me. He knew what he was doing, I thought with sudden admiration; he knew how far to push and when to ease off, and I was excited at the thought of being taken further by him, into territories I had only glimpsed or had intimations of. Then, still keeping one hand on my head, he reached down and very quickly removed first one and then the other clamp from my chest, at which there was a quick flare of pain, making me cry out again, and then a flood of extraordinary pleasure, not sexual pleasure exactly but something like euphoria, a lifting and lightness and unsteadiness, as with certain drugs. He returned his hand to my head and gripped me firmly again, still not moving, having grown very still; even his cock had softened just slightly, it was large but more giving in my mouth. And then he repeated the word I didn't know but that I thought meant steady and suddenly my mouth was filled with warmth, bright and bitter, his urine, which I took as I had taken everything else, it was a kind of pride in me to take it. *Kuchko*, he said as I drank, speaking softly and soothingly, addressing me again, *mnogo si dobra*, you're very good, and he said this a second time and a third before he was done.

He stepped back, withdrawing from my mouth, and told me to lay myself out on the gray carpet facedown, with my arms stretched over my head. It was a difficult position, the carpet was rough and there was no good place for my cock, which was still hard, having never softened, or softened only briefly, though we had been together I thought for a long time. He grunted as he knelt beside me, settling his large frame, and then he placed his hands on my back, not stroking or kneading but appraising. *Mnogo si debel*, he said again, you're very fat, pinching my flesh between his fingers, but I like you, he said, *haresvash mi*, you're pleasing to me, and I thanked him, I said *radvam se*, I'm glad of that, though a more literal translation would be something like I rejoice or take joy in it, which was closer to what I felt. His hands moved lower then, to my ass and the opening there, which he touched, still tenderly, though I flinched as he tested it, he said How is your hole and inched the tip of one dry finger inside. *Kuchko*, he said again, and again I like you, still speaking tenderly to me, so that I felt I had passed some test, that I had proven myself and entered within the compass of his affection, or if not his affection at least his regard. Then he stretched out beside me, not quite touching me, and brought his face close to mine as his hand moved lower still, between my legs, which I spread slightly before lifting up my hips to let his hand snake between my legs and touch my cock for the first time. And you like me too, he said, feeling how hard I was; he gripped me tightly before letting me go. Very much, I said, I like you very much, and it was true, I was excited by him in a new way, or almost new; I had never been with anyone so skilled or so patient. His hand was on my balls now, which he drew together and down, making a kind of ring with his thumb and forefinger, drawing them tighter before folding the rest of his hand around them. He wasn't hurting me yet but I grew tense anyway, and he sensed this, bringing his forehead to my temple, laying it there and whispering again that I was good. And then he began to tighten his grip, very slowly and with a steady pressure on all sides, causing that terrible low ache to build in my abdomen, and I pressed my own forehead into the coarse fabric of the carpet, rubbing it very slightly back and forth. I groaned as he continued to squeeze, and then gasped as I felt his tongue on my cheek, a broad swipe from my jaw to my temple. *Mozhesh*, he said, you can take it, and then I cried out when suddenly he squeezed me harder and let me go.

Good, he said again, whispering with his forehead still pressed to my temple, as I lay there recovering, though the worst thing about that particular pain is that you recover so slowly; the pain welled instead of ebbing, settling in my groin and the pit of my stomach and the backs of my thighs. When his weight shifted next to me I almost protested, I almost said *chakaite*, wait, I had even taken the breath to say it. But he hushed me, making a soothing sound to keep me in my place as he shifted his frame over mine, sliding himself over until he was resting on top of me. It helped, the weight of him, it pressed me down and pressed down the pain I still felt, that ache about which there is nothing erotic, or not for me. I know there are men who like it, who go to great lengths to find others who will hurt them in exactly this way, though I've never been able to fathom the pleasure they take from it. But then there's no fathoming pleasure, the forms it takes or their sources, nothing we can imagine is beyond it; however far beyond the pale of our own desires, for someone it is the intensest desire, the key to the latch of the self, or the promised key, a key that perhaps never turns. It's what I love most about the websites I visit, that you can call out for anything you desire, however aberrant or unlikely, and nearly always there comes an answer; it's a large world, we're never as solitary as we think, as unique or unprecedented, what we feel has always already been felt, again and again, without beginning or end.

He lay on me for some time, not moving or rather moving only to press me down, to ease out my pain and my will; he spread his length along mine, reaching until his hands were at my hands, coaxing free the fingers I had curled, and his feet found their place at my ankles, and then it was as if with his whole body he eased me, stretching and relaxing me at once. It was a delicious feeling, and again I admired his skill, how well he knew his instrument, how much I would take and how to bring me back from it. He was gentle, as he lay there he spoke to me, crooning almost, calling to me again *Kuchko*, the term of abuse that had become our endearment, *spokoino*, he said, relax, be calm. And I obeyed him, I could feel that fluid ache drain as he lay on top of me, moving just slightly, pressing me down and at the same time stretching me, pulling tenderly on each of my limbs, though soon his movement became something else. He had remained hard, though my own excitement had waned, had flowed out as the pain flowed in; and now it was his hardness I felt, he ground it into me, making my excitement return, not all at once but like an increasing pressure that provoked its own movement in response, a movement of my hips upward just slightly and back. It was a suggestion of movement, really, all that was permitted by his bulk on top of me, but it was enough to make him laugh again, that low, quiet, satisfied laugh I heard against my ear. *Iska li neshto?* he said, does she want something, and I did, I wanted something very much. He was moving more now, not just grinding but lifting his hips, which shifted his weight to his knees, which dug into the hollows of my own knees and pinned me more insistently down. He began to move more forcefully, rubbing the length of himself against me, and I could hear his breath quicken with the effort of it. Then he lifted himself more, and without moving his hands from my wrists he positioned his cock to fuck me, though he couldn't fuck me, I thought, he was dry and had done nothing to prepare me, with his hands or his mouth, and I felt myself tighten against him as he pressed forward, moving not violently but insistently. Wait, I said, speaking the word I had almost said before, wait, I'm not ready, but he said again *spokoino*, relax, be calm, he didn't try to enter me now but fell back to that insistent rubbing. He spoke softly as he rose again, crooningly, You're ready, he said, you want it, open to *gospodar*. *Ne*, I said, *ne*, wait, you need a condom, using the word *gumichka*, little rubber. He shifted his position at this, he released one of my wrists to wrap his arm around my neck, not choking me but taking hold of me, pressing the links of the chain into my skin. We don't need that, he said, I don't like them, he spoke close to my ear, intimately, persuasively, and it will hurt you more if I use one. He started to move again, pressing forward though I resisted him, you need a condom, I said, please, there's one in my pocket, let me get it, and I moved my free arm as if to lift myself up, setting it as a brace at my side. *Kuchko*, he repeated, not quite sternly but with disapproval, and then crooned again, don't you want to please me, don't you want to give me what I want? I did want to please him, and not only that, I wanted him inside of me, I wanted to be fucked, but there was real danger, especially in this country; many people here are sick without knowing it, I knew, and knew too that he wouldn't be gentle, that I was likely to bleed, it's necessary, I said, please, I have one, we have to use it. Hush, he said again, *kuchko*, let me in, his voice gentle but his arm tightening around my neck, my throat in the crook of his elbow, let me in, and he pressed forward with real force. For a moment I wavered, I almost did let him in; it's what you wanted, I thought, it's what you said you wanted, I had asked him to make me nothing. But I didn't let him in, I said no, repeating it several times, my voice rising; no, I said, stop, *prestanete*, still using the polite form. Open, he said, but I didn't open, my whole body clenched in refusal, I did try to lift myself up now, but found I could hardly move at all. I was used to being the stronger one in such encounters, being so tall and so large, I was used to feeling the safety of strength, of knowing I could gather back up that personhood I had laid aside for an evening or an hour. But he was stronger than I was, and I was frightened as he held me down and pressed against me, shoving or thrusting himself. But he couldn't enter, I was clenched and dry and there was no forcing himself inside, and he grunted in frustration and said again bitch, spitting the word, bitch, what are you to say no to me, and then he pulled back on my neck and bit my shoulder very hard, nearly breaking the skin, making a ring of bruises I would wear for days.

He lifted himself off me, shoving down so I lay flat again, and said loudly, almost shouting it, *Kakuv si ti*, what are you, *kakuv si ti*, and there was real anger in his voice now, not just frustration but rage, *kakuv si ti*, and then he grabbed a belt from the table, a leather strap, and brought it down hard on my back. The pain of it made me cry out, a womanish cry, and as he struck me he shouted *Pedal*, faggot, as if it were the answer to his question, *pedal, pedal*, each time striking me very hard as I cried out again and again, saying stop, the single syllable, returning to my own language as if to air or waking, stop, I said in English, I'm sorry, stop. It wasn't just the beating that I wanted to stop but the whole encounter, the string of events I had set in motion, the will-lessness I had assumed, which had carried me now past anything I might want, and I said to myself what have I done, what have I done.

He did stop then, and in the sudden silence I could hear him breathing heavily, as I was, breathing or sobbing, I'm not sure which. I gathered myself to my hands and knees, moving slowly, it was the most I could manage; I was covered in sweat again, from exertion and from fear. It was over now, I thought, but then he spoke again, saying *Dolu*, down. I didn't contradict him but I didn't lie back down, I couldn't bear to return to the helplessness I had thought I wanted. *Dolu*, he said again, and when again I didn't obey him he lifted his foot and set it on my back, pressing as if to force me down. But I held firm, and so he reached down, not removing his foot, and grabbed the leash or chain where it hung, and as he straightened he pulled it tight, not with all his strength but enough that I felt it, and felt that he could choke me if he chose. He stepped off me then, moving behind me with the leash still in hand, and I tried to rise, lifting my chest both to slacken the chain and to rise to my feet, to stand for the first time in what seemed like hours. As I began to get up I must have shifted my knees apart, I must have moved in a way that opened myself to his foot, which struck me now hard between my legs, so it wasn't the chain that choked me but pain as I fell forward without a sound, unable to breathe, stripped clean of the will I had been gathering back in scraps; my arms collapsed and I fell forward and curled into myself in animal response. But he didn't let me curl into myself, he fell on top of me, he pushed or shifted me until I was available to him again, so that beneath pain and sharper than it I felt fear, a rising pitch of fear and protest and a terrible shame. He positioned himself as he had before, with his knees in my knees and his hands gripping my wrists, and in my confusion and pain I'm not sure if I struggled, or how much I struggled, though I did clench myself shut; he couldn't enter me at first, and again I heard him make that grunt or growl of frustration. But he was wet now, he must have spat into his palm and slicked himself with it, and when he lifted just slightly and brought himself down with his whole weight he did enter me, there was a great tearing pain and I cried out in a voice I had never heard before, a shrill sound that frightened me further, that wasn't my voice at all, and I choked it off as I twisted away from him, not thinking but in panic and pain, using all my strength. Maybe he was frightened too by my cry, maybe I had startled him; in any case I was free of him, I had thrown him or he had allowed himself to be thrown. He must have allowed it, I think, since he made no further attempt, though he could have done whatever he wanted; after my effort I lay exhausted, watching him where he lay on his back breathing hard.

Bitch, he said softly several times, softly but viciously, *mrusna kuchka*, dirty bitch, get out. It was a reprieve, permission to leave, and I pulled the chain from my neck and stood, after a fashion, hunched as I was around pain. I felt nothing of what I had thought I might feel in standing, I reclaimed nothing, nothing at all returned. I dressed as quickly as I could, though it seemed I was moving slowly, as if in a fog or a dream, I put my socks and my belt in my pockets, I left my shirt unbuttoned. I watched the man where he watched me, sitting now with his back to the wall. I turned away from him finally, I went to the door and felt something like panic again when the knob refused to turn. Like all doors here it had several locks, and I looked at them hopelessly, turning first one and then another and finding the door still locked, more locked now that I had turned more latches, and this was like a dream also, of endlessness and the impossibility of escape; stupid, I thought, or maybe I whispered it to myself, stupid, stupid. The man rose then, I heard or felt him heave himself up and walk to the door. *Kuchko*, he said, not angrily now but mockingly, shaking his head a little, pacified perhaps by the fear that was evident as he reached around me to unlock the door, as I pressed myself as best I could into the wall behind me; there was nowhere to go, the corridor was narrow, and it was hard not to touch him as he opened the door, as I tried to slip past, feeling again what he wanted me to feel, I think, that if I left it was because he let me leave, that it was his will and not my own that opened the door. And then he seemed to change his mind, when as I stepped into the dark hall he grabbed my shoulder, gripping me hard, not to pull me back but to spin me around, making me face him a final time. Things happened very fast then, I had brought my hands up when he grabbed me, to ward or fight him off, though I couldn't have fought him off, I've never struck anyone, really, never in earnest. Still, I lifted my hands, palms up at my chest, and when again as at the beginning of our encounter he spat into my face, which was why he had grabbed me and spun me around, to spit again with great violence into my face, I placed my hands on his chest and pushed or tried to push him away from me. But he didn't fall back, I hardly moved him at all, maybe he staggered just slightly but immediately he sprang forward, with the kind of savagery or abandon I could never allow myself he lunged to strike at me. Maybe he had staggered just slightly and that was why he missed, his aim failing as he lunged or fell forward into the hallway, where I was already moving toward the stairway, off balance myself, almost reaching it before his hands were on me again, both of his hands now grabbing me and throwing me forward so that I fell down the stairs, or almost fell; by luck I stayed on my feet, though I landed on my right foot in a way that strained or tore something, I would limp for weeks. And maybe it's only in retrospect that I think I chose how I landed, though I have a memory, an instant of clearheadedness in which I knew he wasn't finished with me, though he was naked and it was dangerous for him I knew he would follow me, and so I think I decided as I fell forward not to catch myself against the concrete wall but instead to strike the small window there, hitting the pane with my right palm hard, shattering it. The noise did what I wanted, he turned and raced for his door, and in the instant I looked up at him I saw he was frightened. I ran or stumbled down the flights of stairs, and reached the door just as the hallway lights went on, some neighbor above drawn out by the sound.

It was very late, the boulevard was quiet, and if in a moment someone would emerge from the little convenience store (*denonoshtno*, its window said, day-and-night), if in a moment someone would emerge to investigate, I had time to get away, as I thought of it, walking one block and then another without passing a soul. I kept my head down, trying to be blank and unplaceable, trying to calm what I felt, which was pain and relief and shame and panic still, even though I thought I was clear, that I was far enough now to go on uncaught. But I couldn't calm what I felt, something rose in me I couldn't keep down, as I couldn't keep walking at the pace I had set; with each step my foot was more tender and there was something else too, a nausea climbing to my throat, I was going to be sick. I turned quickly into the space between two buildings, an alleyway lined with trash bags and refuse, among which I bent over or crouched, unable to stand. But it wasn't with bile or sickness that I heaved but with tears, which came unexpected and fluent and hot, consuming in a way I hadn't known for a very long time, that maybe I had never known. I raised my hands, wanting to cover my face, though there was no one to see I was still ashamed of my tears, and I saw that my right hand was covered with blood. In the light from the street I could see where my wrist was torn, a small deep wound where it had caught on the glass. Stupid, I thought again, stupid, at the wound or my weeping, I'm not sure which. Why should I weep, I thought, at what, when I had brought it all upon myself, and I took one of my socks from my pocket and pressed it to the wound, wrapping it around my wrist and folding the cuff of my sleeve over it, not knowing what else to do.

It was a fit of weeping violent and brief, and as my breath steadied I felt a sense of resolution, that I had been lucky and must learn from that luck; I wouldn't go back to such a place, I thought, this would be the end of it. But how many times had I felt that I could change, I had felt it through all the long months with R., months that I had spent, for all my happiness, in a state of perpetual hunger; and so at the same time I felt it

I felt too that my resolution was a lie, that it had always been a lie, that my real life was here, and I thought this even as I struggled to climb from the new depth I had been shown. And even as I climbed or sought to climb I knew that having been shown it I would come back to it, when the pain had faded and the fear, maybe not to this man but to others like him; I would desire it, though I didn't desire it now, and for a time I would resist my desire but only for a time. There was no lowest place, I thought, I would strike ground only to feel it give way gaping beneath me, and I felt with a new fear how little sense of myself I have, how there was no end to what I could want or to the punishment I would seek. For some moments I wrestled with these thoughts, and then I stood and turned back to the boulevard, composing as best I could my human face.

Scissors

by Kim Fu

As the curtains open, Dee sits on an empty stage in a small, cabaret-style theater. Black-painted walls, the smell of dust burning on the stage lights, ancient cigarette smoke baked into blue velvet drapery. The spotlight swings to Dee, a garish full moon. She sits in a plain wooden chair, her wrists bound to the armrests and her ankles to the chair legs with neatly torn strips of canvas. Her posture is slumped and casual, her knees open and her shoulders expansive and angled slightly backward, as though lounging in a hot tub. Her white T-shirt dress rides up over her thighs, the radiant heat on her bare arms and legs more like sunlight than moonlight.

The audience sits crowded around tightly packed, circular tables. Lit candles at the center of each one illuminate white tablecloths and sweating highball glasses, while the faces beyond remain largely in shadow. A table in the front row draws Dee's attention: a group that remained rowdy after a hush fell over the rest of the room, the only people she can see clearly in the reflected footlights. Their drinks slosh out of their glasses as they make jokes and jostle for the best view, but one person at their table is quiet, sitting back in his chair, slightly outside the conversation. He toys nervously with the candleholder, testing the hot glass, the tiny flame rolling on its wick. His hands jerk away and draw back. He glows pink, already blushing behind a pair of square glasses.

El enters stage left, dressed in a fitted tuxedo with tails, the black bow tie locking in place her high-necked shirt collar. She crosses in front of Dee. She holds up a pair of scissors, ordinary but large, stainless steel from tip to handle, as one might keep in the kitchen to snip through tendons and butcher twine. The steel catches the spotlight like a wink. She waves them around and gestures toward the audience, a magician with an empty hat.

El usually wears dagger pumps with the suit, six inches of killer heel with her trouser legs jacked up short. Tonight, she's barefoot. Dee stares. She's thrown by the sight of El's feet, their unexpected intimacy, her unpainted toenails like a row of pink pearls.

El grasps the bottom hem of Dee's dress and begins to snip. She takes her time. An inch, a pause. Another inch. The sound is satisfying, the neat clip of the blades coming together, the fabric stretching and shearing. A straight slice up the center, in line with Dee's navel. Dee feels the scissors close and stop at her solar plexus, and then El steps away. The fabric on either side of the split hangs to her sides like a flyaway nightgown, an inverted V of exposed skin between.

El leans in and kisses Dee on the mouth. Dee draws back, to the extent that she can, but El presses forward, the kiss soft and insistent. El has never kissed her onstage before. In the dressing room afterward, yes, during the frenzied, private fucking that used to end all of their show nights, El's sweat-melted makeup smearing across Dee's neck. She can't stop thinking about El's missing shoes. Her giantess persona shrunken to everyday height. Maybe it's nothing. Maybe a heel snapped backstage, moments before El's entrance, but Dee likes everything just so. Her surrender is an act of choreography. She can't do this if she's picturing El at home in her apartment, an apartment like any other. El taking off her shoes in a foyer and rubbing her tired arches, her blistered soles. El eating a bagel standing up in her kitchen, her bare feet on the linoleum.

Someone at the rowdy front table starts booing, but good-naturedly, still laughing. *Get on with it! Don't tease us!* Dee tries to focus on the audience, reorient herself in the moment. Her pupils have adjusted, and when she squints, she can see a couple at the very back, delineate their shapes from the darkness. Two women, their skin and pale hair lit red under the fire exit sign. They're making out distractedly—lazy groping with their attention drifting back to the stage, always one eye on Dee.

El snips through the last few inches of Dee's dress, now cut through from bottom to top. The edges curl outward, hanging over her bare torso like an unbuttoned jacket. When El tucks the flaps back and around her, the sleeves still comically intact, Dee can feel the energy in the room change. El steps back. She doesn't touch Dee. Nothing touches her, which makes the nakedness stranger, more acute, more helpless.

El taps the scissors against Dee's knee, as though absent-mindedly toying with a pen, exaggerating the bounce. She rests the point against the side of Dee's neck. The front table finally quiets.

El surveys Dee's body for a long moment, as though deep in thought, a vein jumping in Dee's throat. She lifts the scissors and presses the flat edge firmly against Dee's left breast, parallel to her body. Not piercing or cutting her, just sinking in, as into a mattress. A presence, a hardness, the potential of menace. Drawing attention to how soft she is, how her flesh indents and depresses to the slightest pressure. Nearly flush with her chest, the blades open and shut without catching any skin between them, snipping through air between her collarbone and nipple, severing an imagined connection.

The closed blades slip across and between her breasts, down to her belly, without a scratch, pressing and skimming like the back of a fingernail. Down farther, to the plushest part of her thigh. The steel begins to warm.

Dee loves the way the audience flinches at El's every movement. Their held breath. Gritting their teeth and clenching on the inside, holding as still as they can, as though if they don't move, if they don't exhale, Dee won't get cut. She knows it's maddening to watch, a sharp edge near skin, on skin, the tension of it, the blood pulsing inside all of them, swelling up like balloons that want to be popped. It's easier to be her, she thinks. She knows precisely where the scissors are, can feel the calm and control in El's grip. She feels as though her skin lifts to meet the metal of its own accord, faint hairs and gooseflesh rising, a slow, magnetic draw.

The scissors are flat against her stomach again, pointing downward, dipping now and again into the waistband of her underwear, colder on the concealed skin. El rotates them slowly until they're perpendicular to Dee's body, still pointing to her center. The blades open, the beak of an eager bird. El snips through the side seams, the elastic at each leg opening, and the front half of Dee's underwear falls forward like a drawbridge. Dee strains against her bindings to lift her butt as El pulls the silky scrap away.

The low stage puts her knees at eye level of the crowd. If they don't raise or lower their gaze, it lands straight between her legs.

El uses the scissors to lift Dee's chin. Their eyes meet, lock. Now El is running the scissors along Dee's body without even looking down, blades all the way open in a narrow X, skimming in long sweeps as though curling ribbon. Her skin pinkens in strips from the friction and heat, though it remains unbroken. Her mind is still clear, restive, trusting, but her body clenches all the same, bearing down with her hips on the chair.

Still without looking, still on instinct, she touches the flat surface of the scissor blades—glancingly—to Dee's vulva, against the outer lips, and someone in the audience moans, a sound of simultaneous dread and desire. The steel is wet. She brings the blades together, only an inch from Dee's tenderest skin, the empty *snip* loud in the pin-drop silence. The same moan emerges from the dark.

El brings the scissors to Dee's mouth, prompting her to kiss them, which she does. She slips the pointed tip between Dee's lips, and Dee draws the closed blades deeper, up to the pin of the pivot point. The scissors feel dull against her palate and tongue, the depth of her mouth filled with metal. Dee is in control of this part, the sword-swallowing, bobbing her head and sliding her lips. She looks up at El, pleased with herself, expecting El's eyes to be glassy with approval and desire, that wild-horse energy of hers, impatient for the next thing, for more.

But El isn't even looking at her. Her gaze is just behind Dee, into the sea of candles and stained tablecloths. Her hand around the scissors relaxes, goes slack. Is she *bored*? Dee lunges upward, indignant, her mouth widening to take in the base of the handles, the tip in the opening of her throat. Without turning her head, she tries to see what's stealing El's attention. The hecklers at the front table? El is smiling in their direction the way she does when someone challenges her, presents her with a bet or a dare.

El takes the spit-polished scissors and cuts a strip from Dee's dress. She holds the scissors between her own teeth as she folds the strip in half, to thicken it, and wraps it around Dee's head as a blindfold. Blackness closes around her. Dee tries to trust what she knows: El tying a tight, neat knot at the back of her head; El tucking the scissors ostentatiously into her hair bun, like decorative chopsticks. A thrilling dread alights in her gut.

"Are you ready?" El stage-whispers.

Dee is supposed to pause and then nod shyly, to appear hesitant but excited. She's surprised to find herself actually hesitating. She told El from the beginning that she needed to write the details of her own submission, and El had understood. That Dee needed to be in control to give up control. That she would tap out over something as small as missing shoes, an unplanned kiss, an unnerving smile. That their lives had to be separate, their roles pure, their daytime selves left at the alley door of the theater. As though a hundred nights of sex and conversation and show adrenaline hadn't revealed more than any other relationship she'd ever had.

El has never nicked her onstage, never misjudged a fraction

of an inch and drawn blood. The scissors remind Dee of a jangling, dubiously constructed roller coaster at the state fair near where she grew up. The two-person car held her loosely as the metal sides bruised her ribs and her head whipped back and forth on her spine, once chipping her front tooth on the guardrail. But she was never truly afraid. She lined up over and over, elated and alert.

The room is humid, hypnotized, heavy with want. In this moment, there's no acute danger, no dips and turns rattling her teeth in her head, no steel edge digging into her naked skin, yet she feels a vertiginous tingling through her fingers and toes. Her carnival fear edged with something real: El, her El, bored with her. What a bored El might do.

El puts her hand on top of Dee's, trapped palm-side up on the armrest, and squeezes lightly in a gesture Dee understands: *It's all me. It's only me. It's always me.*

Dee nods.

"She says she's ready!" El cries, turning toward the audience. "Those who want to play, line up in an orderly fashion. Stay close to the wall and wait until I gesture for you to come forward. Remember, hands only, and your turn is up when I make this signal. We won't have time for everyone. I'll be watching! Rule breakers will be escorted out!"

Dee reminds herself that nothing is happening, that the murmuring and shifting and patter is for show, people are just heading to and from the bar—this has all been explained to them in advance. Dee's brain tells her one thing, that she's a performer in a well-established show with rules of her own making, while her body knows only that it's trapped, blinded and bound, the prickling sensation of being watched. Being seen without seeing. Even when she wasn't blindfolded, she'd only been able to make out a handful of faces—the shy man at the front table and his raucous companions, the couple under the exit sign. She has no idea who's out there. If they look hopeful, worshipful, like supplicants before a queen. If they're laughing, having a fun night out, amused by the whole situation. If they're sneering, impatient, eerily focused, blackout drunk. If they know her from some other time and place. A crowd is more lawless and unpredictable than any one person. A crowd is one of the most dangerous things she can think of.

Behind her blindfold, she pictures El's face, broad-browed, impish, easy to love. Unbidden, Dee remembers an evening, not long ago, when she arrived at the theater and found El in a loose-knit sweater with one sleeve, a ragged skein of wool dangling from her other shoulder. Dee thought that she'd been attacked, but El only laughed in astonishment. She'd been idly tugging on a loose thread, scarcely aware of what she was doing until she'd unraveled the entire sleeve. "I get fidgety when I'm bored," she said.

It's all me. It's only me. It's always me.

The first touch is a jolt. The tip of a fingernail grazing the back of her neck. She hadn't realized that anyone was behind her. The nail is pointed and sharp, the same intimation of threat as the scissors. She pictures a woman with brightly colored acrylics, stiletto tips. Large, teased hair, a bandage sheath dress. The fingers spread and comb upward through Dee's hair, palming the back of her head like a basketball, manicured claws flexing open and closed. Dee leans into it. She likes having her scalp scratched this way. El knows that.

The hand withdraws, immediately replaced by the sensation

of touch on her sternum, slight enough to be chilling, ghostlike. An almost unpleasantly light touch, trickling downward, circling one nipple with a hesitancy that makes her tense. If there were wet paint on these fingers, they'd hardly leave a stain, the contact is so glancing. It seems clumsy, hungry, a little afraid, like a virginal teenage boy. The man with the glasses at the front table comes to mind. (Had El noticed him, too? Is this her imitation of him?) The hand is joined by another, cupping her breasts from the front, and she imagines him standing in front of her, his glasses fogged with sweat, his shirt collar rumpled, his mouth falling slightly open, awed by the sight and feel of her. "That's enough," El says. Leaning back, throwing her voice in that way she does. She hears someone reluctantly stepping away before tweaking Dee's nipple in a spiteful goodbye.

Just as suddenly, someone grabs Dee by the neck, thumb and forefinger holding Dee's chin from below, the flat of their palm against Dee's throat. The movement is swift and sure, and Dee gasps. A little louder than necessary. The hand seems too large to be El's, the middle finger reaching almost to the back of her neck, the base of the wrist resting on her chest. Too slender and too smooth to be El's, missing her lifetime of calluses. Dee's mind draws a pianist's hand, wide-palmed with long fingers, masterful in its manipulation, octave to octave.

The musician gives her throat a friendly squeeze, the way you'd squeeze someone's upper arm in congratulations or comfort—except it's a flash of constriction, a skipped breath. El would never risk letting someone else touch Dee this way. Would she? A firmer squeeze. Dee gasps without meaning to.

It's all me. It's only me. It's always me.

Her throat is released. Two hands settle on her thighs from

the front. Someone is kneeling in front of her, close enough that Dee can feel their breath hot between her legs. They turn their head back and forth, blowing a stream of air from the inside of Dee's knee, up the inside of her thigh, across her pussy, down her other thigh, and back again. This, Dee thinks, seems like it violates the hands-only rule, in spirit if not word. The kneeler giggles, voice high and girlish. El's natural laugh is a big, spirited bark.

Strong hands massage the muscles at the base of her neck, unmistakably El's. Dee tells herself that El—somehow—stood from where she'd been kneeling and moved behind the chair without making a sound, without disturbing Dee's kinesthetic sense of where she was in the room. She tells herself it's El she feels looming over her, that the clatter of footsteps and the scent of unfamiliar sweat and cologne is farther away than it seems. She tells herself it's just El pretending to be other people, tricking the audience into thinking she's tricking Dee, as they've agreed.

She tells herself El would never turn her over to a roomful of strangers. Not even if Dee wanted her to. Not even if Dee begged her to. If Dee welcomed them, offered herself up like a feast. If she felt drunk on their attention, power-mad, giddy at having reduced a packed theater to single-minded animals.

Hands slide over Dee's shoulders, across her belly. Hands squeeze her breasts, climb up her thighs, rest on her hip, slap her cheek, tap the tip of her nose, tug lightly at her pubic hair. Hands palm her ass, cup her mound from behind. Fingers strum and abandon her clit. Fingers pop in and out of her mouth. Quick, darting motions, from all directions, never lingering, like she's swimming with a school of fish, at the lightless bottom of the sea. An overwhelming, disorienting, untraceable amount of touch.

It's just El, of course. Of course. El walking in circles around her, El and her ventriloquism, her disguises, her multiplying, quicksilver hands, able to reach every part of Dee at once. El, who knows her, who can give and take and break her. Or not. Dee will never know, not really, what happens to her as she swims in darkness—she will always have to take El's word for it. Dozens of times on this stage, she believes it was only El, only El's hands that she's ridden and bitten and bucked against, but she can't know.

And it's the not-knowing that makes her core sing.

Maybe people lined up in a theater, out the door and down the block, for the privilege of touching Dee, and it's these faceless figures who are grasping at her now, entering her with their hands, jostling for their turn. Maybe this time, El will lose control of the crowd, and they'll rush the stage, overwhelm her, a force as tremendous as Dee is powerless, strapped naked to a chair, her skin thrumming, death-defying adrenaline electrifying her veins.

Or.

Or El will whisper to Dee in her true, private voice, remove the blindfold, and reveal just the two of them onstage. She'll undo Dee's restraints, help her out of the chair, hold her upright on wobbling legs. She'll take Dee's hand, in her warm, familiar grasp, and raise their arms together, Dee still naked and bruised and soaked and spent, the audience beaming in the seats they never left, wild with applause.

The Lost Performance of the High Priestess of the Temple of Horror

by Carmen Maria Machado

I would never forget the night I saw Maxa decompose before me. I was a young woman, barely budded, but I'd been able to make my way to Le Théâtre du Grand-Guignol by telling my mother I needed to go to church.

My mother was a devout woman, a seamstress, and when I walked out the door she kissed me and said she was pleased I was seeking God's wisdom. When she pulled away, I saw there was a black spot of blood where she'd brushed a pricked finger against the sleeve of my coat.

The entire way to the theater, a crow had fluttered around me. It flew from rooftop to rooftop, occasionally dropping down the cobblestone to fix me in its gaze before ascending again. Its eye looked like an onyx, and an oily prism blazed over its black feathers. My mother, had she seen it, would have told me the devil was leading me. But she was not there, and she did not see that the bird could just as easily been following me, as if *I* were the devil. I kept walking, and it kept leading, or following, until I turned a corner and it ascended to a rooftop and disappeared.

The theater was built at the end of a narrow alley, limned with white, sand-colored buildings pocked with shuttered windows and wrought-iron terraces. For a brief moment, the chatter of pedestrians fell away, and the Grand-Guignol glowed in the dusk. The cobblestones beneath my feet were the same I'd been walking on, but suddenly their unevenness made me aware of every rotation of my hip, every inversion of my foot. I felt like the theater took two steps away from me for every step I took toward it, stretching the space before me to an ever-doubling length.

The crow dove at me from a rooftop, shrieking like a djinn. I ran toward the threshold. The light pouring from the open door throbbed like a bruised thumb.

I had not, precisely, told my mother a lie. The theater had once been a church, though that night the room was hot with spectators instead of congregants, and just as cramped and feverish.

The stage was claustrophobic, like a too-hot whisper from an intoxicated stranger. The cherubs that lined the ceiling had a demonic air, an askew quality, and seemed glazed in our collective oils. The smell of bodies was heightened—women's menstruation and the swampy folds of men. We all breathed in sync and through our mouths. I sat toward the front of the room, pressed between a man who kept glancing at me in confusion and desire, and a couple who gripped each other's bodies like they were about to be borne away by a flood.

When Maxa came onto the stage, it was as if a window had been opened to allow a breeze, and a gale had entered instead. I felt the room bend around her. She was not beautiful in a traditional sense, but her dark eyes beheld all of us as if we were slightly familiar to her. Her mouth was painted the red of clotted blood.

The play concerned a wife who hatched a scheme to murder her husband so that she might live with her lover. Maxa played the strutting spouse with such assurance I forgot I sat shoulder to shoulder with my fellow Parisians; instead, I felt as if I were the play's maid, who appeared at the edge of the stage from time to time so that she might overhear the strategic dialogue, staged to divert suspicion. The plan was so nefarious, so meticulously plotted, I was certain I could reproduce it if I cared to. She turned to the audience from time to time, addressing us with scorn, sounding a little disappointed in our prudishness, our lack of imagination. We did not care. We arced toward her voice like petals to the sun.

In the final act, the wife lured her husband to her bedroom, where a large traveling trunk rested open on a tarpaulin. This was the plan: to murder him and pack him into the trunk, which she would take with her on a long journey. But before she was able to execute her plan, her husband seized the pistol and shot her dead. Her wrapped her in her own tarpaulin and placed her into her own trunk. It was heaved high in the air by an attendant and placed at the edge of the stage. The fiend murmured to himself—"She thought of everything"—and then cackled as he walked offstage. Then, a tremendous bang, as the front of the trunk fell open to reveal her body, twisted in a grotesque knot. The audience let out a collective breath. A woman wept silently in the row before me, and her companion turned to console her.

I waited for the curtain to close on her death, but as I watched, her body began to teem with a living curtain of maggots. Someone screamed—it was me, it was me—as her flesh blackened and greened and sank in around her bones like fallen cake. I felt like a girl-child trapped in a nightmare. Some tiny corner of me knew that the effect was done with something real—lights or clay—but could not convince any other part of me that this was anything but the end.

When the performance was over, I sat there picking at my skirt as the audience stood and shrieked and murmured confidences and eventually departed. I did not wish to return home just yet, when the nightmare of the performance lingered so close in my mind, and I felt warm and drowsy. No one came to move me, and I fell asleep there in my seat.

A slam, wreathed in whispering, woke me. The theater was dark as a tomb, aside from a candle burning in my periphery. I reached for my throat, as though I expected it to be wet or gone or bitten, but only felt my own rapid pulse. I turned toward the whispering and saw one of the confessional booths had been closed, and from within there was a gasping sound, like a woman being strangled. I stood and walked to the screen, pressed my face close. Inside, the dark-haired woman was bent over, a man rutting behind her. Her face turned to the side and she saw me, but instead of screaming, she pressed a white finger to the pillow of her mouth.

I turned and fled.

When I returned that night, my mother asked me what the sermon had been about. I went to her and admired her embroidery. "The sinful Flesh and the living Word," I said. She kissed me on the cheek. Her finger was still bleeding.

————

When my mother died of her wasting illness a few months later, I left our home—thrown out by the landlord, who'd asked for my body in lieu of rent—and found myself in front of the Grand-Guignol once more. I had some money on my person— enough for a few nights at an inn, a few hot meals—but still I turned some over for a ticket when I saw Maxa on the poster from the street. When I entered the theater, I saw once again the fleur-de-lis wallpaper surrounding me like so many seeds, like I was at the center of a large and pungent fruit—something unfathomably exotic.

That night, Maxa gouged out her right eye with a knitting needle. I don't remember why; besides, all explanations and plot contrivances were weak beneath the weight of the violence. She dipped her head forward and her hand twitched with new weight. I thought it would be white and smooth as an egg, but when she pulled her hand away it looked like a stillborn chick; a round mass of wet and gristle. I realized after she let it fall to the stage that I'd been holding my breath, and the influx of air was sweet as summer rainfall.

At the end of the performance, I lingered near the stage, which was covered in gore. A young woman came out with a bucket and began to slop brown water along the wood. She looked up and saw me but said nothing. Feeling bold, I hitched my skirts and climbed up, stepping over a menacing streak of red. I could feel her eyes on me as I walked past her.

Backstage, Maxa was sitting on her chair, looking ravished. Her curls were already half-undone, as if she'd been out on the water. A book was open in the dip of her skirts, and she was glancing at it with her good eye as she unpinned her hair. "Sabine!" she shouted. In front of her loomed a mirror the color of rust. In its reflection, I looked wide-eyed, feral, faint as a spirit.

"Sabine, do you—" she said, and then flicked her gaze toward me. "May I help you?"

Behind me, I heard footsteps, and the young woman, Sabine, appeared. She stepped around me and got very close to Maxa's face. Her fingernail scraped along Maxa's temple like a cat begging to be fed, and as the black peeled away, Maxa's eyelid emerged beneath it.

"I'm looking for work, for room and board," I said.

"Running away to the Grand-Guignol?" she said, her lips twitching slightly upward. "This is not a place for children to escape to. Won't your mother be looking for you?" The effect seized the hairs on her brow, and she hissed a little. Sabine rolled her eyes, kept picking.

"I'm not a child," I said. "And my mother is dead."

She blinked her eyes hard, the one that had been encased

in blood blinking a little more slowly than the other. Then she turned toward me, her whole body leaning from its chair as if she were drunk. Did she recognize me, from that night many months ago? It was unclear. Her eyes were bright, as if with fever. I felt that if all the lights went out, they would glitter like will-o'-wisps and lead me into the darkness.

"Very well, Bess," she said.

"My name is not Bess," I said. "It's—"

"It is now." She hiked up her dress and pulled a flask from her garter.

Something—disappointment, maybe—flicked through the muscles of Sabine's face, but then it went flat, cold. "Don't you have to ask Camille before—"

"I'll deal with him," said Maxa. She lit a cigarette, stood. "If anyone's looking for me, I'll be in the alley." She tipped her head back and sucked at the flask as if it were a teat, and then stood and drifted into the shadows.

Sabine handed me the mop.

Even when the Grand-Guignol was empty, it was never empty. Fat mice waddled casually along the baseboards, searching for what had rolled out of view. We chased bats out of the theater daily, an explosion of fur and leather. Crows—maybe even my crow—were taken to sauntering in casually, searching for food or baubles left behind by terrified audience members.

Camille did not seem to understand why Maxa had hired me—though how could he, as I hardly understood it myself—but since I slept in her dressing room in the theater and Maxa fed me, he did not object. His round glasses did not stay on his nose very well; I offered to bend the wire, but he pushed them up nervously and turned away.

Maxa's vanity was cluttered with what she needed and more: bulbed bottles of scent with sleek lines, a small scissors, mascaras and powders the color of chalk, lipstick and a metal tracer, kohl for her eyes, a hot curler, rouge, a fat brush tipped in pink dust, pencils, old scripts, a pair of bone-colored dice. It seemed like a place where spells were cast, that by scooping up a resident mouse and opening its throat into her wineglass, she might be able to curse whomever she pleased. But there was no need for animal blood; powdered carmine—which Sabine told me was created by boiling insects—arrived in small sacks and I spent my waking hours mixing and reheating the concoction like a vampiress.

At night, before sleep, I stared at the ceiling and thought about my mother—the gap of her, the tenacity of her voice. Every so often someone would come by to the theater's doors, rattling them with a drunken ferocity, and then their footsteps would recede. I understood better than most. I was outside those doors once, but I never would be again. I could have been out on the streets, hungry and terrified. Here, the questions that seemed to follow me my entire life did not seem relevant. I was invisible in a way that soothed me. My identity, my inclinations, my desires—it was all open for discussion.

Before my mother's death, when I performed the duty of pious daughter with rigor, there was a neighbor woman who often watched me from her window. My mother seemed to think of her as a useful eye—keeping watch on our door when she went to the market—but the woman never seemed to be watching with anything besides curiosity and disgust. Once, when I played jacks on the stoop, she came out and stood at the bottom of the steps with a basket slung on her hip.

"Where is your father, child?" she'd ask.

"He is—no longer here," I said, for that was what my mother had said when *dead* could not reach her lips.

She snorted as though she'd suspected as much.

"And who does your mother think she's fooling?"

I caught my ball and looked up at her face, hard with suspicion and even anger. I didn't know how to answer.

"We all know who she laid with," she said. "Look at you." Then she shook her head and walked down the street.

A week into my tenure, I woke to find Maxa sprawled over her vanity, moaning into her arms. I stood, alarmed, and when she did not respond I rushed out to the theater, where Sabine was scraping candle wax off the floor.

"Maxa is ill," I gasped, bent over from my pulsing heart.

Sabine stood with no tension, slowly wiping the blade on her skirt as she followed me backstage. She knelt down and looked at Maxa, who had fallen asleep.

"Wine or opium, Maxa?" she said loudly. Maxa moaned a little. "Both?" Sabine said. Maxa slid from the dressing table and crawled into my cot. She was asleep before she finished her ascent, and her body went soft bent over the wooden frame.

"Come," Sabine said. "If this is the new arrangement, you should know what needs to be done."

We stepped into the sunshine and took off down the road. Sabine withdrew a novel from her basket and read as we walked. I could not see the cover, but when I tried to read the words she twitched and turned the book so I could not see. We didn't speak until we arrived at the pharmacist's, and Sabine located a blue bottle on the shelf. She shook it a little and held it up to the light.

"What is it?" I asked.

"*Recette secrète*," she said.

"What?"

"Just some nonsense, but Maxa gets what she desires." She closed the bottle in her fist. Her expression was flat and cross. "Maxa watches you," she said. "She watches you like a cat watches a bird."

"Jealously?"

She snorted. "Hungrily."

Back at the theater, Sabine lifted Maxa's feet up onto the cot and then dragged her torso upright against the wall. She slapped her lightly on the cheek, and Maxa moaned piteously. Sabine handed me the bottle. I poured out the liquid with a trembling hand and laid the spoon against Maxa's tongue. She bit the metal and swallowed listlessly. Her eyes fluttered open, and I felt like I was at the edge of the mouth of a cave, with every intention of jumping in.

After I'd helped Maxa prepare for the night's performance, I was allowed to sit in the audience, though not to occupy a paying chair. I thought I would become tired or bored of the same rotating sets of plays every night, but I could not stop watching Maxa. She exhibited control over every twitch. She never laughed when she might have laughed, never put a crack in the tension.

Every night, Maxa screamed onstage. Her scream was a magnificent thing, a resonating animal that climbed out of her throat and gamboled around the room. Some nights, if the room was particularly hot, I swore I could see the ribbons of her voice emanating from her. She screamed as she was raped and strangled, disemboweled, stabbed. She screamed as she was consumed by wildcats, shot in the gut, shot in the head (here, accompanied by an uncanny whistling sound, as if the scream were coming through the newly created orifice). She screamed as she was beaten, lit on fire. Audience members would stagger into the street to vomit, and at the end of the night the cobblestone street was studded with glistening puddles.

There were always a few doctors in the audience, sitting at the end of their rows. They were necessary, as fainting of audience members was also a regular occurrence. Mostly men, which caused a great deal of snickering and speculation among us.

The prevailing theory for this fact was that women were always afraid and covering their eyes, and men watched what they could not—and then found themselves unable to bear it. But Maxa knew the truth, and told me the reason for the fainting. Most men, she said, would only see bodily fluids when they caught their ejaculate in their hands, or if their life ended at the wrong end of a brawl. But for women, gore was a unit of measurement: monthly cycles, the egg-white slip of arousal, the blood of virginity stolen through force of hand or the force of law, childbirth, fists splitting the skin of the skull, the leak of milk, tears.

(I once saw a woman in the street who had been knocked about by a lover, or perhaps a customer. Her eye socket looked crushed; the new shape of her head made my stomach curdle.

She was weeping, but the salt tears were pink. She wiped them from her filthy face and looked at them on her hand: the color of a rare diamond. "Even my tears bleed," she said, and staggered down the street.)

"Men occupy terra firma because they are like stones. Women seep because they occupy the filmy gauze between the world of the living and the dead," Maxa said. She was always saying stuff like that. But after watching her perform every night, I began to believe it.

<hr>

Weeks and months, Maxa died again and again. One of them, in the early spring—death by slicing with a trick razor—was among the most dramatic I'd ever seen. I had watched the rehearsals but could not wait to see the final effect. Louis's forehead gleamed with sweat beneath the stage lights. He was more scared than Maxa, I realized. But then again, that was easy—Maxa wasn't afraid at all.

From behind the curtain, I glanced out into the audience. When I squinted, I could see that their collective foreheads were hazy with filth. When the curtains kissed, I glanced out again, and realized that all of their foreheads were crossed with soot—it was Mercredi des Cendres.

I watched Louis slash thin lines across Maxa's breasts, blood seeping down her white slip. She shrieked in pain, her eyes glittering with pleasure. Then he drove the razor into her side. A stream of blood left her, as though he'd punctured a wine cask. The dagger's blade, I knew, sank easily into its handle, and the blood I had mixed and warmed myself, but the effect was alarming nonetheless.

When the play ended, the audience went to their feet, and would not stop clapping until Camille told them to leave.

Backstage, Sabine staggered beneath the weight of her water bucket. She came up behind Maxa. The thin metal handle drew a white stripe across her red hand.

"I want Bess to wash me," Maxa said.

Sabine flinched and then dropped the bucket to the floor. Water sloshed on the wood and drew up what was dried there. I barely heard her receding footsteps.

Maxa slumped into her chair. In her hand, she held her removed eye. I knelt before her and took it—a piece of chicken fat bound in twine and dipped in the carmine and glycerine, because the butcher had no beef eyes for us today—and set it wetly upon the vanity. I knew that the dark dip in her face was merely paint, but still when I approached it with a damp rag I felt something sour swell up inside me.

Maxa lifted her legs and balanced the balls of her feet on another chair. The fake blood had left dark lines down her body.

I rubbed the cleft behind her knee, not wanting to pull on the hair. She watched me, her lips pursed a little as if she wanted to moan but needed to stop herself. My rag felt like a living thing, a snake warmed by sunlight.

"My uncle was a garlic farmer," Maxa said, closing her eyes. "Hardneck garlic. Have you had it?"

"No," I said, wringing out the rag in a bucket.

"It's wild and peppery—the best you can have. My parents sent me there one summer when they worried the city was too wild for me. I would sit in the field and listen to the garlic grow. It sounded like a chorus of insects. I could hear a crackling, like onion skin. The air was green and sharp. They—they had such soft voices."

Though outside the audience was talking, laughing, their voices were muted, as though the room was a womb.

"My uncle would harvest them and dry them braided together and hanging in bundles from the ceiling. The roots were like little hairs, and the bulbs were purple as a man's eggs." She laughed a little. "My uncle would scold me, but sometimes I'd pull a clove and eat it raw. It tasted like . . ." Her mouth parted in memory, and in her mouth her tongue glistened like an oyster. "It tasted like a spell. When I got back, my father said I looked changed, and I think I was. I think the garlic tipped something in me. Kindling for a fire a long time coming."

"Where is your father?" I asked.

Maxa opened her eyes, and her leg twitched beyond my grasp. She ran her hand along her thigh and stared at the pinkish water on her fingertips.

"Where is *your* father?" she replied.

I did not know what to say. She leaned down and took my chin in her hand.

"What was he? Maghrébin? Your skin is gold in this light."

I flinched. "I don't know," I said. Maxa looked at my face like she wanted to bite it. Instead, she stood and examined herself. She seemed pleased. She walked behind me and gripped my shoulders in her powerful hands, and I felt blood rushing into the muscles that had been like stone. She worked her way around my flesh as if it were a spirit board, and her fingers were on the planchette, torturing answers and poems out of my pain. I writhed and twitched beneath her. "Thank you," I whispered, but she was already turning away.

Maxa's flat was a few streets over from the Grand-Guignol, on the hill, in a rickety tenement at the top of a narrow staircase. She did not answer the door when I knocked, but the knob turned with no resistance.

Somehow, I had imagined a room bathed in light—a kind of temple. But it was closer to a courtesan's boudoir. At one corner of the room was a beautiful divan, with plush gold-and-red brocade and a single, sensuous loop of an armrest. The walls were hung with posters from the Grand-Guignol, a daguerreotype of a woman I did not recognize.

The shelf was piled with books, a tiny brass pot, a horsehair brush. An articulated mouse skeleton in a bell jar. Her bed was covered in a fur blanket, on which was draped a massive wolfhound. The dog glanced at me and growled a little, the muscles tensing and releasing in liquid bursts beneath her hide, but Maxa made a barely audible *shush*, and she fell silent, her gaze fixed on Maxa's form.

"This is Athéna," she said, gesturing to the creature. "Hello, my little Bess," she said. "I'm glad you're here. I need to eat and bathe."

When she let her robe drop to the floor, I finally saw the body that I'd only caught glimpses of. Her thighs were round, and the hair between her legs a rusty brown, through which the slit of her sex was visible. Her stomach had a low pooch, like she was early with child, and her breasts were small as apples. Thin white scars clustered near the clefts of her.

I drew a bath for her, and after she lowered her body into the water, I cut her meat pie into chunks and blew on them until they were cool. She wanted no metal, so I fed her by hand. Her mouth was warm and tight. She was careful not to bite but used the edges of her teeth to pull the meat from my fingers.

She let me sleep at her feet, near Athéna. Curled there, I felt the jabs of her feet as she got comfortable, sought pockets of warmth.

In my dreams, she walked down the streets of Paris on a winter night, and I followed behind. Green, waxy scapes pushed from between the fine hairs of her mink coat, and when the wind blew they rustled and, with a creak, reached farther out. Her body blotted out the moon. She was an ambulatory garden, a beacon in a dead season, life where life should not grow.

———

Spring came. One morning, Maxa woke me from my cot by yanking my hair. "I need you," she said. "There's a car out-side." As I stood, she undressed me—removing my nightgown and digging around in my trunk for a day dress. I stood shiver-ing, my arms crossed over my breasts. When she'd finished, she unknotted my braid and gathered my hair into a soft chignon at the base of my neck.

In the car, our knees came together, bone knocking against bone.

"Have you ever had your fortune told, Bess?" Maxa asked me.

I shook my head.

"I hadn't, either, until I came to Paris. As a girl I had a doll who meant to tell little girls' fortunes. She had a skirt made of slips of paper, and you would ask a question and open her skirts and there would be answers waiting for you. I consulted her daily. Once, I asked her if I was meant to be upon the stage, and when I unfolded the slip it said that I should give up, as evidenced by my doubt. So I shredded her little skirt until there was nothing left."

I felt a terrible itch at my neck and reached behind to scratch it. My nails dug into the soft give of my skin, and I drew blood. Maxa leaned in and examined my fingers, dipping her own into the gore and examining what she found there.

"Many years ago, I visited a woman who told me many things that would eventually come to pass. But what happened past those events, she said, was shrouded in mist, and I needed to return to her once I met a *mulâtresse*."

The car stopped at Rue Vieille du Temple, and Maxa paid and stepped out to the street. I followed her down the road, where carts stood pitched against buildings and people of all types stood at low tables covered in fabric.

Maxa did not slow down at their tables; instead, she went to a particular door and knocked. A young girl answered. She tilted her head suspiciously up at Maxa, but Maxa handed her a small green stone, which she examined briefly. She shouted something in a language I did not understand into the house, and from its depths a voice answered back. Maxa pushed past the girl, who pocketed the stone and smiled at me, as if we shared a secret.

The room the girl led us to was dark and narrow, cluttered with bric-a-brac and a narrow table. The woman who sat at the table was young—perhaps the girl's mother—and she sat in front of a brass bowl and a glass pitcher filled with water.

"You've come back," she said.

Maxa gestured toward me. "I want the mist cleared," she

said. I sat in a chair in the corner of the room. A thin white cat leapt easily into my lap despite her ancient gait and rolled her skull against my breastbone.

The woman looked at me, her expression unreadable. Then she tilted her pitcher toward us and filled the bowl with water. She waited for it to settle, and then withdrew a vial from her sleeve. A single drop of oil struck the surface, and after a moment it spread outward. She cupped her hands around the bowl's edge and gazed deeply into it.

I looked over at Maxa. Her face had lost its lazy, indolent softness; she was alert, tense, her lower lip pinched beneath her tooth. The woman looked up at me again, and then returned her gaze to the water. "You are a conduit for violence, but not a host. It passes through you," she said.

"Is that all?"

"You will die a violent death."

I saw Maxa gather the red tablecloth in her hands and feared she would yank the bowl and table over.

"Maxa," I said. "She's just a foolish woman."

The woman's eyes snapped at me, and then drifted back down to her bowl.

"What do you see in there, about my friend?" Maxa asked.

The woman shook her head. Maxa dug into her glove and removed another franc. The woman slipped it into her purse and gazed back down.

"On a distant shore, your lover will find you," she said. She looked back at me. "What are you?" she asked me, and I had no answer.

Back in her flat, Maxa seemed agitated. She spun around pinching the air as though reaching for something, and then finally alighted upon a black box on her vanity. When she opened it up, I saw soft spheres resting in between crumpled cloth. She removed one and held it up.

"A fig," she said, "all the way from Spain." She handed it to me. It was warm and dense and heavy, and a milky drop of nectar clung to the fruit's opening.

"Where did you get these?" I asked.

"Oh, an admirer left them for me after a show," she said. "Eat!"

I did not know whether to bite or split, but Maxa bit into hers, and I did as well. In the bite, I could see hundreds of tiny seeds, shadowed and clustered like orphans at an open door. I pushed into the opening with my finger, and the fruit clung to me like rugae drawing me in.

"It's the flower," she said. "It's grown inward, see? It is less beautiful but much sweeter for the effort. I'm told wasps crawl into its depths and die."

The fruit slid down my throat, but I could not bring myself to take another bite.

I do not know when I first understood that Marcel was Maxa's lover; she never talked about him. Marcel was a queer figure, always fluttering and talking, the opposite of Maxa's languid substance. He was mealy and pale and perpetually damp, something one might uncover by inverting a stone in a garden. His hair was his only redeeming feature, long and soft. But I noticed that Maxa's chin twitched downward in his presence, and his never did. I did not like how he touched her, as if he owned her from her skin inward, the way he tangled his fingers in her hair and pulled as if drawing on a leash and pinched her breasts and thighs as though testing her tenderness.

He did not like me, either. He called me Maxa's little Arab, her whore, her *vase de nuit*. One evening, after the two of them had polished off a bottle of Arrouya noir, he put his cigarette out in my skirts. I yelped and leapt up from the divan, shaking the material so it did not catch on fire. From beneath heavy lids, Maxa watched this performance without comment, even when I looked at her for guidance. Then she yawned, her tongue black with wine.

Only the next day did she take me out to buy me a new skirt and laughed as if we were dearest and oldest friends catching up after an absence.

It was Marcel's idea to take us both to see La Revue Nègre at the Théâtre des Champs-Élysées. It was brand-new, and nearly impossible to attend, but Marcel knew a man who knew a stagehand.

Maxa brought me to her apartment for preparation. The dress she'd found was short, heavy with silver beads, beautiful despite being shapeless. When I reached out to run my fingers through the fringe, Maxa slapped my hand away. "Hair first," she said, pushing me down in her chair.

Maxa let my hair down and tried to take a brush to it. The brush caught, resisted. She instead ran her fingers through from root to tip, lightly tugging at the snarls and knots. "There's no reason to let it be like this," she told me.

In the mirror, my hair made me look indescribably young. I looked away. "It's always been this way," I said.

"We should change that, Bess."

"Why do you call me Bess?" I said.

She lifted my hair up like a curtain and let it drop over my shoulders. I thought she would refuse to answer, but when she spoke her voice curved with a smile.

"Have you read 'The Highwayman'?" she asked.

I shook my head.

"A lover read it to me," she said. "He brought it from Scotland." She fondled the curls that gathered around my ears. "A landlord's daughter falls in love with a brigand, and he is betrayed to soldiers."

She tugged again, and I yelped at the pain. She rubbed my scalp soothingly and then opened a drawer behind her. With a whisper, she looped a scarf over my wrist, binding it to the arm of the chair.

"Maxa—"

"The soldiers come"—she bound the other arm—"and tie Bess—that's her name, Bess—to her bedpost, and place a musket between her breasts." When she lifts the scissors into the air, I struggle against the bonds, but it feels perfunctory. I know what is going to happen.

"She knows that they are plotting to kill her lover as soon as he returns, so she finds the trigger of the gun," Maxa said. "'Then her finger moved in the moonlight'—"

The first cut was crisp and terrible.

"'Her musket shattered the moonlight'—"

Another.

"'Shattered her breast in the moonlight'—"

Again.

"'And warned him—with her death.'"

I hadn't realized how much my scalp had been aching until

so much of me was gone. My hair ended in a jagged horizon at my chin. "I look like an urchin," I said.

"I should leave you like this," she said to my reflection.

I believed that she would, but then she laughed. "I'm not finished." She pulled the chair sideways and sat directly across from me, bringing the blade close to my face. Every dry snip sounded like a mouse setting off a trap. Dozens of snips, dozens of mice scuttling to their doom.

"So she died for her lover," I said.

"He dies for her, too," she said. "At the end. He's shot down on the road."

With the weight lifted, my hair gathered up into the curl I hadn't seen since I was a girl. She oiled it a little, then brought a hot iron to the ends, curling them under. After, she pasted curls to my forehead with petroleum jelly. "Spit curls," she said. "One for every man you've kissed."

"I haven't—"

"Shh."

"Maxa," I said, "are you still upset about the fortune-teller?"

She shook her head as she dragged her finger down her tongue, sharpening the curl by my ear to a point. "No," she said. "You're not a *mulâtresse*. That was my mistake. The reading was similarly in error."

I stared at the tapestry behind her head—some Eastern cloth tacked into the wall; a tableau of tigers and elephants.

"What are you?" she said. "Tell me."

"I don't know."

"What sort of an answer is that? You must know."

"My mother was a teacher," I said. "My father died when I was young."

A bobby pin scraped my skull, and I flinched. Maxa looked slightly deflated, but then she busied herself at her vanity. She lifted up one of her bottles and poured out a spoonful. I opened my mouth obediently, like a child, and the liquid was bitter. I asked her what it was, and she did not reply. The powder puff huffed over my face, and I coughed. I felt a warmth gathering in my belly; the air softened. Maxa had been chewing on fennel seed; her breath was sweet.

"What country did your mother travel to, to teach the heathens?"

I closed my eyes, as if trying to remember, even though I knew I did not. "A warm place," I said. "She was sent back after the war."

"What do you remember, of the warm place?"

"Nothing."

"Nothing?"

"Trees."

"Don't be stupid, Bess. What kind of trees?"

I tried to imagine them, but as soon as one appeared in my mind's eye I saw my mother, laughing, bending down for me, and I felt my mouth tremble.

"Oh, oh, oh, now," she said. "Never mind. Now is not the time. You have to be still."

I clenched my anus and felt my organs settle in me. She drew on my face, and it felt like she was drawing forever, like she was tracing my whole self because I'd faded into myself. Like I'd become a smooth dome of skin and she needed to put back what had vanished.

She lifted her gilded hand mirror and inverted it before me.

I did not recognize myself. My skin was pale as death, paler even, and the cupid's bow of my lips pouted unnaturally. My eyes were smudged dark as if I'd been struck twice. I felt old. Not old as Maxa, nor old as my mother before the illness took her, but old enough to have seen all of time in its infinite cycles, looping over and over again.

She unbound my arms and tossed the scarves back into a drawer. I lifted them and rubbed at the marks.

The dress Maxa had bought for me was oddly square—the style, yes, but beneath it my body's elements were subsumed. My new face now sat atop a neutered body, a body as soft and sexless as an infant's. I shivered. Maxa produced a mink coat and put it on me. The hairs grazed my skin, and I had the uncanny sensation that a living thing was slung over my shoulders, breathing intimately against me.

Marcel came in without knocking, and he bent to the floor to gather the leavings from the haircut. He rasped it between his fingers with an expression of disgust before dropping it to the floor.

Then we were down in the street, and Marcel was opening a door, and a cab whisked us down the street. The car bobbed and weaved and jolted over the cobblestones like we were small, and we were running and I could not tell if we were the escaping prey or the fox pursuing it.

————

Years before we arrived there, the Théâtre des Champs-Élysées had been the site of a terrible riot. I was a young girl, but the stories reached my ears anyway: how Igor Stravinsky's *Rite of Spring* alongside a ballet performance set in pagan Russia had set the audience to madness. They barked like dogs and climbed on their seats; I even heard that one of them tried to burn the theater to the ground. As we approached the façade, Maxa murmured something to Marcel, and he laughed raucously.

Inside, we took our seats, Maxa between us. The stage grew dark. From the ceiling, a platform descended, and as it landed on the stage, I saw a woman, a negress, sprawled on a bright mirror. When she looked up, I felt like she was staring directly at me. Her hair was slicked tightly against her head, and the outline of her body gleamed like light on a river. When she stood, a set of long, pink feathers concealed her breasts and between her legs; she was otherwise nude. The music opened as a shimmer and then went wild; in the same way, the dancer began to jerk and turn as though seized with madness. She seemed multiplied, three women dancing as one. And as she quaked, she sang. Her voice began low and wide and wooden and then lifted to the ceiling, bright and wire-thin. Between, it warbled as beautifully as any songbird. I felt something light up inside me like a candle knocked against a curtain.

"The Black Pearl," Maxa whispered in my ear. "Josephine Baker. They say she has a pet cheetah with a diamond collar."

Around us, the audience leaned closer with every breath. They had, I thought, the same hunger as the Guignoleurs, though they didn't know it.

"Do you ever dream of singing and dancing, Maxa?" I asked.

The smile that came to her lips faded so quickly it was as if I'd imagined it. "I only know how to scream," she said. Marcel placed his hand on her thigh. "And that's all anyone wants from me."

Marcel knew a nightclub and hailed a cab for all of us.

I had never seen so many different people in the same space. Parisians pulsed together, closer than I had ever seen in the streets. Marcel vanished and brought back two fluted glasses.

"What is this?" I asked over the music.

"Just drink it," he said, turning away and gesturing to a man who seemed to know him.

"Maxa?"

"*Le soixante-quinze*," she said.

"Why is it called that?" I asked.

The drink lurched as a man stumbled into my body, and then clutched the fat of my face in his large hands. He leaned in, inches from me. "Because it is like being shot with a field gun!" he howled before Maxa pushed him away. Even as he stumbled into the crowd, I could see his glistening mouth and yellowing teeth, smell his rank breath. I closed my eyes and drank.

The drink bubbled in my mouth, an unexpected explosion of botanical sweetness. I drained it to the bottom, and Maxa handed me hers and gestured for more. Marcel lifted his own glass toward the jazzmen in the front and laughed raucously. He fumbled beneath Maxa's skirt, and I looked away.

One young woman, a negress with high cheekbones, danced with a white girl I'd seen in the Grand-Guignol many times. They held each other close, kissed each other's wrists, moved as if the room were empty. The familiarity between them made me ache. Maxa followed my gaze.

"Tomorrow they may pass each other in the street, and it'll

be like they never met," she said softly into my ear. "That's always how it goes."

"But they have what they want," I said. "Even just for a night."

"Well," she said. "One of them, at least."

We returned to the apartment in the earliest hours of the morning. Maxa gave me a glass of sherry, and I stared at it for a moment before crawling onto the divan and falling asleep. I heard her set it down on the nightstand, and the murmur of their voices.

I woke up to hear the sound of Marcel's open palm on Maxa's skin. With every *crack*, I imagined where his hand was going—her face, her buttocks—and when I turned my face ever so slightly I saw he was hitting glistening cunt. At every beat, she gasped and writhed, and tears leaked to her pillow. I closed my eyes, but the musk of her hung in the air, and I could not make myself leave the room, even in sleep.

———

On a warm evening in May, Maxa invited me to take a walk with her. We drifted away from Saint-Georges, down past the Théâtre Mogador. She held my arm with an uncanny intimacy, as if we had been friends since childhood.

"I have seen you write," she said. "Have you ever considered writing a play?"

"I've never written a play," I said. "I enjoy your performances, but I don't know if I could write anything that could rise to them."

"It isn't about that," she said. "It's a pairing of power, not a transfer of it. The actress and the authoress meet in the middle."

I picked up my skirts to avoid a pile of horseshit.

"You know," she said, "I like that you still wear this old-fashioned thing. I bet you still wear a corset, too." I flushed.

"I only wear it because I can't afford anything new," I said. She pulled me around another pile of dung, and when I was clear of it—but could still hear the buzzing of flies—she did not remove her hand but ran it along the line of my shoulder. I shuddered with the familiarity of it.

Then we were at the Seine, past Champs-Élysées, and I blinked at the river, which had come up so suddenly. It flowed with an aggressive swiftness, and I suspected that if there'd been light in the sky, the motion would have made me dizzy.

"Have you ever noticed how the buildings become less crowded as you get closer to the water?" Maxa asked me. "It's like the teeth of a young girl as she ages into an old woman. One day she has too many, and eventually she will have too few, a mouth of glistening gums."

We began to walk over a bridge. Halfway through, Maxa turned to look out to the water. I did as well. The river unspooled before us like a line of spilled ink making its way across a table. Along the shore, we saw something moving in the shadows.

"When I was a girl," she said, "a mad dog bit the neighbor's child. The dog was shot dead, but the girl became ill. My mother and I went to visit her, and in her bed she saw me and began to scream. She howled and kicked and acted mad herself, as if she would have rather torn through the walls with her bare hands than be in the room for one more moment with me."

She fell silent, and I worried a chip of stone that had been resting on the railing. She did not say anything else, and after a few minutes we continued walking.

When we reached the Nymphs at the center of the bridge,

Maxa turned my body toward her. The stone railing was cold against my back. She bent my torso backward over it and wrapped her hand lazily around my throat, like a sleepy man clutching his member to piss. Behind me, the black river was a starless sky, and the sky a star-filled river, and she pulled up my skirt and stroked my sex with her fingers. I hung there like a strung-up game bird, blood vacillating between my legs and my head, until I felt a swell like the air before a storm. My abdomen spasmed, and the more I trembled the more firm her grip became, and somewhere in the space between darkness and darkness my cells expanded outward and I bore down against her hand as if my muscle wished to vacate my skin.

"Thank you," I said. "Thank you, thank you."

She pulled me upright and drew my shaking body against her breast. Then she kissed me as if extracting snake venom from a wound.

Back in her room, she removed her stockings and pulled her skirt to her waist. I went to her with my mouth, but she pulled my face toward hers and slipped my fingers inside. She circled my fingers, all muscle and fold, drew me in, and I moaned into her collarbone. It felt like I was pushing into a closed fist.

"Write me a play, Bess," she said, panting and pushing against me. "Write the filthiest, foulest, most tremendous play, and we will put it on."

That night, I dreamt that I was spread-eagle on a ceramic platter larger than my body, glossy and white as the moon. In the sky, a blazing star grew larger and larger, coming toward both of us. Maxa sat down before me, and began to swallow me like a python, and I was gripped by the muscle of her until she'd taken me in entirely. The air grew white and hot, and even as we were unmade, I was coming. When I woke up, nude and draped at Maxa's feet, I knew the play that had to be written.

"It's ready," I said to her the first day in September. Around us, the cast gathered for rehearsal. Maxa took my face in her hands and kissed me, long and slow.

"Wonderful," she said, her mouth twisting up into a smile. "I crave the experience of reading it next to you. Wait for me after tonight's performance, and we will read it together."

That night, I let myself in and sat on her bed, the play resting on my lap. The show had recently ended, and when enough time had passed for Maxa to change, I expected to hear her footsteps on the stairs, but there was nothing. Athéna chewed on a butcher's bone in the corner, but after a while she ambled up to the bed and laid her silky head on my lap, on top of the pages. As the hours wore on, my back became stiff, and I drifted into shallow half dreams until my wilting body woke me with a jerk.

Well past midnight, I heard voices on the stairs—Maxa's sotto, Marcel's reedy as a girl's. When the door opened, I saw Maxa's surprise soften into remembrance. They were both drunk; a haze of anise surrounded them. Athéna growled lightly at Marcel.

"Your little dog is here," he slurred at her, and I realized he did not mean Athéna. He walked up to me and grabbed my knee through my skirts. "Will you service us both? Or are you as useless a hole as you are an attendant?"

"Marcel," Maxa said. He turned and grabbed her wrist.

"What, my love?" he sang, his voice shot through with

threat. Athéna barked, a ridge of fur raised along the back of her neck.

She twitched and twisted her arm away but said nothing else. Marcel looked at me again, and while arousal was in there, somewhere, it was mostly anger. He kissed Maxa gently on the cheek. She did not look at him.

"Good night, my queen," he said, and left.

Maxa stood there in the darkness of the room. I could not see her face. I thought of a doll I'd had as a child, a faceless doll my mother told me had come from my grandmother. A young girl who lived nearby drew a face on my doll in charcoal, and after that I would not touch her.

"Bess," Maxa said finally. I stood there, the pages tight in my arms. She tried to take them; after pulling hard, I relented. She sat on the bed and flipped through them, reading with the kind of sustained focus I normally only saw on the stage. When she arrived at the climax, her eyes glittered. "Oh, Bess," she said. "Bess, my Bess."

I got down on my knees, but she drew me up and laid me on the bed. "I am so sorry," she said, stroking my hair. "I am sorry for Marcel. He's a slug and a bore, and you're like lightning that turns sand to glass." She rubbed her thumb over my pulse.

"Why do you stay with him?" I asked.

"You're so young, Bess." She lifted my skirt with a rustle and leaned her mouth into my ear. "You simply don't understand. The world is terrifying for women. For us."

She began to massage my sex with her thumb, and when my body acquiesced she slipped inside. Her thrusts were saturated with need, as if her hand were a cock. I whimpered and felt myself curl around her, and she sealed her free palm over my face. "Bess, Bess, my little Bess," she whispered. "Do you want to go to Greece with me?" Her hand did not move from my mouth. "We could leave this theater and take a train to Thessaloniki. We could tell people we're cousins and no one will pry. We can have goats and sheep and plant garlic and never have to labor outside our own walls."

I felt pleasure from far away, like a horse cresting the horizon. The door to her flat rattled loudly, and Marcel's slurred voice drifted in from behind it.

"Maxa," he said. "Maxa, come with me."

My back arched, and she pressed her hand against my mouth. The sound that had nearly escaped moved back and forth between my cunt and my head, with no release.

"I come to you, my king," she chirruped bright as a bird, and then whispered in my ear, "I will check the train schedule, I promise." She slipped her hand out of me, whisked her coat around her body, and was gone.

When the door shut, the sound that had been staggering through my body came out in a ragged sob. The candle on the table guttered, even though there was no wind.

The troupe gathered and read the play together, and when it was over a pall of silence descended onto the room.

"This play is profane, even for us," Sabine said. "The police will come."

Camille looked helplessly at Maxa, but she was smiling at me. "Don't be afraid, loves," she said. "This is going to be the best show we've ever performed."

The night of my play's debut, I arrived at the theater early only to find Maxa and Marcel drinking on my old cot.

Maxa's eyes glittered. "I've had an idea, Bess," she said. She lifted up a cigar box and opened it; inside were lines of francs.

"Maxa," I breathed.

She sent me down into the house to place the bills on the seats. I did, and when I had leftovers I turned and showed them to her. She made a scattering motion, so I swung around and released the bills everywhere. When I had rid myself of every scrap, I returned to the stage and to the peephole where Maxa stood.

The audience began to enter. The Guignoleurs moved with swiftness, and others flinched and rolled their eyes upward, taking it all in. Then, a woman in a beaded dress noticed the franc on a chair and lifted it to her eyes. She turned to her companions, who were laughing. "It's real!" she said. "It's real!"

Her musical voice ran through the crowd like a swift illness. Others began to echo her, unthinkingly at first, and then it took, as they saw the paper scattered at their feet.

"Let me see," said Maxa.

Marcel, Maxa, and I stood there, taking turns at the peephole. Maxa laughed wickedly, and when Marcel looked I saw his muscles tense, like a cat about to pounce.

"Please," I said, and pressed my eye socket to the peephole.

In the audience, the patrons tore at one another. The ladies abandoned their hats and handbags, crawled over one another, their skirts riding up. The men punched one another in the jaw, cracked chair backs against skulls. They did not look human, but rather like a group of feral cats I had once seen swarm over a horse who had fallen in the street—liquid and animal both.

Maxa's breath was hot in my ear, and I felt her pressing against me. It was only when the pressing became rhythmic that I realized that Marcel was behind us both, and Maxa's skirt was drawn up to her hips. My breath quickened, and I braced myself against the wall, so that I might slip away. Maxa grabbed my wrist.

"Please don't leave me," she begged into my ear. "Please don't."

A woman who had been rummaging about on the floor sat up, a fistful of francs in her hand like a wedding bouquet. But instead of pocketing it, she threw it back above the crowd, refreshing the chaos. I heard Marcel make his groan of culmination, and then he was done, disappeared into the back of the theater. I turned around and saw Maxa there, looking disheveled. Sabine came running up to us—"Maxa, you need to change!"—and then I went and sat in the audience.

And so the play began.

———————

I had, as Maxa commanded, written the most degenerate play I could have imagined.

Jean—a kind and solid man I'd forgotten existed before this moment; a man whose face I would not remember after this night—walked to the center of the stage. "I am your host for the evening. Tonight, we will not be showing *The Blind Ship*. Instead, we have the debut performance of a new play, by a playwright brand-new to our stage. A virgin, if you will. The play is called *The Star*."

The audience tittered. Jean lifted his arm and walked to the edge of the stage, bowing as he did so.

"The village of Roquebrune-Cap-Martin," he announced, "at the end of the world."

When the curtain rose, Maxa was standing atop a swelling slope, a falcon on her arm. Behind her, a servant lifted bits of bloody meat to the falcon's beak, which the falcon seized with a quickness. Beneath the stage, attendants used water and mirrors to send soft and glittering orbits into the room, as though she stood on the ocean's shore. She smiled. Her lip curved like a hooked finger drawing a viewer into a room.

"It is the end of the world," she said. "See, the comet in the sky. It tears down toward us, threatening. I am the last queen that reigns over man."

Jean dropped to his knee. "I'd do anything for you, my queen."

"A comet in the sky," Maxa repeated again. "I thought it was the moon, but it is coming to end us. It bears down on us like a disapproving eye. It reveals truths and dispels illusions. It causes us to remember what we never knew we forgot. It causes us to forget what we never knew. We are small, we are small. Mankind's theater is wasted on our smallness."

We arrived at the part of the play where the dialogue and stage direction ceased. The actors were instructed to turn to the audience.

"What do we do with our final queen?" they said, in unison.

There was silence among the audience. I waited for five breaths before opening my mouth to command: "Worship her." I imagined an orgy of bodies. Indeed, even Jean was unbuttoning his cuffs, preparing for the audience's lust.

But in the same instant, a deep voice bellowed from the audience, swallowing my own. "Strike her down." There was a beat of silence, and the actors did not respond.

Another voice, higher this time. A woman's. "Subdue her."

"My people," Jean said, rolling up his sleeves. "The comet arrives. The end of the world is nigh. Perhaps . . ." He flicked the edge of Maxa's breast suggestively. Beneath the fabric, her nipple hardened to a pebble, but she did not move. She continued to stare at the audience, impassive, her face slack as dough.

"Beat her," said another man.

Jean looked at me, but I did not know how to intervene. My play felt alive, less created than born, and I had no more control over it than any being.

The first blow was soft, like a parent wishing to frighten a child instead of hurt them. Maxa barely moved; the hand seemed to sink into her. Jean turned back to the audience, a troubled expression moving across his face like clouds before the moon.

"And now that she is softened," he began, "perhaps we—"

"Again," said a young woman who barely looked old enough to be in the audience.

Jean looked at his hand as if he did not recognize it, as if it was some creature that had climbed onto his limb for a ride. He struck Maxa again but did not look at her.

Now the audience was silent, but the command rose from them like a collective thought. Their white faces bobbed in the blackness like so many corpses in the river. Jean hit her again and again. As she fell, the falcon took off from her arm and swooped toward the woman with the scraps of meat. She shrieked and tossed them to the ground; the bird landed and swallowed them one after another.

Jean grabbed Maxa's hair and lifted her to her feet.

The fifth time he struck her, a woman stood up in the audience. "Stop!" she screamed. Around her, a few glazed eyes turned upward. She grabbed the jacket of her escort, a dewy young man who looked at her as though she was making an observation about the weather. "Stop," she cried again, and stumbled over the legs of audience members so that she might make her way to the aisle. "He's hurting her, he's truly hurting her!" she said, pushing over the bodies in her way. "Make him stop!"

Jean struck Maxa again, so hard I heard a *crack*, and she collapsed to the stage for a final time. The woman kept pushing her way through the audience, and in one swift motion a group of men stood and bore her body aloft. She shrieked in fear, and once again cried, "Stop, stop, he's hurting her!" and the men passed her back, and men and women alike pushed her into the air, her body contorting like a puppet, and they passed her around, pulling the clothing from her like the skin from an orange. Segment by segment, her garments fluttered to the floor. Her body was white as pith.

She began to scream anew—no longer for Maxa, but for herself. The actors stood there, waiting out the stage direction that had so delighted Maxa: *When worked into a frenzy, let the audience play out their desire until their exhaustion and natural submission.*

Then the crowd opened up like an orifice and drew the woman into itself, and she sank as if in quicksand. There was a sound—a slurping, a yawn, as if she had entered into a giant

mouth. Then, as suddenly as it had began, the audience returned to their seats. The woman was nowhere to be found.

Jean's eyes were soft and wet as rose petals. He staggered
past his cue. "It comes," he said, though what was coming he
did not say. "It comes."

The effect of the comet striking the earth was twofold: light
and sound. When the stage cleared, the actors had dropped
down flat, and the falcon continued to eat, a hard eye turned to
them all. Of course, they should have been nude, having fallen
directly from whatever sexual position they'd been imitating.
But instead they dropped from violence to death with nothing
in between.

The audience sat there, as in a trance. Then they began to
clap, and clap, and they stood. Cloth from the woman's dress
was strewn over the seats and their arms, and they clapped and
clapped and clapped. It was only the lights coming up that
stopped them from clapping unto blood.

Camille met me backstage. "We will switch back to *The
Blind Ship* tomorrow," he said. He pushed a pile of scripts into
my hands.

When the audience had departed, I walked up the sides of
the aisles, looking for the woman. I saw white scraps of dress,
but no naked, crawling thing, not even a corpse. I walked the
perimeter of the theater, but she was simply gone.

Many years later, when Paris was a distant memory, I asked
myself if I had known that the audience would not encourage
the actors to descend into an orgy, but would instead demand
Maxa be taken apart before them? That only the intervention

of a woman in the audience, a stranger who then lost her life at their hands, had prevented such a thing? I do not know.

———

When I arrived at Maxa's flat that night, I found Athéna looping around the street, whining piteously.

I ran up the steps to the flat and leaned my ear against the door. Marcel's reedy voice floated toward me. "I love you, my demon, my sweet," he said. I heard the sound of leather on skin, but was not certain if they rang with rage or pleasure. Then, the *crack*ing sound ended with the faintest of chimes—metal. I began to throw myself against the door.

"Bess," Maxa screamed from inside. "Bess, help me, help me, please, God, help me."

As the door gave beneath my shoulder, the belt buckle struck the side of my face. I spun blindly and pinned Marcel to the wall, yanking the belt from his hand. I struck his groin, and he crumpled.

"Get out of here," I said. He stood and ran.

I closed the door and turned back. Maxa was sprawled on the divan, weeping. Her dress was torn, and welts bubbled on her skin as if she'd been burned. I wetted a cloth with water and brought it to her.

"Oh, Bess," Maxa said, clutching tearily at my skirts. "He was mad, he was mad. I did this. I lit some wicked fire in him. He wished to purge my sins—"

"You'll be all right," I said, dabbing at the welts.

"I lit some fire in you, too. I created you, turned you into a monster."

I lifted the cloth and let it drip onto the floor. Maxa gathered herself from her weeping and stared at me as if she did not recognize me.

"I am not a monster," I said, "and you did not create me." I confess here that my voice wavered a little, for I thought of my mother, and for the first time in a year longed to hear my name, my true name, in her voice.

Maxa laid her head against my stomach as if she were an exhausted child. I stroked her hair. "You love me, don't you, Bess?" she asked. She looked, the goldfish of her mouth trembling. She smelled like *le fruit défendu*, like overripe apricots fallen to the earth, bitter smoke. I held her face in my hands; it was lovely and cold. "I must go," I said, and she did not stop me.

As I left, I opened the door, and before I left whistled for Athéna, who loped up the stairs and went straight to her mistress.

The next morning, Maxa was gone. No one at the theater knew where she was, though she'd left a note, and Sabine was preparing to fill in. Marcel, they told me, had been arrested in the night for his drunkenness—he'd assaulted a woman outside a hotel after he'd left Maxa's flat. An officer lingered in the doorway, having been making inquiries about a disturbance, and a young woman who had not returned to her dormitory.

"What kind of theater is this, exactly?" he asked, squinting nearsightedly at the poster on the wall.

"We perform religious plays," I said breathlessly. "Excuse me."

When I arrived at her apartment, I found it full of her possessions and empty of life. It was only when I asked her landlord that he procured a piece of paper with her thick, cramped hand-writing—a forwarding address in Rouen, and several months' rent. I caught the next train.

When I arrived, I hired a driver. A steady rain obscured the details of the landscape except for turning of the wheels and the road unfolding behind us.

It seemed like an age that I stood at Maxa's door, my wet hair wrapped around my throat like a noose. The yard was quiet as a cemetery. Beneath a willow tree, loose soil bulged with new death. A shadow slipped across the window, and I knocked. She did not answer. I threw myself against the entrance but slipped and fell into the mud. I stood and lifted a stone, intending to break the lock, and the door opened. I saw a single, liquid eye. She opened the door farther and took me in. She looked at me as if she'd never seen me before. I pushed past her and into the warm little villa.

"What are you doing here?" she asked me. She looked frailer than I remembered her, wrapped in a bloodred kimono limned with blue-and-gold cranes. She turned toward her window, and then her eyes seemed to land upon the grave in her yard. "Athéna died. Her back legs went soft and she shit herself and then she left me in the middle of the night. Sickness follows me wherever I go."

My jittering fingertips missed the buttons before it found them. I undressed before her and pressed her hands against my gooseflesh. I thought they would be warm, but they were cold, even colder than me.

"Strike me," I said.

She stared at me as if I were mad.

"No," she said.

I grabbed her hands and placed them around my throat. When I released them, they fell limply to her sides. Water dripped down my body.

"You asked me if I loved you."

"I—"

"I don't need you to tell me you love me," I said, "but you do need to tell me that I will not be limping after you for our entire lives. That my humiliation is not your only pleasure. I don't want your performance or your persona. I just need to know that you need me, or some part of me."

Her eyes filled with actress's tears, and when my face did not soften, it hardened to real anger. "Need you for what?" she said flatly. "I'm not an invert."

The slap I delivered to her cheek was not hard, but she crumpled to the floor like a kicked animal anyway. There, I heard a high, keening sound, and I realized that she was weeping. I had never heard her truly cry before. She clawed listlessly at the wooden floor, as if it were earth and she could bury herself there. I pulled up my dress. She stayed on the floor, curled into herself. I would never see her stand again.

"I'll find you, Bess," she said. "On the distant shore, remember? I will find you, when I can be better than I am."

"My name is not Bess," I said, leaning down to her. "And you will never know what it really is."

As I walked back to the train station, the rain began to dissipate, and the clouds faded like breath dissolving into the winter air. When I arrived at the station, the bustle of it was strangely muted. I looked up into the sky. A bright new star glittered next to the waning moon, and the people on the platform pointed to it in wonder, faces all turned equally toward this new sight.

Watching the countryside flit past the fixed window, I remembered something I hadn't thought about in a long time: the first time I saw Maxa, decomposing on that stage. How she had let herself dissolve away.

———————

I drifted west, to London, where I worked as a seamstress like my mother had and spent what little discretionary money I had on the movies.

I loved silent films—perhaps because the dark eyes and expressive faces of the actresses, which commanded with so little effort—but when sound arrived I felt a fluttering moth of excitement. The world was advancing forward, in its own way. I did not know then, sitting there in the darkness, that under the dialogue I was hearing the death knells of the Grand-Guignol from across La Manche, one pleasure traded for another.

Then the war came—men doing what men did. When it was over, and the newspapers were filled with humankind's unspeakable horrors, the Grand-Guignol had nothing new to show us anymore.

———————

I emigrated to the United States a few years before Hitler's occupation of Paris. My life settled into some manner of routine. Montmartre was in my past and would remain there.

One afternoon, a letter arrived for me from Algiers: my aunt, searching for me.

I have sent a dozen letters after you, she wrote. *Many years have passed since we have laid eyes on each other. It was terrible to lose you, beloved creature; I hope to find you soon.*

The letter was soft from its travels and, when I placed it against my nose, smelled like incense. My mother had dabbed an oil onto her wrists when she was alive, at night, after I'd always gone to bed, though it lingered on her in the morning. It smelled like this, like a fire in a cedar grove. I had not smelled it in so many years. My body seized up with distant grief, and that was how my lover found me—sitting in an armchair and clutching the letter to my breastbone, spasming with anguish. She brought me a pen and the stationery with my name embossed at the top. "Write back," she said.

———

The next afternoon, as I carried my letter to the post office, I felt something on my neck—the sensation of Maxa's gaze. Though she was decades past, I flinched and reached up to smooth the hairs that had prickled there. I turned. It was a bright, matte day. The sky was the color of strangulation; the streets glittered like crushed glass. Beneath them, New York's creatures teemed and strutted like they'd all been loosed from their circus.

Then I saw her face, looming up from the cover of a magazine. The vendor who was selling it smiled toothily when I handed over my money.

At home, I spread the magazine open on the table. "I Am the Maddest Woman in the World," the headline read, and what followed was a first-person account of what Maxa perceived to be her life. I read that she had returned to Paris after her time in the country, and about the series of doomed love affairs she'd carried on then. One man, a Paris businessman, had made her line the walls of her flat with black velvet. I pictured her on the bed, curled up there, like a tiny brooch at the bottom of a jewelry box. She had, it seemed, returned to the Grand-Guignol for a final performance, in which she screamed so loudly she ravaged her voice, and could now do nothing but whisper. The article did not mention me, except for a single reference to the "degenerate women" she had power over.

My lover read the article over my shoulder, her breasts grazing my back. She did not speak as I flipped the pages, only huffed a little through her nose when she arrived at certain lines. When it was over, and I set the magazine down on the table, she said, "Come, my little degenerate, let's go for a walk."

When I didn't move, she slid her fingernails along my scalp and gripped my hair at its base. When she gently pulled my head back, she delivered a kiss to the naked arc of my throat. I felt a spasm of joy.

"Now, Aisha," she said into my skin, her voice acid and sweet, and my skull vibrated with my name. I stood and followed her into the street.

The Voyeurs

by Zeyn Joukhadar

The Peeping Tom had left a pair of gray men's briefs under the sugar maple behind the house. The underwear lay rumpled across the fresh crust of snow, the kind of crust Omar loved to watch Belén crunch with her boots when they went out for their morning walks. It was a Sunday. These walks had become a daily ritual, even in January. On their first date, Belén had told Omar that winter was the most beautiful thing about New England. She loved the unspooling aloneness that walking in the snow made her feel. Omar had been nursing a bitterness toward Connecticut when they'd met, an undigested resentfulness about staying put after his divorce, but Jordan was happy in his school, and he'd made friends here, which allowed Omar to withstand the judgmental silence of his neighbors, who had known his ex-husband and gawked at his transition. A little more than a year after his divorce, he'd met Belén. The winter he really wanted to escape, Belén had suggested to Omar after a few dates, snug inside a corner of the town's only coffee shop, was the winter of other people's eyes.

Belén used the rubber toe of her boot to kick free the frozen curve of the briefs, a cotton mélange with a thick brand-name waistband. The waistband was stiff with frozen sweat, weighted down by it in the snow. She said, I told you there was somebody out here last night.

Omar looked up at their bedroom window. The briefs must have been slipped off on purpose; the peeper wanted them to know they had been watched. The night had been exceptionally cold. The wind would have pinked the tip of the erection—with the exception of Omar and Belén, this was a white neighborhood—the voyeur would have puffed his way, red-faced, up into the maple that held the old tree house, its boards mossed and warped with age. The watcher must have felt the planks groaning in the dark.

They debated. Omar wanted to trash the underwear—they were an eyesore on the snow—but Belén was disgusted by the idea of touching them. In the end they left the briefs where they were and went inside to run a bath. Jordan was upstate this weekend—what would he have done for child care without their chosen family these past few years, Omar thought, my God—so he and Belén had a chance to reconnect, a chance to see where their bodies might take them with a good night's sleep and fresh sheets on the bed. Omar found he was relieved to not have to explain the appearance of the briefs to his child. Soon Jordan would be older, he would ask questions.

Belén unwound her red scarf from her hair and shook it out while Omar filled the tub. How he'd used to love to watch her undo her hair the first few times they'd undressed each other. Belén had been partial to braids during the early part of her transition, had dressed up her dark curls with velvet headbands and butterfly clips. Every trans person has a second adolescence, she'd told Omar: *We have another chance to get it right.* These days she wore her hair down, tucked into her coat in the winter to keep her neck warm, and she tied it up now into a bun. She got into the tub with Omar, and he maneuvered himself between her legs to rest his head on her chest, letting the kelp of his pubic hair sway. Belén took the strawberry-shaped sponge and daubed at his scars, the still-raw spot under his armpit where a keloid was forming, the hardened patch beneath one nipple where the incision had dehisced. He'd had to slather medical-grade honey on that spot for weeks, until the white pus spat out the knot of a surgical suture, fine as fishing line.

Since his top surgery, bathing each other had been their most reliable intimacy, often their only one. Belén had been the first to identify his postsurgical depression. She'd had a bad bout of it herself, years ago, after a hernia operation. Of the days immediately following his surgery, he remembered Belén's hands most: her hands squeezing the blood from his drains, her hands lifting a glass of water to his mouth. He had always loved her hands. After they'd slept together the first time, he'd seen her in the Price-Rite on Main the following afternoon and thought, the blood surging between his legs, *Those elegant hands were inside my body.* Omar had missed fucking Belén in these last weeks, but it wasn't quite the sex he missed, or maybe it was another kind of missingness, less a lack of intimacy and more the anticipation of something he hungered for, like a first invigorating run after a period of rest.

Intimacy was what he'd missed most during his postpartum depression, after he'd given birth to Jordan six years ago, and that was how he was able to differentiate this kind of missingness from the many kinds of human missingness he'd learned to live with since his transition, the missingness of privacy and safety chief among them, along with his faith in the kindness of strangers. Belén was the one who'd taught Omar to forge a life from this new reality—no-nonsense, double-Virgo Belén, who hated when people apologized to inanimate objects (*Cis people apologize when they bump into a table but not when they bump into me*, she would quip, *explain me the sense of this*), the Belén who found him a new route home from work to avoid the speed bumps that worsened his dysphoria. When he'd wanted to lock himself away from the world, she had managed to get him up and out of the house. Last summer, his dysphoria at its peak, their walks had carried Omar through one of the darkest periods of his life. One evening they'd come across a family of turkeys in the woods, and he and Jordan had hushed while Belén pointed out the mother fluttering up into the low branches of a beech tree, followed by the fluff of each of her chicks. The mother turkey spread her wings and gathered her babies into her body until they disappeared under her feathers for the night. It reminded her of a picture of the Madonna that hung in her parents' house when she was a girl, Belén said, Piero della Francesca's *Virgin of Mercy*, all the sinners gathered like chicks beneath Mary's blue mantle. In the tub, Omar turned his head, wanting Belén's eyes on him. He had never stopped wanting her—the wanting pulsed under his skin—he only had to find the way back through the gate of his desire.

She kissed the top of his ear. The bathroom window was

shut, but the curtains were open to let the light in. Omar wanted to say something about the Peeping Tom but didn't want to upset Belén. Beneath that feeling was another feeling, the sinister sense of being watched, a discomfort they survived by forgetting. He didn't want to make Belén remember it.

Do you think it was the Harris kid, Belén asked.

It was plausible. Mitchell Harris, the neighbor across the street, had a kid in high school, and everyone knew Mr. Harris used his connections to shield his son from the consequences of his own mischief. Mitchell Jr. had been caught setting fires in abandoned factories; driving drunk; once, driving down Rosemont with his friends in his father's Audi, the kid had shouted a slur at Omar as he walked home from the store. But why should it be him? The whole neighborhood had made it clear that Omar and Belén weren't wanted, and it could have been any of them, really, or their children, to make it known.

Whoever it was, Omar said aloud, I'm sure he didn't see anything. He stroked Belén's knee. He wanted to make her forget. He wanted to say that he, too, had begun to enjoy the aloneness of the snow.

The housing market will be better in the fall, Belén said. She took her hair down and let the water darken the curls. We could talk to a realtor, cariño. We could look for something else.

But Jordan, Omar said, wincing at the whine in his voice, he walks to school, he has his friends, it took years for him just to sit with other kids at lunch.

He's a kid. Belén wasn't looking at Omar; she directed her voice into the sponge as she soaped her dimpled thigh. Kids adjust. Didn't we adjust, she added at the end, and her voice caught there. Omar knew she was thinking of the year they'd spent in New York, of the dreams they'd had for a new life in that studio apartment, and also of the man who had followed them home from the subway that first winter, the one who had jerked off on them on the R on their way to work the next morning. He came all over the wool coat Omar had given Belén for her fortieth birthday, ruining it. Belén had made a strangled cry; nothing like that had ever happened to them on the subway before. It was the strangeness of her voice that snapped Omar to attention. He'd tried to punch the masturbator, but the man had run off with his dick bouncing. Perv, the man had shouted from the platform, tr—

Everyone in the subway car had squinted their eyes at the cum on Belén's coat as though she'd ejaculated on it herself.

———————

Omar tried not to look toward the back of the house when he went outside to check the mail, the warmth of the bath still on him, that clean feeling. Mr. Harris was outside when he got to the mailbox, jiggling the lock on his own front door, his phone on his shoulder. It was colder now than it had been at dawn, and the sky was a smooth, threatening white. A drift of snow had piled up against the beige siding of the house, and Mr. Harris kicked the powder from the tops of his slippers. He clutched the Sunday paper under his skinny arm, bulked by the looping knit of a fisherman's sweater. Harris was a white man in his early sixties, fat around the middle, his red cheeks and the tip of his nose peeling from a constant sunburn. Most days Omar saw him in his crisp navy suit and camel car coat, sporting sunglasses and leather driving gloves, though as far as Omar knew he only worked in Hartford, in upper-level management at one of the city's insurance companies. There was a perpetual haughtiness in his posture that, mixed with a stoop in his shoulders and a briskness in his gait, reminded Omar of an Italian comedian whose films he used to watch with Belén. Fantozzi, that was the character's name. Mr. Harris fighting with the lock brought to mind the tragicomic Fantozzi, the scene where he suspects his wife of cheating with the baker, the way the narrator takes voyeuristic pleasure in watching Fantozzi open cabinet after cabinet of stashed bread, the wretchedness with which it all dawns on him. That scene had always made Omar sad, or maybe it was the shame of watching more than sadness.

Omar called out to his neighbor from the mailbox. Mr. Harris startled and looked around before answering, as though Omar had shouted an obscenity. He'd locked himself out of his house, Mr. Harris said after a moment. His wife was away on business, he'd have to wait for the locksmith. He said this in a hurried way, as though Omar were intruding. It's cold out, Omar called back, you can come and wait inside if you want.

He regretted this as soon as he said it, but Mr. Harris wouldn't be there long, and anyway he was an ordinary cis man with ordinary cowardices; he wouldn't dare say anything in Omar's own house. Mr. Harris didn't come right away, and when he did come he came reluctantly, picking his way through the snow in his slippers like someone's aging father. Unsure of himself, he hesitated ten feet from Omar. Belén was at the upstairs window. She wouldn't come down, Omar was sure, but when he got inside, there Belén stood in the kitchen doorway in her pajamas. Mr. Harris sat down at the kitchen table. Omar put a rakweh of coffee on the stove.

Belén and Omar had crowded the small kitchen with bits of themselves: evil eye charms, the silver ayat al-kursi plaque Omar's parents had bought them from their last trip to Lebanon, the avocado pits that Belén speared with toothpicks and left to sprout on the counter in the sun. They'd put a playlist of queer R&B on Belén's phone while making breakfast, and a song pulsed now, warm and slow. Mr. Harris wrapped his sweatered arms around himself like a cornered bear. They made small talk—Jordan was away for the weekend; work often took Mrs. Harris to Phoenix; had Omar ever been to Arizona (he hadn't); his wife liked the desert, but Mr. Harris was afraid of going too near the border with Mexico. All the while Mr. Harris avoided Omar's and Belén's eyes, and after a while Belén drifted away into the living room without saying anything, cracked open the door to the screen porch, and lit a cigarette. Mr. Harris kept glancing up and down Omar's body, lingering around his chest and his groin. At first, Omar pretended not to notice. It was a compulsive kind of looking, one that cis people indulged in when they believed they could do it without being seen, though it was so common to catch them looking that their lack of shame was obvious. Omar poured coffee for them both, but Mr. Harris sipped from his cup without looking Omar in the eye, not even when he sat down at the table across from him. Omar thought now of the times he'd caught his neighbors watching him, not only Mr. Harris but nearly all the families on the block, that crawling feeling of being stared at from a curtained window, the way Omar had convinced himself he'd only imagined he'd felt it. Sometimes it was subtle like that, but mostly it wasn't. The week before, Belén had driven Omar to the leather shop forty minutes away to buy him his first X-harness. He'd wanted one for so long, had fantasized about the way it would feel to slip it on like armor over his scars. The first two months after Omar's top surgery, they'd both worn pajamas around the house, had gone out only for groceries and to walk Jordan to school. That day, Belén had dressed up, though: a pair of black overalls and a body-hugging turtleneck in maple red. They hadn't noticed the two cis girls at first, the giggling and staring, and Omar had tried to assume they were pointing at the row of butt plugs across the room, or to the leather-upholstered spanking bench. But there was no mistaking it. What the fuck is their problem, Omar had said, all the sex in this shop and they can't find anything better to stare at? But then it was irrational to be so upset, he thought; he had always managed to stuff this anger down in public, because after all it didn't do any good to glare back at cis people, they never lowered their eyes. As with animals in confinement, there was no shame or danger in staring. Mr. Harris didn't know that Omar had learned this, and most likely he would never know, but the anger grew in Omar, and the smallness of the kitchen pressed on him as Mr. Harris stared at his body, unflinching, as though they were not really in this room together. On the screen porch, Belén spoke Spanish on the phone to keep Mr. Harris from eavesdropping. The table was small, forcing Omar and his neighbor to angle their bodies to keep their elbows from touching. Omar caught a whiff of sweat on the collar of Mr. Harris's sweater, a primal smell he recognized without being able to explain, and then the locksmith's truck pulled into the driveway across the street, and Mr. Harris darted out the door, clomping across the crusted snow in his slippers.

The tension remained in the house all through the daylight hours, and for most of the day neither of them spoke. When it was getting dark, Omar soaped the day's dishes. He let the water run—it took a while to get it good and hot, the water heater always labored in the winter. A twitch had started at the base of his shoulder, a trembling that ran all the way up his neck and into his jaw, where he'd clenched it. The red light was fading on the ice in the backyard. Omar massaged the tightness out of his scars, and lightning shot through his left nipple. It was a good sign, his surgeon had told him at his last follow-up, a sign of sensitivity returning, of nerves reconnecting. In order to feel pleasure again, he had first to feel pain.

When there was no longer enough light to see the frozen briefs, Omar went into the bedroom and found Belén propped up on a pillow, reading. With the dark a different kind of tension had crept up on him, the knowledge that tomorrow Jordan would be back and this moment, which the shadow of Mr. Harris's presence had squandered, would be replaced by another moment, another day's panicked concerns. Omar crawled into bed and curled himself around Belén, who stroked his hair as she read. *Stupid*, Omar thought to himself, *you've wasted this day, you've wasted your time together.*

I had to invite him in, Omar said without meaning to speak. He wouldn't have done the same for us, it's not like I don't know that, but what am I, a fucking monster? It was freezing out. Belén looked at him over the spine of her book. He looked at me like an animal, Omar continued, even in *our* kitchen drinking *our* coffee he still wanted to know if I had a dick. It's like it turns them on to make us feel like meat.

Belén brushed the back of his hand with her fingers. Baby, she said, I know.

It wasn't the first time they'd had this conversation. Early on in their relationship, there had been no gay bar in town, so Omar had taken Belén to a straight bar vouched for by a friend, a place that was supposed to be safe. The men's room was a onesie converted into a stall, two urinals crowded by the door. Omar had just pulled his pants down when the door slammed open. What the fuck is going on in here, a man had yelled, slurring, what the fuck is going on? He planted his body between Omar and the door, trapping him inside. Omar held the stall door shut by its flimsy chrome lock. The music in the bar was too loud to shout for help. The thought had crossed Omar's mind—more an image than a thought—that if this man raped him here it would matter to no one, they would say his body had provoked the attack. He'd been frightened by the ease with which his mind shifted to calculate his chances: which was the sharpest fingernail he could drive into an eye; if he offered to suck the guy's cock Omar might get the chance to bite once, hard, and run. *Please, God*, Omar prayed, *please, God, please*, but there was no rest of the prayer, only a desperate plea not to die on the floor of this dirty bathroom. As Omar was thinking of this, the man's voice had changed, so that he growled his refrain with what was almost pleasure, no longer pounding on the door but grabbing and tugging at its lock as if it were a belt buckle. The guy was getting off on it, Omar realized; he was getting off on trapping him in here, on the fear he could smell from the other side of the stall door and from the tremor in Omar's hands that shook the lock. The man unzipped his fly, taking his time to choose the urinal visible through the gap in the stall door. He wanted Omar to see his dick, to watch its pink softness when he shook the piss off the head, to remain frozen in that filthy bathroom after he'd left, after the door had slammed.

Please, Omar said to Belén, and at first he didn't know what he was asking for. He pulled his shirt over his head, collar first; it would be another few weeks before he could lift his arms all the way up. Belén laughed and set her book aside, then took rosehip and bio oils from the bathroom and warmed them in her palm. She sat behind Omar and used the mini vibrator from the bedside drawer to massage the oil into his scars. His whole body hummed with her touch. He still remembered having drains in after his surgery, the tightness of the tubes under his skin arcing toward his sternum; though practically everything had been numb there wasn't a moment he hadn't been aware of them. When his surgeon had yanked them out, there'd been no pain at all, only the giddy, fluttering high of relief, and he'd laughed in a way that had scared Belén, had scared even himself. Belén massaged his chest in whorls, pressing the length of her belly against Omar's back, and he almost laughed again now, it felt that good. Omar's nipples tingled in a way they hadn't since he'd come home from the hospital, and he began to make little mewling sounds of pleasure. The ring of muscle around each brown nipple pulled taut. Does it hurt, Belén was saying to him, do you want me to stop, and he turned around and took her face in his hands and kissed her. They fell onto the bed and laughed into each other's mouths. He was already wet when she opened him, so wet that she slipped her fingers into his mouth to give him the sweetness of the juice. Omar tried to remember if he'd closed the bedroom curtains, it was getting dark now and someone might be able to see in, but then he didn't want to know; the world beyond this room was all snow and eyes and Omar shut himself against the thought of it.

Belén slipped off his pajamas. It felt strange to be naked before her. Of the two, he was usually the one to pleasure her first, he loved to put his head between her legs for hours; but tonight there was a need in him, he couldn't get Mr. Harris's face out of his head. Belén cupped his little cock in her hands, rubbed it in wet circles and tugged it up between her pinched fingers. He was panting, straining. Please, he said, I need your hands, I need you inside me. She smiled then and lubed her fingers before she eased him back onto the bed. She kissed the inside of his thigh. I love you, she whispered to him, do you know how much I love you?

Then make me invisible, Omar said.

He pressed toward her as she entered him, first one finger and then another. The single bedside lamp cast gaping shadows over Belén's thighs as she knelt between his legs. Omar shut his eyes and reached for her wrist. She had three fingers in him, then four. More, he said again, I need you. She had fisted him once before, but it had been so long, and his hunger made it hard to tell if he was opening to Belén or if it was she who was opening him, she had always been the only one who could open him this way. She curled her fingers against the rough spot beneath his clit, making him strain for his pleasure against her slicked hand. Still, there was the window, and his gaze kept wandering back to the dark strip of glass where the curtains could not reach. He wanted to be hidden. He pulled Belén up to him until she partially covered his body, gathering him into herself, and then she covered his eyes. She said into his ear, Stop looking.

The darkness beneath her hand amplified his ragged breath, the chill of the mattress under him, the pulsing cluster of her fingers. They were committing a sacred act, sewing him back into his body. Omar imagined his ancestors engaged in this same straining, this same rhythm, generations of lovers reaching into that same hot center. I love you, Omar said into the dark, and then all that came out afterward was Please, just that one word again and again, please, as though with her hands she could show him the self that only she could see, and when he came he let out a cry that became a laugh of release, and Belén held him to her until the shaking had passed and Omar opened his eyes.

There was a loud crack from the back window. A second passed. A thud. Belén reached for her robe, and Omar pulled on his pajamas. They raced downstairs and out the back door. Mr. Harris was sprawled in the snow beside a broken plank of the old tree house. He crawled away from them, dragging a twisted ankle. Let me take you to the hospital, Omar said, but Mr. Harris snarled at him to keep back, like a wounded animal. Don't touch me, he said, repeating the command when Belén appeared beside Omar in her slippers. The cold had crusted the snow into a silken sheet of ice, and Belén stood atop this crust in her red robe, shivering, as Mr. Harris crawled toward the road. Everyone on this street knows what you are, perverts, he said with venom, do you think we're all stupid? He was really in pain now, even in the dark it was clear in his voice. Though it was absurd, Omar thought again how much he resembled Fantozzi. There was no actual affair between Fantozzi's wife and the baker, Omar remembered, only an unrequited infatuation and the moment the baker laughs and calls Fantozzi's wife a monster, not knowing she is listening. Omar stood over his neighbor. Mitchell, Omar said, though it felt strange to use Mr. Harris's first name, we need to get you to the hospital. Mr. Harris recoiled from his hand. Don't *touch* me, he said again. They were close enough to the road now that the streetlight illuminated the scrape from a branch on Mr. Harris's face, an angry red that was sure to scar. Other people would see it one day, after the cut had healed, and wonder. Their eyes met. Mr. Harris must have seen something in Omar's eyes, the concern mixed with pity that dulled Omar's anger, or maybe he was only repulsed by Omar's looking. What are you looking at, Mr. Harris hissed, stop looking at me. He struggled to his feet and covered his face, and Omar and Belén could hear him repeating this as he limped toward the light of his front porch, Stop looking at me, stop looking at me, stop looking.

Retouch/Switch

by Cara Hoffman

She talked about money and how she didn't have any, but this was fiction. Said she was terrified of losing her job, but the truth was she didn't need it.

The job was retouching: making skin look smooth on the screen, making flesh lean, eyes bright, faces pale. She talked about the crime of it. How it wrecked your head. How you wanted more. She swore it was the money that kept her there. Money made our lips full and rosy, our bellies smooth and taut, our thighs slimmer. Money sanitized our faces and bodies of the moments that built us.

Her eyes were gray like concrete, and she never said *I*. She said *we*. *We can't sleep at night*, she said. *We're hungry again*, she said.

She sent pictures of herself alone and said, *This is a picture of us*. Sent pictures of horses, pictures of parking lots, pictures of an open wound, a pocked stone. *Here we are*, she said. *And here we are again*.

She said when she lay beside me, she retouched me in her mind. Those eyebrows the wrong shape, that lip too thin. Arms should be slimmer, breasts higher, no one has a birthmark like that.

When she came to me in Aveyron, I had been alone for months, not speaking to anyone. The town was surrounded by fields of yellow rapeseed flowers; elder trees bloomed their hot breath out into the empty courtyard. I'd been eating one meal a day.

There were white horses grazing and black moths clinging to the screen doors and kingdoms of frogs in the mud. And I was silent, ecstatic in the cradle of real things.

I'd left the States and the noise of people talking about who they were. I'd left the tyranny of their camera-ready faces. It was when people began to say they were "on brand" that I lost the power to speak. I left because there was nowhere to rest my eyes and because at home in solitude, a machine stared back at me. I left because I had nothing to say to anyone who stayed.

I loved her because she knew the membrane between this world and that one was thin.

That one, faery land. The smell of his skin.

———————

Bent over, the fur of him, the knots in his spine, the flesh and meat of his ass. Opening him. Smooth and strong, tender and deep, exposed. His face in the pillow, the weight of his body pressing back. The sound of his breathing like suffering. The salt musk alkaline smell and taste of him. Smell like mango, moldering pages, linseed oil, leather, ice.

His back streaked red and the stretch marks at his shoulders where new muscles pushed against the skin and made tears in his body.

———————

When he was her, she said she wanted to turn me inside out.

In the apartment above the bar. In the closet at work.

In the basement when she first lost her job.

Her whole hand inside. And she sucked me until I was bruised.

I took it on my back, in the dressing room, on my knees, on the street. She said it was like biting into a plum. It was like running fast down a hill so light you might become airborne.

"That's what it's like to fuck you," she said.

———————

Asleep in her studio. Asleep on the couch by my desk. Asleep near the ruin. In her bed—nothing else in the apartment; no furniture, not a scrap in the kitchen, a single bottle of fig leaf perfume in the medicine cabinet. On the beach, her hair bleached white in the sun. In the ramble. Asleep on the lawn in the park when the hawk came down to strike beside me, so close a clod of earth from its claws struck my face. And she brushed it away. Put her wet lips on mine.

Driving with her in summer while her wife cried in the back seat. Each of us retouched by her.

———————

Back in the States, where I can't taste a thing, you push my face hard up inside until I can't breathe. Your heart a little coffin that you've lined for me with satin.

———————

For a time, I lived alone where things grew everywhere; there were shale cliffs and waterfalls, rich moss and beds of fern along the forest floor. Long-dead industrial buildings perched at the edge of the gorge, their roofs cratered and trees growing sideways from their walls.

You could scale the cliffside if you were light, you could stand on the roof, you could jump from the ruins into a deep pool the width of a fat man's body. Touch the bottom to bring up fistfuls of silt and stones and bullet casings and fossils.

There is solace and comfort in the long-abandoned place, in the golden hour. No one's voice and no one's touch to intercede between you and the world. It doesn't matter where this was. What the place might have been called at that point in time. Borders are unrecognized by wind and water.

———————

I lived here quietly, until another showed up, butch this time, a marathoner.

People thought his house was haunted because the TV antennas were from the fifties and the doors swung open and slammed shut in the wind. And the barn looked like it had been smashed by a giant fist. I loved how he ruled this emptiness and he knew it called to me like no other.

But inside there were more objects still, and he, chief among them, cultivated his body. David with a Gorgon's head, turning to stone in front of his mirror.

———————

It didn't matter who you were. I wanted nothing more than you.

———————

We slept together on the Greyhound bus and shared our clothes and people had no shame in asking what
we were.

Were we this or were we that? Cruising or sleeping out, safer together. The music loud from the street and the city sprawling white below us. You were the purest form. The one I liked best.

Our devotion and our poverty and our whole future clear.

You were the only thing between me and nothing.

And we went down to the canal where those little boats were moored and crept inside one of them to sleep. The light from the flares and the light from the fire burned all night.

I left you with your hand pressed against the glass.

I left you amid the noise of the terminal.

That first time—the rush of bare life—the ecstatic loneliness. Like the world was going to tear right through me at last. You were the door in the dollhouse that led to the kingdom of the real.

You were the one. You were the only one.

If I could have left you forever I would.

Emotional Technologies

by Chris Kraus

Los Angeles, sometime in the late 1990s; I've been living here a year or two, and the landscape is an empty screen of white-sky days. There's nothing here except for what you're able to project onto it. No information, stimulation. No digression. No references, associations, promises and so your own reality expands to fill the day. And this is freedom. Driving from the GlenFed bank to FedEx to the library to the type designer out in Pasadena, I have become an independent contractor of my own consciousness. There is no social web here, only single units, and one is more efficient. Los Angeles is a triumph of the New Age.

The only experience that comes close to the totalizing effect of theater now is sadomasochism. "It's so . . . theatrical" is about the worst thing you can say about anybody's work in the contemporary art world. Theatricality implies an embarrassing excess of presence, i.e., of sentiment. Because it's more advisable to be everywhere than somewhere, we like it better when the work is cool. And so S/m emerges as the most utopian effect of diaspora, because anyone who wants to can consent to play. Contained within itself, S/m does not rely on urbanist associative meaning threads that were once described as "chemistry." It's portable, it's emotionally high-tech—the most time-efficient method of creating context and complicity between highly mobile units.

I am kneeling on the floor of the downstairs studio awaiting the arrival of a man I met over the telephone named Jeigh. For the past five weeks, Jeigh, a graduate of EST and participant in the men's movement, has been training me to be a "woman." Jeigh's ideas are absurd, but as I've observed from being in the LA art world, ideas and meaning are completely arbitrary. He tells me what to wear, what to do, what to say. While I wait, a bowl of ice cubes are melting on the wicker table by the window. I am very nervous now about those ice cubes. Forty minutes ago, Jeigh called from Santa Monica to say that he'd be leaving in ten minutes. Tonight's the first time that he's ordered ice cubes. It's a hot September night, and Santa Monica is about twenty-two miles away. It's difficult to time this right, because if I go downstairs too soon the ice will melt, but he wants to find me kneeling, in position, the moment he walks in the door. My mind's already split in two: I'm halfway here, the other half of me is hovering about the 10 East freeway, following the likely progress of his car.

I've been kneeling here about ten minutes in the sheer black blouse, the crotchless panties. I don't dare get up long enough to check my makeup. My back is straight, and my palms and cunt are trembly. The motion-sensor light outside the house blinks on, and then the door swings open. My eyes are lowered like he told me, looking only at the black jean legs below his waist. He shuts the door, I take the timing of his footsteps as the cue to speak the line he gave me. My voice comes someplace from the swirl between my downcast eyes and the tension of his footstep. Modesty and fear commingling like a cocktail of two complementary drugs, NOW: "My body is yours. You can do what you want with it." I'm speaking in a voice I never used before.

There is no experimental theater in sadomasochism. That's why I like it. Character is completely preordained and circumscribed. You're only either top or bottom. There isn't any room for innovation in these roles. It's a bit like what Ezra Pound imagined the Noh drama of Japan to be: a paradox in which originality is attained only through compliance with tradition. Tonalities and gestures are completely set, and so exactitude is freedom. His black Levi's, my slutty outfit, his black shoes. S/m's a double flip around the immanence of objects in the theater: the objects aren't blank and waiting to be filled with meaning by the actors. The objects here are meaning cards; they hold all the information. He says, "Hold out your hands." "Yes, sir," I say, blood rushing to my face. He's given me a choice of two responses to his utterances. The second is: *I understand*. He puts a collar round my neck and slaps me. Handcuffs, blindfolds, gags, and whips. The objects tell us who we are and what to do. S/m is like the sixteenth-century improvisational theater of commedia dell'arte: a stock repetoire of stories, bits, lines, and gags. He chains my handcuffs to the door. I'm Columbine and he's Pierrot.

The first thing she did when she moved into the house in Mount Washington was install dark green shades to keep the light out. She'd become so sensitive to light. Birds woke her up at six, followed by this gray seepage of pearlescent light through the two half walls of windows where she slept. There was a feeling then, that everything was hovering, and she needed to remain there long enough to remember what she'd dreamt. Dreams steered her through the day, and she needed the slight weight of morning vapor to protect her. She was trying to become a writer. Since she'd never been especially creative, the only way that she could think to do this was to transcribe the pictures in her head. She found that sometimes in the darkened room, the pictures moved outside her head and into her entire body, and these, she realized, were the good times. This was what she sought. Sometimes the pictures moved so fast that she could not keep up. Her temperature dropped, and her breath got short. She needed to find words to delineate this thing that moved inside her body like a small, buried animal. She knew it would take a long time to get the animal out, and sometimes she thought she might die before she did this. It didn't matter that she was not particularly a good writer. If she could just remain within this state for the time it took her to transcribe it, the whole thing might work out.

Like everything about LA, this goal of filtering the light was difficult but not completely unattainable. She'd found a bin of dark green window shades at Virgil's Hardware Home Center in Glendale. Left over from the 1970s, they cost less than twenty bucks apiece. They were totally opaque and had old-fashioned crochet pull strings. She'd seen shades like this before in New York City and East Hampton. There, these kind of shades were custom-made, expensive, and high-concept. But in LA, there were so many pockets left of midcentury Americana that had not been commandeered by style masters. Things forgotten, parts of the city no one wanted. Oh, there were upscale malls and concentrations of conspicuous consumption, but in LA, wealth was blindingly direct. Wealth was manifested just by size and newness. Wealth did not insinuate itself by references to values of the past, symbolized by transom windows, onyx doorknobs, wide-plank Shaker floorboards. Whoever planned things here seemed quite happy with the things themselves. There was nothing there to break your heart, and nothing gelled.

The house was her sanctuary and her brain center, an asbestos-shingled wreck teetering above a canyon on the slummier side of this mixed, bohemian enclave shared by second-generation Okie immigrants and artsy types who valued the "authentic." Mount Washington, they said, was "the Brentwood of the ghetto." Still, like every other LA neighborhood, it was zoned strictly "residential," and there were no corner stores, no reason to walk anywhere unless you were dressed in spandex sweats and carrying three-pound dumbbells. The road outside her house led to a secondary service road, which in turn led to a four-lane service road next to the freeway. Here, on Figueroa, was the Lucky Supermarket, Mobil, the Pick 'n Save, interspersed with body shops and tire workshops, shacks and bungalows inhabited by the exclusively Latino poor. There were no trees along the streets, no, as the urban planners call it, "infill."

While Mount Washington had the vague charm of Appalachia butted up against West Coast expat English Hinduism, there was no evidence that Figueroa Street had ever existed any other way. That is, there were no tugs of memory. Back east, she liked to move across the sprawl with X-ray eyes, conscious of four hundred years of history. Driving on the 87 Thruway through northern Westchester County, the exit sign for "Spook Rock" always gave her chills because it made her think of lynchings. As a child in Bridgeport, gazing out the window of her parents' car, she pictured mail carriers hunkered down in horse carts on the Post Road between Boston and New York City. "Neither wind nor snow nor sleet," her dad intoned as they passed the Dunkin' Donuts.

But Figueroa Street and San Fernando Road, as far as she could tell, had never been anything but a string of stores that doubled as a residential dumping ground for the poor, who gathered every morning at the five-point intersection on Avenue 35 in an unofficial shape-up for day labor. Men in scavenged clothes who pounded on car windows, flexed their muscles, and shouted, "I work good," and "Hire me," which were probably the only English phrases that they knew. The first time that she witnessed this, she caught her breath and sobbed, not believing this could be. Later the same week, at the opening of MOCA's Claes Oldenburg retrospective, she was amazed that there was not a single black person or Latino in the crowd that milled around the corny giant pencil. Los Angeles, she thought, was like Johannesburg. Everyone was white, except for several Asians. Eventually, she got used to it. Later still, she picked up some of these same men to rake her yard and help her strip and bag the old asbestos shingles.

After a while she stopped looking for shots of content from the landscape.

It was the first house she'd ever bought and lived in by herself, without her husband. It was what she could afford. "It's perfect for her," her long-ago ex-boyfriend had reportedly said to her then-boyfriend, an ex-filmmaker-turned-carpenter who was renovating the house. "It's a real shithole." She imagined the two of them chuckling. But who'd laugh last? Neither boyfriend past or present had ever owned a house; both were heading into middle age with artistic aspirations and boring jobs they had to keep, while she was living on her own now, for the very first time since she'd been destitute and single.

"My goal," she told everyone she met upon arriving in LA, "is to become famous in the art world." Since everyone she met was somehow in the art world, they failed to get the joke and regarded her with some embarrassment. "I figure it will take two years," she added, deadpan. Because who gave a shit? Unlike NYC, no one in the LA art world struck her as especially admirable or smart. There was just one game in town, and that was neocorporate, neoformalist conceptualism.

Back in New York, when she was still trying to become not famous in the art world, but an actual artist, she had no reason to believe she wouldn't die in her rent-stabilized, two-room slum apartment. Desperate about her situation, when she turned twenty-eight, she worked extra shifts of night word processing in order to consult an astrologer and a psychotherapist. "What's all this scarcity shit about?" the astrologer asked, and offered her a discount rate on a prosperity consciousness workshop. "You are a masochist," the therapist sighed when she confessed to hoping she could eventually support herself as an experimental multimedia theater artist. Meanwhile in the building, the old Italian lady died across the hall. When Social

Security learned of her demise and stopped emitting checks, her fifty-five-year-old son became a crack dealer. Downstairs in #1E, Frank, a retired featherweight pro boxer with no known relatives, contracted Alzheimer's. Within a year, she saw him smearing handfuls of his shit across the hallway wall, but there was no one there to stop him. Eventually, he died, and his body rotted for five days before the Turkish super finally showed up with a cop to break the door down.

But in LA she had a part-time job teaching at a rich prestigious art school. The LA art world was starting to be considered "hot," and since it revolved entirely around the schools, the job conferred an instant credibility. This particular institution was at the forefront of a movement to expunge identity from contemporary art. It was a two-year hazing process that utilized Socratic modes of instruction. That is, when the students weren't tearing one another's work apart in carefully orchestrated "theories of construction" seminars, their time was spent in private meetings with instructors, whose job it was to draw them out in "discourses" about their "practice." Faced with roomfuls of acrylic paintings of computer chips and monochromes, she learned to cultivate a dreamy vacant stare, to verbalize non sequiturs, and finally to drop the names of first-wave minimalists with a slight inflection upward at the end, as if these names themselves were challenges or questions.

Black security guards in golf carts crawled around the lawn while she and other part-time faculty sat beneath the pepper trees discussing the technological sublime, spatiotemporal realism, Kant, and Hegel. None of the other part-time faculty were any more or less qualified than she to talk about these things. No one had any formal training in philosophy, much less a PhD. It was a kind of heaven. Better still, unlike the other part-time faculty, she didn't have to teach at other schools in order to get by. Her husband was still living in New York, and he was nominally employed as an advisor to the institution. Every other week, two checks—a large one in her husband's name, and a small one in her own—arrived, totaling $2,500. She cashed them both. And so at forty-one, she had the thing she'd always secretly known to be her birthright: independence and enough money to walk into a store and buy a Chanel lipstick without calculating how many hours of word processing it would cost.

The house was up a flight of seventy-three cement steps. (A Guatemalan laborer's son had counted them one day when they were hauling bricks to build a patio.) Scrunched between two rubber trees, it looked out across the canyon. Lying in the bed she'd set up in the living room was like living in a tree house. It was the perfect house for Pippi Longstocking. Except she didn't feel like Pippi Longstocking, because there was hardly any promise of adventure beyond the house outside.

She was trying to become a writer and was discovering that this required large blocks of empty and unstructured time. She drew the shades and read and masturbated and lit a candle at her desk. At night sometimes she used the automated sex ads on the phone. She liked that they could link her up with other outposts of loneliness around the city. She was living entirely within her head. For a while she experimented with keeping pets.

———

Half a century ago in Poland, the director Jerzy Grotowski began developing a technology through which his actors could attain heightened states of performative extremity within the framework of dramatic texts. Because he sought a confrontation between the actors and the text, the plays he chose were always mythic, because by that time myths were dead.

The Polish Laboratory Theatre techniques were exercises aimed at pushing actors into states of pure intensity. It was the kind of "cruelty" Artaud envisioned in the 1930s, inspired by traditional non-Western forms of dance in which performers enter into trance states simply by repeating ancient gestures. According to the American Lee Breuer, it works this way: "The Kathakali gestures reverse their way up through the stimulus system of the body. The movement of the hands transmits sensation to the nerve centers of the brain, and this creates emotion. There is a loop." But Artaud had never studied Kathakali, and he was mad, and the only person who he ever could enact this "cruelty" on was himself.

And so for fifteen years in Warsaw, the Polish Laboratory Theatre devised a system that would make these heightened states repeatable and teachable. They devised a set of exercises called *plastiques*: exercises that pushed the actor beyond ordinary endurance, in order to break down the gap in time between cognition and response. After several hours, "[impulse] and action are concurrent," Grotowski wrote. "The body vanishes, burns, and the spectator sees only a series of visible impulses." And in this way, "[the] actor makes a total gift of himself."

Grotowski, a midcentury Eastern European, never saw the "self" as a buried treasure, waiting to be probed and finally revealed. This came later, in America. To the Poles, the "self" was more like a translation, the energy that flows between the dialectics of behavior. A moving thing. Acting was releasing, and yet it never was a matter of "release." Like the ancient Kathakali gestures, the movement patterns of *plastiques* left no margin for improvisation. They were rigid, codified. "We find that artificial composition not only does not limit the spiritual but it actually leads to it." Years later, he spoke scathingly of the experimental theater orgies staged by his US imitators as "wretched performances . . . full of a so-called cruelty which would not scare a child."

Working in small cities in midcentury Eastern Europe, Grotowski saw theater as a technology through which we might "transcend our solitude." It is hard to get a picture of just what that "solitude" might have been. Grimy, dark cafés and baggy overcoats; unspoken yearnings underneath a fixed circle of routines and friends? Rehearsal and performance both involve "an utter opening to another person . . . It is a clumsy way of expressing it, but what is achieved is a total acceptance of one human being by another."

When the carpenter boyfriend, who she'd seriously considered impoverishing herself to marry, dumped her for a woman he described as "a really nice girl," her truck flipped over on an icy highway in the desert. For half an hour she was trapped inside the cab, feet forward like an astronaut. She thought she was an animal. For two days, she was trying to explain this on the phone to anyone who'd listen, her husband and her therapist, her friend Carol Irving in New York, until she finally passed out. The hospital diagnosed concussion and sent her home. Shortly after this she decided she was much too old for conventional romance.

"Tonight," Jeigh said, "I am going to teach you the difference between pleasure and pain."

I'm curious to learn this. I'm curious to learn just about anything he wants to teach me. Today the television said it was the 159th straight day without rain. I can't remember when they started counting. For weeks or even months the leaves of all the eucalyptus trees along the 110 freeway have been a brittle brownish green. The sky is white, and nothing breathes. It is a kind of summer hibernation, hovering like the smoggy air.

All summer long, Jeigh and I'd swapped sexy voice mails before we ever talked. I listened to his voice mails from the ferry terminal in Canada; I listened to them in New York. His messages intrigued me, turned me on. His Dom voice reminded me of a freakish grade school teacher who we all called Snagglepuss. The kind of guy who might describe himself as a "gentleman." Low-class, middle-aged fag trying to play butch. In his phone ad, Jeigh described himself as "intense, creative, and, oh yes, very dominant," and that he was. He didn't seem to be afraid of me, so I figured he was smart.

I think it was his second visit when this happened. He'd instructed me to undress at seven thirty and kneel, naked, by the phone. Sometime within the next half hour he'd call with more instructions. The phone rang at 7:59. Well, I found this pretty fucking witty. How many times have I, has every heterosexual female in this culture, spent evenings mooning around our houses and apartments, psychically stripped bare and on our knees while waiting for "his" call? Why not take the courtship ritual literally? And then there was the psychophysical part:

thinking it was silly but suspending disbelief enough to do it, and then waiting on my knees until I felt a queasy, shuddering anticipation, like being in the car that's at the top the moment the Ferris wheel stops.

He arrived to find me kneeling naked in the studio downstairs. He said: "We need to have a little talk." I didn't look at him. My eyes, as he'd instructed when he called, were focused on the floor.

"There are three stages in a relationship between a dominant and a submissive. The first stage is to play together once. The second is to agree to play together on an ongoing basis. And the third—do you know what the third stage is?" I shook my head incredulously, imagining scenes out of Pauline Réage. "No." He laughed. "I didn't think you did."

He told me he would put me on probation. If I consented, we were entering the second stage. The rules were: He'd decide when and how often we would see each other. He'd decide when and how often we'd talk on the phone. I would not know his address or phone number, but I was free to leave as many voice mails for him on the service as I wanted, providing that they made him hard. I found this very liberating. How many hours had I spent in "normal" dating situations, pondering the etiquette and timing of the post-fuck call?

And then his voice turned mock-solicitous. "I've even thought about your safety. If when we're playing, any of this becomes too much for you to take, you'll say, 'Enough.' And within thirty seconds of your saying it I'll pack my bag and be out the door."

Because we were listening to each other hard, the room seemed small.

For the first few months after she moved into the house, she rented out the downstairs studio to a girl named Aimee. Aimee was the girlfriend of an artist she'd met outside the institution, a hippie guy who painted Disney characters humping one another in the woods. In terms of art-world discourse, the guy didn't have a clue. At twenty-two, Aimee was a goddess: tall and lean, with masses of blond hair. Born in a redneck desert town, she was brilliant and completely fearless. Aimee'd spent a good part of her sixteenth year in a mental institution, like most of the other working-class girl geniuses the woman knew. Every boy that Aimee met fell instantly in love with her, and Aimee loved boys, too. Reading Charles Bukowski, she'd arrived at a goddess vision of the world that echoed the belief system of Hasidic Jews. It went something like: men should have all the power, run the world, because they're spiritually and biologically inferior to girls. Still, they became good friends.

Aimee'd just dropped out of Cal State Northridge to become a full-time singer-songwriter. The woman hired her as her assistant and let her have free rent. Together, they produced a philosophy rave in the Nevada desert. For nine months, they sold tickets from their office in the tree house and chatted up the press while Aimee elaborated her existential views on being and becoming: "You're born into the setup . . ." The event was finally a huge success. There was a gorgeous shot of Aimee singing on the stage in a cocktail waitress outfit, towering above a short, fat, famous French philosopher on the front page of the *Los Angeles Times* that day—a thing, it seemed, so easy to achieve it hardly counted. Aimee had drinks with managers, sat in with famous NY bands, but then she got depressed, spent days in bed. She stopped working, couldn't find another job, and then she started borrowing money. But on sunny days that winter, Aimee would get up for a while and sit on the steps outside the studio, writing songs on her guitar. Music pouring out across the canyon. Aimee's vibrant brash soprano voice, singing strings of words about spiders and machinery. The woman was so certain Aimee was about to become a star.

But as the months wore on, things just got worse. Aimee started smoking pot with Travis, the idiot savant next door whose mom had been a manager for Devo. And then Travis went to jail for spousal battery, and Aimee took to dumping bags of garbage in the yard. She hid behind the curtains when the woman timidly approached to ask about the rent. Eventually, the woman kicked her out. Months later, Aimee moved to San Francisco with another boy. She could not remember any of the songs she'd sung that winter. None of them were taped or written down.

The thing that struck the woman most about living in Los Angeles was how things happen but nothing ever quite adds up. The way it's possible to be in regular contact with another person, to talk on the phone, to maybe see each other once a week, and then for no discernible reason the contact stops, the person drifts entirely out of range. Perhaps it was depression? The guy at the bookstore, the photographer, the woman living in Marina del Rey, were all like the mythic agent or producer who suddenly stops returning calls.

And that's the end of our discussion. This is pure romance, as in *roman*, a story that's contained within itself. Like theater or pure math, S/m is a self-generating system large enough to reference everything that it excludes. Romance, desire, context, expectation loop back and forth between us through our roles. Multiple paradoxes yielding triple penetration. The game is totally complete within itself. Unlike ordinary sex, it is an act, and not a metaphor, of love.

Montage of Irony was the title of one of the courses offered at the institution where she taught. Like most of the discourse about contemporary art that went on there, the meaning of it narrowly escaped her. She recognized the words, but the meanings of the words in these new combinations drifted out beyond the range of anything she knew. Given that "the work of art as such . . . exists to manufacture ambiguity," the trick was to create an *atmosphere* of meaning without the burden of any *particular* meaning. Disparaging asides about one's enemies (the "left" and "feminism") are infinitely more effective than a confrontation. "When considered as action rather than idea, in other words, the categorical intentions contained in the word 'feminism' may be seen, sometimes, sadly, to have effects which add further testimony to the case for describing the signified as unstable, and therefore to how it is pointless to attribute to categories the kind of stable and collective benevolence which is their common due on the *left*" (Jeremy Gilbert-Rolfe, *Beyond Piety*, 1995). Subordinate clauses are your friends. It's best to drop the poison at the end, when the subject of the sentence has been buried in the drift and can no longer be refuted because it is impossible to decode.

Minimalism, Heidegger, Kant, and beauty. The categorical imperative and monochromes.

It was possible to make up a story about anything, she supposed.

———————

Grotowski sought out mythic texts because he wanted to demolish subtext. There are no internal conflicts within an allegory. Everything's direct and on the surface. When Death confronts him, Everyman seeks out strength and friendship, goods and kin and beauty. None of these can help him. But can't there be a way of translating allegory into psychological realms? The master and the slave, the monster and the slut. All the little dramas of romance get batted back and forth between these poles.

———————

Because she didn't care if people liked her and seemed to notice what went on, most people saw her as a monster. In S/m, she liked that somebody else could play that role.

———————

To make a metaphor so big and bold that you drain it of its subtext, create an overarching irony where all the codes of romance are exposed. S/m is a parody, a carnival, of het dating.

When Jeigh announces that he's going to teach me the difference between pain and pleasure, my muscles jump. I'm scared, but still excited, because since coming to LA no one's taught me anything at all. I'm blindfolded, listening to the rustle of his bag of whips. I'm so startled I've forgotten that he's told me to respond to everything he says. He grabs me by the hair. "What do you say?" And I repeat one of the lines he taught me: "Yes, sir. Whatever pleases you the most." The line's a trope, pure *Punch and Judy*, an S/m cliché, and yet it's *not*, it's totally alive because by saying it I know that I'm inviting him to really hurt me if he wants. (When I use the other line, "I understand," my pussy dilates 'cause my mind is opening.)

He says, "Get up." "Yes, sir," I stumble. He clips my handcuffs to some device he's mounted on the door. "Legs spread. Hands against the wall. That's right." He leaves me there. I feel him watching. This must be love because I feel myself expanding in his gaze, and so I say, "I want you to know I take this very seriously." He listens, takes this in, and slams an index finger up my cunt. "Heh heh. Just as I thought." There are only two criteria for success within an S/m performance: wet or hard. And then his whip comes down across my back abrupt and sharp. "We'll start with ten. You'll count them off." There's nothing sexual about this. The pain shakes through my back around the room and then there's two and three then—"Oooops. You forgot to thank me for them. We'll have to start again."

Grotowski complained that his American imitators and successors were more concerned with working with the "I" than with the "self." I think the difference is important. In the last scene of *Diary of a Mad Housewife* (1970) the Carrie Snodgress character submits herself to "group therapy"—a pack of stupid dogs yapping at their prey with one eye toward the bone, an approving nod from the leader of the pack, the therapist. That's pretty much how I remember experimental theater acting in New York. Art schools bring this practice back to junior high school, because it's not the person who's confronted, but their coolness: their ability, or not, to learn a secret set of rules.

_____

Toward the end of his life, Michel Foucault began to write about "technologies of the self." He was interested in how the "self" creates itself within a framework defined entirely by the institution. He only got as far as ancient Greece, and there he saw how individuals became "citizens" by internalizing codes of ethics, investing them with subtext.

Interestingly, Foucault loathed American feminists and dykes. For many years in Paris, and later on in California, Foucault played S/m. It's only in his interviews with the American gay male press that he began to talk about what it felt like, what it meant. He described S/m as the "reterritorialization of pleasure." Foucault's biographer David Marcy does not repress this information, but casts him as the top. He apparently admires the philosopher so much he can't admit that Foucault played the bottom.

Grotowski criticized his American followers for seeking out security in the group, creating false familial situations. "A director," he once said, "is not a father. A fellow actor is not a lover. These are elements of a banal sentimentality which is irrelevant to creative work."

I think stupidity is the unwillingness to absorb new information.

_____

The first time that we met, Jeigh handcuffed me to the passenger seat of a rented Ford Aspire. We were in the parking lot behind the Dresden. On the phone I'd told him I was more turned on by people's energy than by their looks, so he decided not to let me see him. In the restaurant I was told to keep my eyes down. Then outside, the blindfold.

In the car, he pulled my dress up and slapped my thighs until they bruised. This hurt more than I expected. With every slap I moved a little deeper down inside myself, associating this hurt to all the other hurts I've known and witnessed. It was a bad trip down the well of psychotherapy. I was a thousand miles outside the car, but then he brought me back: "Don't pout." "It hurts." "Then find some way to tell me." I started gasping, moaning, and then eventually I came. It was a micro-moment of intense theatricality.

> *Let me tell it to you all . . . But no, the lines*
> *the rhythm forced . . . the heart is larger!*
> *The collected works of Shakespeare and Racine*
> *are not enough for this occurrence . . .*

> *Misery! There are no shores, no roadmarks!*
> *Yes, I agree, losing score,*
> *okay, by losing you I lose whatever*
> *whoever or anywhere never was!*

> *It's useless—she's in me, everywhere—shut*
> *eyes, she's bottomless, no day—and the date*
> *on the calendar lies . . .*

> *Through what seas and cities*
> *Should I look for you?*
> *(Invisible man to a visionless*
> *spectator)*

> *Leaning up against the telegraph pole*
> *I hand down the ritual of the road to the wires.*

Exiled in Paris in 1923, the Russian poet Marina Tsvetaeva projects herself headlong into submissive space. "I was born carried away," she wrote, and then she was. Running between countries, using strange punctuation, dashes, exclamation marks, ellipses to write poems like telegrams, the most advanced technology of her time, she was a ball of longing projected onto the European landscape.

There isn't much I want here in Los Angeles because without a context everything's the same. The streets of Manhattan are a *Where's Waldo?* map of personal shortfall and inadequacy, but here I don't envy anybody's children, cars, careers, or houses. I think it's 'cause the dead are missing from the landscape.

In a disembodied floating space, S/m offers little pockets of theatricality and connection. So long as they are playing, two people are totally accountable and listening to each other. S/m radically preempts romantic love because it is a practice of it.

To see this fact as cold or cynical is as naïve as thinking writing ought to be "original" or that speaking in the first person necessarily connotes any kind of truth, sincerity.

AFTERWORD

I wrote this piece almost twenty years ago, improbably for the school magazine at ArtCenter College of Design, where I was then teaching. I'd moved from New York to LA a few years before. Partly, the piece was an attempt to normalize and explain my interest and delight in kinky sex to old friends in NY who were horrified, and partly it was an attempt to locate myself in this new environment. Looking back, I realize the whole adventure was also an attempt to hold part of myself back from the wholehearted and gleeful pursuit of an art-world career, which was what everyone around me seemed to be doing. None of the dominant partners I met through the Telepersonals ads were in the art world, and none of them seemed very invested in their careers. They were highly intelligent people who were choosing to channel all their best energies into these games, which seemed like a great gift to me and their other submissive partners. BDSM was the most important thing in my life for a few years, and then it was over. What I didn't recognize then was that most of the dominant partners I played with had recently suffered the loss of a partner or spouse, and I was feeling and writing about loss then, as well. The whole thing may have been a collaborative ritual that was driven by grief. I see this in the work of the late photographer Brian Weil . . . his trajectory from BDSM clubs to violent crime scenes to Hasidic communities in upstate New York. I hope to reconsider these experiences as an exorcism of grief, sometime in the future.

Acknowledgments

With deep gratitude to Ellen Levine, Martha Wydysh, and Nora Rawn, and to Anna Stein. To Ira Silverberg, for his heartening faith in this book. To Zachary Knoll, for his ever staunch, wise stewardship. To Heidi Meier, Kassandra Rhoads, Elizabeth Breeden, and the rest of S&S, especially David Litman, Lewelin Polanco, Janet Robbins Rosenberg, Yvette Grant, and Kimberly Goldstein.

To MacDowell, where this book started. To Jennifer Baker, Piyali Bhattacharya, Rowan Hisayo Buchanan, Manjula Martin, Claire Rudy Foster, Andrea Lawlor, Ingrid Rojas Contreras, Lauren Markham, Rachel Khong, Andi Winnette, and Tony Tulathimutte for invaluable advice and help.

To Brontez Purnell, Esmé Weijun Wang, and Lidia Yuknavitch for the generous support. To M., always. To everyone who's ever felt out of place because of what your body wanted, this book is for you.

About the Authors

CALLUM ANGUS is a trans writer, editor, and former bookseller currently based in Portland, Oregon. His work has appeared in *Nat. Brut, West Branch, LA Review of Books, Catapult, The Common, Seventh Wave Magazine*, and elsewhere, and he has received fellowships from Lambda Literary and Signal Fire Foundation for the Arts. His first book, *A Natural History of Transition*, is forthcoming from Metonymy Press.

ALEXANDER CHEE is most recently the author of the essay collection *How to Write an Autobiographical Novel*. He is a contributing editor to the *New Republic*, an editor at large for *VQR*, a critic at large at the *Los Angeles Times*, and an associate professor of English and creative writing at Dartmouth College.

VANESSA CLARK is an intersex trans fem author that has been featured in *Harper's Bazaar, POPSUGAR, Vice*, and *Them*, and has written articles for *Vox*. Pronouns: she/they. Even though she lives in New Jersey, she is more than likely spending her free time at some of the best indie bookstores, parks, museums, and record shops in New York City. On social media, you can find her on Facebook (@vcerotica) and Twitter (@FoxxyGlamKitty).

MELISSA FEBOS is the author of three books: *Whip Smart*, *Abandon Me*, and *Girlhood*. The inaugural winner of the Jeanne Córdova Prize for Lesbian/Queer Nonfiction from Lambda Literary, her work has recently appeared in the *Believer*, *McSweeney's*, *Granta*, the *Paris Review*, *Tin House*, and the *New York Times*. She is an associate professor at the University of Iowa.

KIM FU is the author of the novels *The Lost Girls of Camp Forevermore* and *For Today I Am a Boy*, as well as the poetry collection *How Festive the Ambulance*. Her first short story collection, *Lesser Known Monsters of the Twenty-First Century*, is forthcoming from Tin House Books. Her writing has appeared in *Granta*, the *New York Times*, the *Atlantic*, *TLS*, and *Hazlitt*. She lives in Seattle.

ROXANE GAY is a writer, splitting her time between New York and Los Angeles, but she will always, always be from the Midwest. She has written several books, comics, and other things.

CARA HOFFMAN is an American novelist, essayist, and journalist. Her work has appeared in the *New York Times*, the *Paris Review*, *Bookforum*, *BOMB*, and *Rolling Stone*, among others. Her most recent novel, *Running*, was a *New York Times* Editors' Choice. Her fiction has received numerous awards and accolades. She lives in Athens, Greece.

ZEYN JOUKHADAR is the author of the novels *The Thirty Names of Night* and *The Map of Salt and Stars*, which won the 2018 Middle East Book Award. His work has appeared in *Salon*, the *Paris Review*, *[PANK] Magazine*, and elsewhere, and has been nominated for the Pushcart Prize. Joukhadar has received fellowships from the Montalvo Arts Center, the Arab American National Museum, the Bread Loaf Writers' Conference, the Camargo Foundation, and the Josef and Anni Albers Foundation.

CHRIS KRAUS is a writer and critic whose novels include *Summer of Hate*, *Torpor*, and *Aliens & Anorexia*. Her first novel, *I Love Dick*, was adapted for television. She is presently working on a book about the Iron Range in northern Minnesota. She lives in LA and teaches writing at ArtCenter.

CARMEN MARIA MACHADO is the author of the bestselling memoir *In the Dream House* and the short story collection *Her Body and Other Parties*, which was a finalist for the National Book Award and the winner of the Lambda Literary Award for Lesbian Fiction and the Shirley Jackson Award. Her essays, fiction, and criticism have appeared in the *New Yorker*, the *New York Times*, *Granta*, *This American Life*, *Vogue*, the *Believer*, and elsewhere. She holds an MFA from the Iowa Writers' Workshop and is the writer in residence at the University of Pennsylvania.

PETER MOUNTFORD is the author of the novels *A Young Man's Guide to Late Capitalism* (Washington State Book Award), and *The Dismal Science* (a *New York Times* Editors' Choice).

His work has appeared in the *Paris Review*, the *Atlantic*, the *Southern Review*, *Granta*, the *Sun*, and the *New York Times Magazine*. Currently on faculty at Sierra Nevada University's MFA program, he also teaches at Creative Nonfiction and Seattle's literary center Hugo House, and is a developmental editor.

LARISSA PHAM is an artist and writer in Brooklyn. Born in Portland, Oregon, she studied painting and art history at Yale University. Her essays and criticism have appeared in the *Paris Review Daily*, the *Nation*, *Art in America*, *Poetry Foundation*, and elsewhere. She was an inaugural Yi Dae Up Fellowship recipient from the Jack Jones Literary Arts retreat. She is the author of *Fantasian*, a novella, and the essay collection *Pop Song*.

BRANDON TAYLOR is the author of the acclaimed novel *Real Life*, which has been shortlisted for the Booker Prize, longlisted for the Center for Fiction First Novel Prize, and been named a *New York Times Book Review* Editors' Choice. He holds graduate degrees from the University of Wisconsin-Madison and the Iowa Writers' Workshop, where he was an Iowa Arts Fellow in fiction.

About the Editors

R.O. KWON's first novel, the national bestseller *The Incendiaries*, was published by Riverhead and is being translated into seven languages. Named a best book of the year by more than forty publications, *The Incendiaries* was a finalist for the National Book Critics Circle John Leonard Prize for Best First Book and the Los Angeles Times Art Seidenbaum Award for First Fiction. Kwon's writing has appeared in the *New York Times*, the *Guardian*, the *Paris Review*, on NPR, and elsewhere. She is a National Endowment for the Arts Fellow.

GARTH GREENWELL is the author of *What Belongs to You*, which won the British Book Award for Debut Book of the Year, was longlisted for the National Book Award, and was a finalist for six other awards, including the PEN/Faulkner Award, the James Tait Black Memorial Prize, and the Los Angeles Times Book Prize. His second book of fiction, *Cleanness*, was published in 2020. His fiction has appeared in the *New Yorker*, the *Paris Review*, *A Public Space*, and *VICE*, and he has written criticism for the *New Yorker*, the *London Review of Books*, and the *New York Times* Book Review, among others. A 2020 Guggenheim Fellow, he lives in Iowa City.

Previous Publication Information

"Best Friendster Date Ever" by Alexander Chee

A version of this story has previously appeared in *The Best Gay Erotica 2006*, edited by Richard Labonté and Mattilda Bernstein Sycamore (Cleis Press, 2005), and *The Best American Erotica 2007* (Touchstone Press, 2007).

"Safeword" by R.O. Kwon

A version of this story previously appeared in *Playboy* (2017).

"Reach" by Roxane Gay

A version of this story previously appeared in *A Is for Amour* (Cleis Press, 2007).

"Gospodar" by Garth Greenwell

Versions of this story previously appeared in the *Paris Review* (issue 209, Summer 2014); *The Unprofessionals: New*

Fiction from the Paris Review, edited by Lorin Stein (Penguin Books, 2015); and *Cleanness* (FSG, 2020).

"The Lost Performance of the High Priestess of the Temple of Horror" by Carmen Maria Machado
A version of this story previously appeared in *Granta* (February 2020) and will appear in Machado's forthcoming story collection from Knopf.

"Emotional Technologies" by Chris Kraus
A version of this story previously appeared in *Video Green* (Semiotext(e), 2004).